CARIBBEAN WRITERS SERIES

7

God the Stonebreaker

CARIBBEAN WRITERS SERIES

Alvin Bennett

GOD THE STONEBREAKER

Introduction by Louis James
University of Kent at Canterbury

HEINEMANN
LONDON

Heinemann Educational Books Ltd
48 Charles Street, London W1X 8AH
P.M.B. 5205, Ibadan · P.O. Box 45314, Nairobi
EDINBURGH TORONTO MELBOURNE AUCKLAND
SINGAPORE HONG KONG KUALA LUMPUR NEW DELHI

ISBN 0 435 98100 5

To
SIR ROBERT KIRKWOOD
and
DR GUIDO GRIMALDI

Reproduced and printed by photolithography and bound
in Great Britain at The Pitman Press, Bath

INTRODUCTION

by Louis James

University of Kent at Canterbury
Formerly University College of the West Indies

Granny Brown, known as GB to her many friends and enemies, was tenant of 'one of the king-size dustbins constructed and filled with rubbish' in the slum area behind Montego Bay, Jamaica. She was a stonebreaker by profession and by genius historian of all the scandalous gossip of the community. Her all-absorbing passion was 'Drop Pan' or 'Peaka Peow', the local illegal gambling game. The novel plots her ascending rake's progress from Swine Lane to a neat detached bungalow in the suburbia of Kingston. The area is familiar. From the beginnings of the Caribbean novel with the work of Tom Redcam, De Lisser and Claude McKay, its writers have explored the life of the black and poor in the shanty towns. Yet Alvin Bennett's story of GB stands on its own.

The first chapter, with its uproarious confrontation between GB and her landlord Quashie, who struggles with his hammer to demolish his own property in revenge for GB's refusal to pay rent, at once sets a tone foreign to any literary parallels. If one looks for comparisons, it is rather with the knockabout bitter-sweet farce of Jamaican popular pantomime and the dialect character sketches of Louise Bennett, which themselves have their roots in the explosive miniature dramas of Caribbean yard life. At its best, Alvin Bennett's book is anecdotal and dramatic, with the flash of street invective. 'None of us should say anything bad about Fanso . . . he come up a long way to reach low class like us. It was not the poor man's fault that his mother died of fright when she saw his colour near white.' (p. 2)

At the centre stands GB, larger than life, and herself a figure out of the popular imagination. She cheats, lies, and wheedles her way from one crisis to another. In her world of amoral deceit she resembles the Caribbean folk-tale hero, the spider-god Anancy. The comparison is significant. The slaves selected Anansi from the pantheon of West African folk-tale heroes because trickery was also the one way they had of combating the overwhelming odds of their oppression. Both Anancy and GB express a reaction to deprivation. Both lie instinctively, as a defence and a way of manipulating a hostile social structure.

Deceit becomes a form of attempted magic through imagination. C. L. R. James quotes a slave who is found with stolen potatoes in his shirt, who cries 'Eh Master, the Devil is wicked. Put stones, and look, you find potatoes.'[1] In a slave story Anancy steals Mongoose's cow, then cuts off the tail and puts it on the ground, crying that the cow is walking into the earth. Cornered with illegal lottery tickets, GB protests:

'Me hate to see pieces of papers flying about the streets, that is the reason why me picked up these papers. Since me open the l'il shop, me notice that children came with dirty 'ands to buy eatables. Me teach them sanitation by using the papers me picked up, to wrap t'ings.' (p. 96)

Significantly, both the slave and GB use the oppressor's morality in an attempt to overturn it. The former appeals to the master's religion ('the Devil is wicked'), and the latter, to the British reverence for hygiene. Neither of these attempts is successful, but GB's upward progress through society is a measure of how far it can work. GB's first major success comes when attending Parson Allen's services. In reality she is searching for clues to the winning numbers for that week's 'Drop Pan', but her earnest gaze and jotted notes convince Allen of her religious fervour, and she becomes part of the respectable church society. When she is installed in Parson Wallis's rectory, her pious attitudes make the running of a major stolen goods

[1] C. L. R. James, *Black Jacobins* (N.Y., 1963), 15.

and drugs ring appear to be the poor coming for spiritual counsel from a latter-day saint. She makes respectability her weapon against respectable society.

GB uses religion, but is also the victim of her own version of it. She is deeply religious—biblical phrases and images are always on her lips, often with sincerity. She inhabits a world ruled by God like a gigantic Drop Pan game. 'God is like a man sitting over a pack of cards, and we blind sinners never knows when God is going to deal aces.' (p. 7) He is a God of money. On 'the walls of her heart' were written 'Money is the source of life, my hope and salvation'; 'blessed are the rich'; 'they that wait on the Lord shall receive money'. (p. 79) He is a cruel God. Her greed for money and praise blind her to the deceit of the religious brothers she entrusts with collecting for her departing present from Swine Lane, and when settled in Kingston with Kate, anxiety over money lent to her daughter shadows the pleasures of success.

Bennett even attempts to give GB a theological role. She takes the title 'B.A.', Born Again, with the suppressed addition, 'B.D.', 'Born of the Devil' (p. 138), and her activities seem to be related to those acted out by Panty, who impersonates the devil in a curious Sunday School entertainment—she is the spirit of greed and discord. But this theme does not work out. There is no opposition of good and evil. The 'good' Christians are as unloving and hypocritical in their own ways as GB, although they may be more self-deceived. Parson Allen and his wife dominate the gallery of English do-gooders that batten spiritually on the hunger of the Jamaican poor. At first there is some sympathy for Mr Allen. He is committed to his vocation, and when confronted with the evil-smelling, pot-bellied Panty, straight from the slum gutters, he recoils but has him taken in—although actual relationship with his daughter would be unthinkable. But even this virtue is undermined. He is a fool, and his acts of charity are ways of gaining prestige from his parishioners and for his own self-esteem. His anti-racialism is only a front for the worst forms of racial prejudice. He tells Panty:

I am only one of the millions of open-minded Englishmen who do not believe in the nonsense called race-prejudice. I personally like your people and, as a clergyman, regard them all as God's children. . . . Race-difference was ordained by our living Father in Heaven and it is presumptuous of some to want to alter the divine plan and law. (p. 210)

To which Bennett adds that Jesus was a descendant of a mixed marriage contracted between the Jewish Ruth and the Moabite Boas.

All complexions and groups of Jamaican society come under Bennett's unsparing eye. The clergymen are fools or lechers, respectable society is hypocritical, the common people are criminals. The points are often tellingly aimed. The social climber from poor black society, Russ, 'needed class barriers to protect him from his past'. (p. 177) Mrs Allen remarks smugly 'We English are famous for our charm.' (p. 104) And GB hopes the judge will not ask questions, for the British are characteristically too proud to admit ignorance. (p. 91) Such observations are straight satire, and can legitimately be given without a compensating picture of the good side of life. Indeed, it is Mr Bennett's attempts to diversify the fable and invective of his story that lead to the book's weakness.

Especially in the latter half of the novel, the story focuses on Panty. Dr Ramchand, who rightly points to the failure of this sub-plot,[2] sees Panty as the stereotype of the mulatto in Caribbean society, fitting neither into the white nor the black worlds. But although his light colour is important, it is not the key to his tragedy. Abandoned by his mother, given grudging protection by GB, at once taken up by the Allen family and rejected by the wife as a slum-child devoid of any human value, Panty grows up without any real personality. 'His heart was sterile, unable to conceive true and deep affection.' (p. 206) He turns to promiscuous sex as the only human relationship

[2] Kenneth Ramchand, *The West Indian Novel and its Background* (1970), 41–4.

possible to him. When he strikes down GB as a hindrance to his own aspirations, justice—as far as justice exists in this book —has been satisfied. Panty is also a retribution to the society that fostered him. He has no social responsibility or moral sense. The portrait is predictable, but not without conviction.

Unfortunately Panty's story, and the passionate love that grows up in Kate for her lost son, jars with the comic, satiric mode of much of GB's part. We accept it when Quashie gets thrown into gaol for picking up his lucky number at Drop Pan watched by the police; or when Parson Pendance dies of heart failure when being shaved by a barber threatening to murder the man who has seduced his daughter—who happens to be Pendance. But when Panty has an affair, and the girl dies of an overdose of sleeping pills in a gambling den waiting for him, other tones emerge that the story cannot take. And the language Bennett uses to try to realize the tragic elements for the reader becomes forced—as when Panty imagines 'the terrible words "gutter-rat" . . . written on his forehead in red'. (p. 128)

These however are but weaknesses in a story dominated by the splendid figure of GB, even when lust for money and an intermittent sense of insecurity in her Kingston eminence prevent her from enjoying some of the rewards of a life of hardworking deceit. Her dedication to herself and to money gives her a certain integrity the 'good' elements in society lack. ''Tis 'ard to get money in this country unless you get a fair and honest chance to steal it' (p. 164), she says with complete sincerity. There is logic if not victory in her plea to the court: 'She pleaded guilty but insane. She said that if she must admit guilt, it was a sure sign that she was not mentally normal.' (p. 95)

Harry's final statement 'God Almighty is a great stonebreaker . . . GB was a good stone' (p. 248), surely denies the spirit of the book. There is no God above GB's universe, only money and respectability created by a materialistic society itself. Harry is closer when he says: 'The world we live in is a stone. We all are stones.' Until this world undergoes radical change there can be no heroes, only anti-heroes. Like Anancy. Or GB.

Alvin Bennett was born in March 1918. In 1954 he came to England as British correspondent to *The Gleaner* group of newspapers in Jamaica, and became involved in the problems of the immigrant community. These form the basis for his novel *Because they Know Not* (1961), set in London and Kingston, Jamaica.

Louis James

I

Middle-aged, Jamaican spinster Beatrice Brown demanded the title 'Granny B' as a mark of respect since she could not be designated as Mrs. In her view, social respect was also due to unmarried women who reached a certain age, especially if they had offspring. She considered herself deserving of social honour, being the grandmother of an illegitimate descendant.

According to her, grandmotherhood was a social rank, hence she insisted that anyone calling her should put a 'handle' to her name. She thought the title of 'Miss' humiliating for one past thirty.

All her workmates who broke stones in the Rockhill quarry in rural St James, near to Montego Bay, affectionately addressed her as 'GB'.

A fervent gambler, GB was obsessed with a lottery known as Drop Pan which was very popular amongst her set.

She lived in a slum area appropriately called Swine Lane, where she was tenant of one of the king-sized dustbins constructed and filled with rubbish.

A self-appointed local historian, GB knew embarrassing secrets of almost everyone in the district, her malicious knowledge being frequently sought as reference whenever her colleagues were engaged in verbal hostility. She readily supplied oral ammunition replete with forgotten scandals and pernicious slanders to all contenders. This was only one of the many reasons why she was very popular in her social group.

All her fellow stonebreakers at Rockhill quarry hated their supervisor Fanso Smith, who came fortnightly to inspect and watch the measuring of the broken stones. The women nick-named him Pharoah, and amongst themselves exchanged end-less bawdy jokes about him. They claimed that he should be treated like a pair of stockings—never passing a woman's knee. His abrasive yellow skin was likened to a hedgehog afflicted with chicken-pox, while his voice was said to sound like that of a rhinoceros suffering from nasal catarrh.

It was from GB that these stonebreakers learned all the unhappy facts regarding Fanso's antecedents, making him the target of the women's ridicule whenever, with assumed airs and graces, he came to supervise and pretend superiority to the stonebreakers.

'None of us should say anything bad about Fanso,' she would advise. 'He come up a long way to reach low class like us. It was not the poor man's fault that his mother died of fright when she saw his colour near white. It could happen to any of us. It was just her bad luck to be living with a man that was the colour of tar.'

Assuming the attitude of defending Fanso, GB produced earthy chunks of slander of Fanso and his family, while her companions hammered their stones and listened to her.

To Fanso, GB was excessively charming, always bowing respectfully while offering him the warmest smile to light her dark, drawn face.

Impressed by GB's manner, Fanso recommended other stone-breakers to follow GB's example of politeness and good breed-ing. GB would give a clandestine wink of the eye to her colleagues on these occasions when Fanso was not looking at her.

As unofficial midwife of the slums, GB suffered loss of fees due to Fanso's promiscuity and irresponsibility. Because he was her supervisor, she received no fees for delivering babies fathered by him and, knowing her operation to be illegal, she could not make loud claims for payment. Because Fanso was in her debt many times over, she hated him. However, she flattered him although everyone but himself knew she was insincere. To her co-workers she expressed her diplomatic policy thus: 'If you hand in tiger's mouth, take time draw it out . . . otherwise . . .'

Fanso was always glad to hear her speaking of the nice man he was and how handsome and important was his father. For her kind remarks, Fanso gave GB the chance to measure her stones without supervision. No sooner was he at safe distance, than GB would say: 'Me can't stand the ugly brute. His mout' resemble crocodile with yaws. De father stole from de mother, and that's how Fanso came to be born, and he is just like his pa: a criminal.'

GB idled many evenings, loafing in a Chinaman's grocery shop in the futile hope of getting clues about the Drop Pan game operated by the Chinese grocer.

From the time, a few years aback, when her landlord Quashie made an unsuccessful attempt to rape GB's daughter Kate, GB immediately stopped paying the 1/6d. per week rent for her shack.

Quashie hid for a long time during which he kept an accurate account of GB's growing indebtedness. The rent for the shack was skyscraper-high when Quashie reappeared to collect his rent.

His weekly attempts at persuasion were frustrated by GB's procrastination and insincere promises. In due course his patience was exhausted and he gave GB one week to pay or get out.

At the expiration of this period, GB hearing his approach like the rumble of thunder, sent Panty her five-year-old grandson to lock the door from outside and to tell Quashie that she had gone to collect money to pay the rent.

The frail, malnourished youngster rushed to carry out his grandmother's instruction and, forgetting to lock the door, ran to meet Quashie half-way.

Rushing madly to the shack, Quashie took a claw-hammer from his canvas satchel and struck the flimsy panel a mighty blow.

3

Panty began to cry: 'You will kill mi granda!'

The first crashing sound sent GB scurrying underneath her low wooden cot. The second bang caused her to run out to deliver herself up to Quashie and beg for mercy.

Heedless of her pleas, supplications and promises, Quashie was determinedly continuing the demolition when, in a frantic last effort to stop him, GB thought of a dramatic act. She must have suddenly remembered that she had an old knife in her hand. She looked at the weapon, turned the back carefully and proceeded to pretend to be cutting her throat.

'This is the end of it all now. Me will be no more trouble to nobody no more.'

The psychological emollient had immediate effect on Quashie. He stopped breaking up the house and turned his head away so that GB would not suffer any lack of privacy in her last desperate deed.

Through the corner of her wizened eye, GB noted Quashie's indifference. She changed her act and resumed her pleas for mercy, but Quashie interrupted her: 'Pity you didn't think of it sooner. It is better for everyone if you kill yourself. All me is begging you is that when you kill yourself, you lie down in the grave and not let your damned duppy come back to haunt the place.'

GB promised that her ghost would never return to Swine Lane. 'Dead or alive, if me gets a chance to leave Swine Lane, me would never come back.'

She now called his attention to Panty, saying that it was because of the child that she was unable to meet her commitments.

Quashie became more furious. He cursed Panty and his mother, who he said was too high to go with her own colour and instead gave herself to a 'no-good mulatto' man who would not look at his own offspring.

GB agreed with him but assured him that it was not Panty's fault.

Now Quashie continued his destructive work with redoubled

4

energy whilst GB sought desperately to calm and restrain him.

'Cousin Q, if even me owes you till me die, the Almighty God knows I would never rob you out of a penny.'

'Woman, shut your cockle-mouth. You takes me for a damned fool! How could I collect when you dies?'

Upon GB's assurance that God pays the debts of the poor, Quashie retorted that there was no money in heaven, otherwise the Church would not have to do so much begging.

GB insisted that God pays all debts in the end: 'It is only that Him is a slow worker. If you want anything done in a hurry you 'ave to ask the devil. Massa God takes years to do what the devil can accomplish in a minute. We must 'ave faith!'

'Faith makes you remain in the house although it is falling down. What you want is ambition. You complain that it leaks when rain comes, and yet you won't go.'

GB protested that she would never run away from her responsibilities. It would be dishonest to leave owing the money. 'What would you think of me, Cousin Q, if I go away secretly with the money I owe?'

'Nothing, just as me think now.'

Seeing that all efforts had failed to relieve her perplexing situation, GB sighed: 'Oh God, make me win a few pounds in the Drop Pan game to pay my honest debts. I'd give Cousin Q a nice gift.'

With eyes sparkling with unpleasant surprise, Quashie exclaimed: 'Ahoah! Now I know where all your money is going! Now I know why you can't pay the rent! You gamble out the money. You give it to the Chinaman and then give me only prayers and sweet words. I see!'

'Cousin Q, the Bible says we must persevere to the end. Me can't stop buying now; me invest too much in it already.'

Quashie puckered his accordion lips thoughtfully, burning his rolling red eyes into GB. GB squeaked; the frail thread of her vocals seemed ready to snap: 'Me pray every night, but the damned Chinaman hides the winning number from God Almighty himself. Me pray for you too, Cousin Q, that God will help you never to need to 'ave to come and bother me.'

Directing a malicious gaze at her, Quashie advised: 'Pray for another 'ouse tonight. God 'ave plenty mansions and you can owe God, if him will trust you.'

Vigorously, he continued to tear down the hovel, shouting at the top of his voice: 'Many of your betters sleep under piazza at nights. You don't 'ave to pay rent.' Quashie flapped his lips like a lobster fighting for life, then he added: 'Deep in my heart, deep down, me love mi own coloured people, no matter what me say or do. When a white man take advantage of any of my people, it hurts me to mi very bones.'

He recounted a tale about the brutal white landowner who instructed his agents to remove a house whilst its delinquent tenant was away: 'They put the woman's few jeng-jeng outside and moved the 'ouse on rollers. The woman had to sleep on piazza where she caught a bad, bad cold and died of a broken heart. That is how white man cruel to black people. Me feels to cry when me think of the story. Me could never do a thing like that. Me prefer to break up the 'ouse before your face. My heart is too soft to do wicked things.'

GB pointed out that the shack was in too poor a condition for him to remove it.

Quashie rebuked her for wasting his time with silly arguments, but GB assured him that he was wasting his own time when he could fold his hands and get all the money he wanted.

'Buy number fourteen today for all you can afford,' GB advised, reminding him of the Bible saying that to him that hath more shall be given.

Quashie resisted the suggestion violently, assuring GB that he never gambled in his life and that he loved his money more than he loved women.

Persuasively, GB told him about a vivid dream she had had, and then directed and urged him to go to the Drop Pan vendor's house. As GB spoke, Quashie remembered that he himself had had a strange dream the previous night. It could be luck, he thought to himself. GB saw that Quashie was considering the matter deeply, so she said:

'God is like a man sitting over a pack of cards, and we blind sinners never knows when God is going to deal aces. God is always shuffling his pack, and me believe it is your turn today, Cousin Q.'

Before going on the winning mission, Quashie swore that if GB caused him to lose his money, there would be plenty trouble. He hurried away, promising to return.

GB raised her hands to heaven in silent prayer of thanksgiving for the deliverance, then immediately began repairing the shack.

'That infernal brute must have bought his 'eart at a butcher shop. Him is the dead stamp of a tadpole.'

Suddenly, she remembered that Panty was around, and addressed him, 'You damned li'l idiot. Is you make Quashie know that me was inside.' Panty denied the accusation but GB upbraided him, advising him that he must never tell lies, unless she told him to.

With all her energy she continued the repairs to the shack and as the hours passed she did not even wonder why Quashie did not return.

On his way to buy number fourteen as GB had instructed, Quashie made a brief stop at a rum bar where he had a large white rum.

Whether GB had deliberately misdirected him or whether he had mistaken her directions, it is not known, but Quashie went to the wrong house.

When told that Drop Pan lottery tickets were not sold there he asked for direction. A man came out of the house to accompany him and during their search for the lottery house Quashie told of his dream and coming good fortune.

Having found the correct house, Quashie threateningly admonished the vendor of the ticket:

'Get it straight, me don't want any cock-and-bull story if

me win today. Me don't make fun with money and so me expect to get pay if I win. Any foolishness, I go to the police and put the lot of you in gaol.'

Having bought his own ticket he introduced his companion, whose name he did not even know.

'My friend want to buy some numbers too. He is just like myself, won't stand for any chicanery. We both will make trouble if we don't get paid when we win.'

The transaction completed, Quashie was now inducing his companion to hurry from the place lest there should be a police raid.

'There is one on right now,' assured Quashie's companion.

'One what? If you delay to make joke, you might be caught indeed. If police catch us in here we will get into plenty trouble.'

'Don't worry yourself about that,' assured his companion, 'I am a detective.' He took his card from his pocket to prove his statement.

'Well, today must sure be my lucky day. It is a good t'ing I come along with you. Now there can be no cheating. I hope you win too. With you, I feel protected.'

'I will have to get someone else to protect you. I'm arresting you and the vendor for breach of the gambling law. The government protects everyone who is in prison. Don't worry yourself. That's what governments are for—protecting prisoners!'

Quashie's bottom lip fell like a trap door on his chin whilst his facial muscles began a spirited St Vitus dance.

Realizing the extent of the trouble he was in, Quashie began to beg for mercy, pleading that he himself had a most urgent work of mercy to perform. He said that he was repairing a shack for a poor homeless and sick old woman in the slums. He was sorry for her plight and if he didn't go to help her she would have nowhere to sleep.

'We must all 'elp each other. We is all the same colour. We must not be too 'ard to one another.'

8

The other arrested man said nothing.

On reaching the station, Quashie vividly volunteered his life's story to show that he was hardworking, honest and an entirely good man, not like the other fellow who sold lottery tickets and robbed the poor. His tender supplications for mercy could only be made by the merciless.

Apparently, he convinced the gullible detective of his goodness, because the detective assured him that his talents would not be wasted if he went to prison.

'Prison is now very short of good men. They need them in there badly. There is hardly a better place for a good man than a prison. There he has the greatest opportunity to be an example for the not-so-good chaps. If you get a long term, you might accomplish a great deal for the community by your example to the bad men.'

Quashie pointed out that any superintendent of police or magistrate could give evidence on his behalf for they knew nothing about him: 'If me was a bad man, they would know me.'

He promised that if given a chance, he would never buy any more illegal lottery or do anything wrong again.

'Don't say that,' rejoined the detective. 'If you and the rest live righteously, there will be no work for the police and we could lose our jobs.'

Ironically, when the result of the game was known, number fourteen indeed was the winner.

Unfortunately, the game was played without Quashie's stakes being received by the proprietor who on hearing of the vendor's arrest, conducted the game without returns from him as there were many other purveyors of the illegal lottery tickets who had done business normally.

The result proved beyond doubt that GB indeed was a good dreamer.

2

An ardent believer in the God of Luck, GB mumbled a prayer of thanksgiving when she heard the news that the number she had bought was the winner. She took the opportunity of promising to honour and obey her Creator if He would only reveal to her the winning lottery numbers daily in advance.

Taking credit for being a very reasonable person, she held to the principle that one good turn deserved another whether it was God or man doing the first turn. Indeed, she believed the principle even applied to the lower animals for she always remarked on the dog's habit of turning twice before it lies down. Here was patent proof that one good turn deserved another.

It grieved her deeply, however, to think that her enemy Quashie won on his first attempt. He would have to do a good turn to her, she resolved. He had no right to win, because he never prayed like her, never studied the game, never lost his money in it. It was hard for her to appreciate his success. This caused her to soliloquize: 'Massa God should practise more division and less multiplication of money.'

She now definitely decided to pay no more rent since it was her dream which was responsible for the fortune which she thought Quashie had won.

In the midst of her contemplation, whilst she vacillated between joy and sorrow, her fellow Drop Pan addict and close collaborator Sue Browley, a buxom matron a few years GB's senior, arrived with the news of Quashie's arrest.

'Thank God!' GB exulted. 'God is a just and righteous man.'

Addressing Sue directly, she said: 'Well if you brought me money, I could not be gladder. Me shall pray tonight that the good Lord make them hang Quashie or send him to prison for life. Prison is like the Sabbath, it was made for man. God will 'elp me to make Quashie come to grief. God can do not'ing wrong. If God even kills a man, it is not murder and in any case nobody can ask him about it.' Sue inquired if GB had won much. In a rather poorly voice, GB complained that the small amount she won would be entirely devoted to Panty's needs which were legion.

She was thus making sure that Sue would not beg her any portion of her winnings.

'As soon as you're gone, me is going to collect the little mite.'

GB was hinting that Sue should depart. When she lost she wanted Sue's company for consolation, but now she had won, she found the company embarrassing. She wanted to go alone to claim the fairly large sum she had won.

Sue now disclosed that she had already collected the 3/- which she won, the vendor having brought it himself to her. Sue said that the vendor did not want people to come to his house for their money as there was trouble in the air.

GB had bought from another vendor, who according to her, was too proud to take around the winnings to his clients.

'Me prefer to go for it myself anyway because whcn people see him come here, they will want to borrow if they know that me win somet'ing.'

Picking up the hint and wearing a triumphant smile, Sue now assured her that there would be no money for her to collect as the vendor had been arrested along with Quashie.

The shocking, disappointing news rocked GB so much that she forgot the secret she was keeping and confessed that she had lost over £7, which was the share of her winnings.

Without regret Sue encouraged: 'Never mind, GB, it proves

that you are a good dreamer, and me sure that God will give you more dreams.'

GB did not need much cheering, since she had the good news of Quashie's arrest. She also drew comfort from the fact that he had not profited from her guidance.

Sue regretted that her 'age', station and lack of beauty prevented her from getting hints, known as 'rakes' in the Drop Pan jargon. Almost querulously she said that the young girls received all the favours from the Chinaman: 'Some mothers send their teenage gals to make the Chinaman play with them and give them Drop Pan rakes.'

GB pointed out that she had delivered many half-Chinese babies resulting from these 'rakes', but she praised the Chinaman for his honesty in paying the midwifery fees: 'If all the men were like him, me would not 'ave to work and fret so hard.'

The next evening GB was jubilant. Perhaps only the celestial joy can surpass the mundane ecstasy which sinners know at the defeat and misfortunes of their enemies—and sometimes of their friends.

GB heard that Quashie was imprisoned for six months and described by the judge as an incorrigible ragamuffin who initiated and supported numberless vicious activities in the community. Quashie's appearance was his undoing. Had he been possessed with the heart of an angel, it would do little for him, since he owned the face of a thief.

Believing that God was on her side, and herself rid of rent-paying for six months, GB neglected everything to dedicate herself to the Drop Pan game. Her grandson Panty, a thinly covered skeleton whose pot-belly GB likened to that of a frog pregnant for an elephant, was not growing normally. He was rather being stretched on the rack of slow starvation, his stomach becoming a self-inflated windbag. He often supplemented his irregular and inadequate diet with assorted refuse, eating everything he laid hands on in his truly hand-to-mouth existence.

13

Commenting on his performance, GB admitted that what was hidden from the wise was revealed to babes. She declared that she had never known such things could be eaten, but God had revealed the secrets to Panty to save him from starvation. Seeing him eating something dirty, she merely said that dirt didn't kill anyone unless it fell on them.

'Dirt is medicine,' she said. 'My mother use to give dirt and water as cure for bitter-cassava poisoning.'

Evidently, a general immunity was mysteriously conferred on Panty, enabling him to eat infected material without any worse effect that mild diarrhoea.

With other little scavengers from Swine Lane, Panty rummaged garbage-bins over a wide area in the suburbs of Montego Bay nearly within reach of the luxurious world-famed hotels.

Saturday was their festive day, when these starving, ragged urchins, the bane of street-cleaners, scrambled for their richest spoils of offal to sustain life in them.

When Panty complained of hunger, GB gave him food for thought in multi-course lectures, telling him of the generosity of God. When hunger pains convulsed his stomach, GB terrified him that such was the punishment of God.

Fairly regularly, GB attended the Anglican church. In her own way, she trained Panty to be godfearing, never allowing him to eat anything without first giving thanks. If and when Panty was reluctant, she warned him not to trifle with a God who would choke him to death with the food in his mouth.

At nights, she left Panty alone in the unlighted shack in order to save burning paraffin. She went in search of Drop Pan discussions or attended meetings of the Pocomania group, a pseudo-religious, superstitious cult who worshipped at nightly saturnalias with revelries of praying and dancing to drums.

GB made it a rule never to go to bed with a full stomach in order not to impair her faculty of dreaming. Panty was also made to conform to the odd practice. Usually he was awakened at about 6 a.m. forced to accompany GB in a long, foolish morning prayer in which he was given the solo part near the end thus: 'God bless Granda and make her win the Drop Pan today for Christ's sake. Amen.'

On being asked about his dream, Panty related a vision in which he saw GB dead.

'Death in dreams mean long life,' GB interpreted. 'In Drop Pan it is number three.'

When Sue called later on, GB whispered to her the dream, urging her to buy number three, but to keep it a secret.

In the evening when they heard that number three was the day's winner, GB and Sue were on their way to collect their money when they met an excited crowd using violent and threatening language.

GB collapsed to the ground like an empty sack when she heard the news. So many people had won, that it was impossible to pay them all.

The crowd now gathered around GB. An old woman smoking a chalk pipe took charge of the fallen GB. Touching GB affectionately, she announced to the crowd that there was no need to worry. She diagnosed GB's case as nothing serious: 'It is just her 'eart that fail, and if it start up again she will live.'

In order to restore GB's apparenly lost breath, this woman asked for something to fan the air into GB's nostrils. Whilst she was fanning GB and mumbling jargon, a vehicle stopped to take GB to hospital.

Sue was doubly sorry—both for her friend's collapse and for the fact that it was she who had advertised the number three against GB's good advice.

Regaining consciousness in hospital, GB looked up into two deep, blue crystal eyes and felt scared that God was looking into her heart. The eyes, however, belonged to the Rev. Michael Allen, a naïve, young English clergyman with less than two years' residence in the island. In his wear-polished black suit, the pious minister was unaware that his presence and serious demeanour nearly frightened GB to death. Instantly remembering Panty's dream, GB suspected something funereal in the clergyman's presence and strongly assured him that she never felt better in her life.

The fear of death accentuated GB's recovery, and when next Parson Allen visited, it was to find a GB who appeared as if she had successfully completed a course in calisthenics. The muscles of her speech organs were apparently renewed. Following a few words of cheer and consolation, Parson Allen told GB of the great help she was to him in his ministry. The shock nearly caused GB to relapse and the ensuing perplexity drove her into dumb silence.

'I watch you when you come to church. You are very attentive to everything I say. You take notes of the word, and it gives me pleasure and confidence to know that all the seeds are not falling on stony ground. I often wish that all the people were like you: we would have a great spiritual revival in the Church. I know that the words you write will bear fruits a hundredfold.'

'I pray it will, Parson,' said GB earnestly. However, she deemed it impolitic to enlighten the clergyman as to what she wrote in church. She admitted that the parson's words and sermons had helped her. In her mind was the particular occasion when she bought number twenty-three in the Drop Pan game and won on a Monday through the hint she received from the pulpit. On other occasions she had juggled with numbers with favourable results.

Parson Allen told her that life was indeed a two-way operation: 'You give me encouragement, hope and power to help your people and you get back blessings and comforts. How truly wonderful has our Father in heaven arranged things!'

Before Parson Allen departed, GB begged him to pray that her dreams would come true. Not understanding the peculiar meaning of 'dreams' in GB's request, Parson Allen promised faithfully to accede.

During GB's stay in hospital, many new buyers were brought

into the Drop Pan game, and GB herself won more than usual, a fact she related to Parson Allen's prayers.

Parson Allen was very pleased to note GB's popularity at the hospital and inferred therefrom that she was a special kind of missionary whom God had chosen to spread the word amongst her people.

She mentioned her concern about her grandson Panty, who could not visit her for lack of suitable clothes. Parson Allen volunteered to help, advising her not to worry herself as everything would be put right in God's good time:

'God loves you and will solve your problems for you. The same God who brought man redemption by way of the cross, life by way of death, will work out your welfare in a way you cannot now see.'

'Me know that, Parson,' assured GB. 'Me never imagine that in hospital me would have so much good luck. God 'elped me in a mysterious way since I come to the hospital, and even before I came here God showed his love for me.'

Of course, GB referred to Quashie's imprisonment and her freedom from paying rent for six months.

3

Sue Browley had a feline appearance as she closed her eyes in prayer:

'Please, dear Lord, make GB get well quick so that she can come and take her damned fair-skin gran'pickney. Thou knowest, O Lord, that me is a poor woman and cannot afford to feed strangers.'

Her welcoming words to Panty were: 'Your mother was a damned fool to bring you into the world since she didn't know your pah. She only caused unnecessary trouble for innocent people like me. Me might as well tell you that me don't like your colour. If you was pure black or pure white, it would be much better; but you come-between mulatto people is always ungrateful. GB can afford to bring up a bird to pick out her own eyes. Me is different. Me know that if you once gets a chance in life, you won't notice poor me; you will despise your own black gran'mother.'

After this energetic welcome, Panty humbly adjusted himself to Sue's shack which was nearly as bad as GB's. He liked it, however, because there was no restriction on his movements and no questions asked about his comings and goings.

During the Christmas season, he excitedly returned to tell Sue that he had seen God. Seven-year-old Panty had known nothing about Santa Claus, hence inferred that the man with the flowing beard, giving things to children, was of heavenly origin.

In defence of God, Sue screamed at Panty's unwitting blasphemy: 'I will teach you to respect Massa God.' She slapped

Panty across his face with her fat hand. 'God is not a man to make fun with, you little idiot. He will take away his little blessing and prevent me from winning anything. If you say any such thing again, outside you go and I know that God will be pleased with me.'

Panty's diet was drastically reduced. Sue gave him nothing without murmuring and indeed the insults were more than the food was worth.

Panty was absent for two days. Sue thanked God for the relief. Never being a mother, she was destitute of maternal tenderness. As a result of Panty's disappearance, she ceased visiting GB in hospital, excusing herself by saying that she was saving GB from needless worry. After Panty had been gone a fortnight, Sue met Parson Allen whom she tearfully informed of the boy's abscondence, making an insincere show of affection for the missing boy.

Parson Allen's high cheekbones, bushy eyebrows and prominent nose depicted solemnity normally, but now Sue's information caused a disfigurement of the clergyman's face.

By the time he reached home, his slightly hunched back seemed to be carrying the burden of Atlas. Rashes of sad thought pimpled his brains, and more than ever he resembled a built-in load in his shabby black suit.

He told his wife Marcia the depressing news and, with much interest, Mrs Allen sympathized with the plight of the unfortunate waif.

That evening, Parson Allen's golden-haired daughter Paula, a seven-year-old, asked her perplexed father what was wrong when he was kissing her good night at bedtime. Parson Allen was near to tears but he assured her that all was well.

For a long time afterwards, he sat pondering the inequities of the world as the inquisitor inside him flung a fusillade of double-barrelled questions at his brain.

Why are some children born to neglect, destitution, crime, disease while others, like Paula, have everything?

Who made some children dead to rapture and only alive to

agonizing starvation? Were children such as Panty included in the invitation to heaven? Is heaven a kingdom populated with teeming ragged, half-naked urchins killed by the neglect and injustice of the world? Was God really concerned about all children of all races, classes, colours, and creeds? Was compensation claimed from the privileged and recompense given to the incapacitated when they all reached over yonder? Will millstones be hung around humanity's neck and they all be cast into the sea for the perpetual offence caused to the children of the poor?

Representative of manger-born Christ, Mr Allen now experienced uneasiness regarding his own comfort. He thought of Panty roaming the street, importunate, hungry and homeless. It made him sad.

Humming softly, thirty-year-old, mouse-brown-haired Marcia Allen entered the sitting-room to keep her husband company as usual. She was plainly dressed in a thin, light-blue cotton frock. She adjusted the cushions before sitting in the large, soft throne-like chair in front of her pensive husband.

'I'm very worried about the little boy,' said Mr Allen, looking intently into his wife's homely face. There was no semblance of glamour about this young woman, evidently bred from austerity. Her short upturned nose, small downward-curved mouth and thin lips gave her a Medusan aspect.

'My dear, don't put it on your conscience. 'Tis a pity for the poor child, but he is not the only one in the world like that.'

'You see, I had promised his grandmother to help and while I procrastinated, this should happen! I feel quite guilty of neglecting him. His grandmother is such a fine Christian that I'd like to do something for her.'

Mrs Allen suggested that slum kids were hard as bricks and that the devil takes care of his own. She did not see how it would help the boy if her husband sat and fretted about him. She imagined that some of the boy's well-off compatriots would rescue him.

Mr Allen expressed further fears at this suggestion. He said that it was possible that someone would enslave him under the guise of rescuing him: 'Some of these people rose from slavery to be slave-masters and they have no pity for the oppressed.' He admitted, however, that the boy's chances were much better because of his light shade of skin. He made a passing comment on the practice of shade prejudice whereby people are socially graded in ascending order of lightness of skin. He said that he thought the practice very stupid.

Returning to the matter on his mind, Parson Allen exclaimed determinedly: 'I must find the boy. It is my duty.'

The rectory was a twelve-roomed cut-stone colonial mansion of two storeys with side-verandas on both floors. Luxuriously furnished, it stood a few yards back from a main street on spacious grounds defined by neatly trimmed hedges. A beautifully-kept garden glorified the front, whilst the back court-yard had an amply-paved barbecue on the edge of a large lawn. A big mango tree shaded the range of out-houses providing a natural barrier between the rectory tenants and the domestic staff.

Traditionally, this rectory was a cathedral of class- and colour-prejudice, black and poor church-members being forbidden to use the front gate. Jesus the Carpenter would have been introduced into a back room but a dashing, dapper Judas would be sumptuously entertained in the upper room with the best Christian hospitality.

Successive English religious sophists highlighted the lack of discrimination in the church, where poor blacks could sit anywhere in the back, without causing raised eyebrows. But a clergyman's home was a private institution, not subject to the rules of public Christianity. A few sensible people in the community described the English clergymen who came to live in the rectory as direct descendants of St Peter, and their particular resemblance to the saint was the fact that they too 'Knew Not the Man', their master.

Thinking aloud, Parson Allen informed his wife that he

would visit Ragged Sunday School in Swine Lane on Sunday afternoon to seek the lost sheep of a boy.

Mrs Allen supported the decision, telling her husband that his efforts were certain to increase his prestige in the community:

'They will realize how much you love coloured people when you go to so much trouble to rescue one of the least of them.'

4

In Swine Lane, heavenly hope was the product of earthly desperation. Hungry, naked and perplexed people were forced to wait with philosophic passivity on the second or third coming of the Unknown God to sort things out for them. Gods of gold have always appealed to man, but Swine Laners expected a spiritual entity with a Midas touch—he needn't be made of gold, so long as he could make things golden.

In the balmyard was a big hut for chapel, where Swine Laners worshipped and where mothers sent their fatherless or many-fathered or wrong-fathered children for Father God to bless them and Brother Christ to accept them, as there was no one else who particularly wanted them. Some children misunderstood the use of the collection plate, thinking it was the means whereby the rich unseen Father sent small coins for his needy children. These took what they could, but hoped that the unseen Father would be more liberal.

Education at Ragged Sunday School was the only sort possible for Swine Lane children, as they seldom had proper clothes or enough food to permit regular attendances at an ordinary school and, in any case, there were never enough places at day schools for the ever-increasing number of children.

The teacher at Ragged Sunday School was a fat man of medium height, with a large shining bald head and in his early sixties. He had a broad pleasant face and his kindly eyes twinkled every time he smiled. His cheerful spirit and love of religion compensated for what he lacked in formal education. They called him Brother Sanko, alias the Founder. He was happiest when talking about 'de Lord', but he also derived considerable satisfaction from discussing world politics in spite of his limited literacy. In the severe tropical heat, he never considered himself properly dressed without a thick black waistcoat which formed an indispensable part of his Sunday attire. As often as not, he was without a tie and sometimes even without shoes.

With gusto he led the group of children in the theme song of the Sunday School:

> Around the throne of God in heaven,
> Thousands of children stand.
> Children whose sins are all forgiven,
> A holy happy band.

Then buttoning his eyes tightly in prayer he repeated:

> Here we suffer grief and pain;
> Here we meet to part again,
> In heaven, we part no more. Amen

It was his unfortunate experience over the years to see many whom he had taught to sing about the happy heavenly band, standing in the prisoner's dock. On one occasion he wept bitterly to see one of his former Sunday School graduates on a murder charge. Between sobs, he then vocalized: 'Everything grows in the slums, except what is good. Sweet fruits and pretty flowers may grow in stinking manure, but no human virtue can grow from a bad heart poisoned by slum air.'

Brother Sanko was a widower for many years and, having no children, was a veritable godfather of all slum kids. From his small wages as a street-sweeper, he gave frequently to little charities benefiting destitute children. 'Me was one of them myself,' he said each time he made such a donation.

His tidy little room on the edge of Swine Lane was always

open to juvenile guests. In spite of what the more orthodox religionists claimed, Brother Sanko knew that it was futile for the hungry to ask God for bread. He told his pupils that God was no baker and heaven had no oven.

When Parson Allen visited Ragged Sunday School, Brother Sanko inferred that it was a definite sign that God appreciated his work. Parson Allen inquired about Panty, but Sanko, anxious to engage the clergyman in discourse, spoke of the incident when Jesus absconded from His parents. He suggested that Panty might be on his Heavenly Father's business. Parson Allen was not amused. From what he saw, he was sure that Jesus would never have visited Sanko's temple, nor would God give such an illiterate man as Sanko a religious message to deliver. The modern God of Parson Allen's acquaintance preferred to send the wise and prudent to preach the Gospel.

The children were all excited at the sight of their visitor, some of them thought that he was Jesus, whom they were told to expect any moment.

One boy, however, said: 'It is not no Jesus! Jesus don't wear trousers; 'im wear frock, like in the picture.'

Information about Panty was sadly lacking. His closest friends Chichi, Ragoo, Psyche, Bobo and Trim said that they had not seen him.

Parson Allen felt insulted when Brother Sanko asked him to talk to the children. Like the Levite Priest, he walked on the other side of duty. 'Tell them that God loves them all,' he advised Sanko and rushed away.

He returned home to pray to the One who counts the very hairs on the heads of mortals.

Discussing the matter with his wife, he was told that in prayer we sometimes contravene divine will. 'What if God has chosen this way of removing the child from the slums?' asked Mrs Allen. 'It is presumptuous to ask for his return!'

'I shall ask God that His will be done for the boy.'

Mrs Allen thought that such a prayer would be stupid: 'God's will must prevail. God does not need our permission to

27

do His will. I think that if we can be concerned about the boy, God in His mercies surely is more interested than we are.'

Mrs Allen did not think this was a matter to pray about. It was one of those problems which the Almighty should handle on His own without human interference, help and advice. If the boy even died, it would be God's way of bringing him relief from the terrors of slum life. She agreed, however, to ask members of the Daughters of the King Society to look out for and help the boy if they saw him.

At evensong, Parson Allen's sermon was based on the parable of the Good Samaritan. He felt self-righteous and proud of himself to be showing such keen interest in an unimportant negro boy:

'And if ye salute (or help) your brethren only what do ye more than others? Do not even the Pharisees so? Christianity demands that we do not limit our goodwill to our own class. Whatever we do for those in our own station is nothing but a friendly exchange. The same will be done for us, sometime to come. If we do good to those above us, it might be that we are paying tribute, seeking appreciation or under some obligation. But when we do good to our inferiors, those people who cannot reward or compensate, and our good is apparently lost, sometimes seeming unappreciated, that is when heaven owes us, and the saying applies that in as much as you have done to the humblest, you have done to me.

'I believe,' he continued, 'that God can do all the good needed in the world. But mortals were not created just to be idlers and self-servants. God expects us not only to wait to do good when it comes our way, but to go out in search of opportunities to serve all men regardless of race, creed, class or nationality.'

As he made his points he told the story of the missing boy and at the end of his sermon invited the congregation to join in prayer for the lost child.

The prayer must have found a short cut to heaven where it received priority, breaking through all the celestial red tape which entangles human affairs on this plane.

Opening the door on Monday morning, the sham-charm smile vanished from Mrs Allen's face as she beheld a dirty, ragged and smelly coloured boy desecrating the semi-sacred steps of the rectory.

'Go around the back, boy,' she snapped, shutting the door as if to prevent the entry of a plague. Holding her nostrils, she shouted a cry of alarm for her husband who instantly came rushing to see what was wrong.

'Your prayer is answered,' she told him. 'Look around the back and you will see.'

Parson Allen obeyed mechanically, rushing as he was directed.

'Oh my goodness! Gracious God! Oh dear! Oh dear me! Boy where on earth are you coming from? . . . I mean where are you going . . . ?'

'Nowhere, sah,' Panty answered both questions correctly. 'Me hear that the police wanted to lock me up because I ran away from Aunt Sue, so I was hiding under a house. But Ragoo told me to come here.'

'Have you eaten lately?'

'Yessir. I found biscuits and cheese in a dust-bin and Ragoo and my other friends help me, sah.'

Parson Allen rubbed his jaw with one hand, shaking his head regretfully as he gazed intently at the bundle of rags covering the skeletal form of Panty, who resembled a half-plucked chicken which had died from starvation or had passed through a fire.

Commanding Panty to stay where he was, the perplexed Parson Allen returned inside to consult with his wife.

Marcia Allen had slumped on a chair in a state of shock as if she had seen a ghost. 'What are we going to do with him?' she asked dejectedly, adding: 'That brat must be infested with all the bugs in the island.'

'We must find some clothes for him. We can't throw him out like that. These things are sent to try us.' Parson Allen remembered the words of his sermon on the Good Samaritan.

Mrs Allen suggested that the boy should first have a bath or perhaps be sprayed with disinfectant. 'Tell the maid to arrange it; I have no strength to rise up now.'

'He looks hungry to me!'

'Food won't be his problem here. The cat has more than enough. I think we had better ask for a transfer. We might as well go back to England. It is impossible to keep a slum boy here to grow up beside our daughter. There is no evil in the world that this boy doesn't know already. Our daughter is innocent, we don't want her corrupted. I'm a mother; I must protect my own child.'

'Things will work out. God never gives us more than we can bear—for long.'

Mrs Allen, whose faith was not as strong as her husband's, tended to panic: 'What have we done to deserve this?'

Again Parson Allen remembered quotations from his recent sermon: 'I was hungry and ye gave me no meat . . .' He kept silent and went outside to call the maid to give her instructions regarding Panty.

Ruby the maid showed Panty into the junk-room, a palace compared with his former dwelling, and whilst he stood in amazement contemplating his great good fortune, Ruby brought him clothes, saying, 'Ya boy, me donno why Parson brings you 'ere. Slum pickneys are thieves and vagabonds. Go bathe your dirty self in that room there. Use Jeyes to wash out the place when you finish. Me don't want disease or insects to lodge on me. If you want me, call me MISS Ruby, understan'!'

This short, slim, dreamy-eyed dark girl in her early twenties considered herself a *doyenne* of domestics and, like the moon, took her light from the sun as represented by her employers. Looking disdainfully at Panty, she said, 'You look like a Swine Lane pickney. It is the worst sort of people live there.

If you steal any of my things, you go to gaol without your feet touching the ground.'

Unperturbed, Panty had his first shower-bath and, after carefully washing his hands in the sewer bowl, dressed himself in Parson Allen's old clothes. He looked ridiculous, although he was feeling like a prince, as he went to the kitchen for food. In the meantime Ruby prepared the junk-room for him, protesting as she did so:

'Look what me gal come down to in life! Domestic servant is one degree lower than a dog. The damned puff-belly pickney should be my servant. Me is not going to slave for a half-breed, copper-colour, slum cur. Few days' time it will want to give me orders. People of that shade don't know their place although they're neither fish nor fowl when it comes to colour!'

Panty ate ravenously, feeling absolutely convinced that God was really a lover of children, regardless of their birth, state or colour.

Ruby, whilst passing, looked at him with the same lack of love with which a washer-woman with a hand infection looks at a heap of dirty clothes on a Monday morning.

Mrs Allen convinced Panty from the start that he was inferior to 'Miss' Paula. Although they were in the same class at Sunday School, they were forbidden to sit beside one another. Even divine democracy had to draw the line somewhere. Mrs Allen took great motherly precaution to prevent any effluent slum-bred ideas from seeping out of Panty to corrupt her unblemished daughter over whose morality and welfare guardian angels presided.

Paula was, however, allowed unbridled freedom to play with eight-year-old Ronnie Carpin, the son of an English clergyman from the neighbouring parish. Ronnie's father was a very close friend of the Allens and was a widower whose love for his departed wife was surely making a saint out of him.

Despite her obvious antipathy for Panty, Mrs Allen showed great interest in coloured children in general and did many kindnesses to them. She could not make herself love them as

31

equal members of the human family, but she excused herself by admitting that love is not man-made and if God wanted her to love them, He would make her do it. She could only make herself kind and dutiful to them within limits.

Because Mrs Allen passed no opportunity of emphasizing the social difference between Paula and Panty, she caused her daughter to be unduly curious about coloured people as a whole and Panty in particular.

Panty was working in the garden one Saturday morning when two little hands covered his eyes from behind. On turning around, he saw Paula running away as stealthily as she had come. Fear prevented him from reporting the matter to Mrs Allen.

Paula's action was the first of a series of probes and friendly overtures. Although her mother kept a strict eye on her, Paula conducted a very successful counter-espionage campaign more efficiently because she was deemed to be guileless and innocent in all respects.

She slipped out of her room where she was affectionately tucked away and made a dash for Panty's room whilst her parents were entertaining important guests. In spite of Panty's objection, Paula taught him a game which she said she had learned from Ronnie Carpin. It was Panty's first sex-experience, and after his eyes were opened, he experienced man's pristine remorse at eating forbidden fruit. His guilt made him feel uncomfortable in the veritable paradise he inhabited. Fear haunted him constantly thereafter.

5

Coming from the hospital to join her grandson at the rectory, GB was like the biblical thief who was taken by holy hands into paradise. Her delight was increased because Panty was also there, clean, neat and well fed.

Ambitious and versatile, GB utilized her convalescence to learn domestic routine secretly from the maid Ruby. Soon as she was well enough, GB volunteered to spy on Ruby and carry unfavourable and incorrect reports to Mrs Allen. Ruby became resentful of the volume of Mrs Allen's perfectly un-justified criticisms, which caused her work to deteriorate, thus providing Mrs Allen with grist for her fault-finding mill.

In this time of trouble, Ruby leaned heavily on GB, from whom she received spontaneous sympathy. Daily, she un-wittingly gave GB more material to use against her. With deep confidence in her apparent friend but secret foe, Ruby repeatedly rallied GB's ostensibly ever-ready support: 'We are the two blacks in the house. We must unite together be-cause white people don't like us. They depend on us to work for them, so we can unite and spite them.'

GB was in complete accord, advising Ruby not to kill her-self with work for any white foreigner. 'That Mrs Allen,' said GB, 'is a blasted miserable woman. She's just covering up the fac' that she can't do nothing for 'erself. She's not a good servant. She's not used to hiring servants and if she was even a good servant, I say that servants should not 'ire servant.'

Assured of GB's dependability, Ruby whispered confiden-tially:

' 'Tis just since you came 'ere that she is showing off herself. Firs' time she never complained about not'ing. She never knew that a fowl wasn't cooked with its feathers.'

'Me know all that,' assured GB. 'She is a dolly-baby. No use at all in a 'ome. Stop teaching her t'ings. If you didn't train 'er she would not be so smart now.'

Ruby agreed. She would curtail Mrs Allen's domestic education, but she opined that she liked Parson Allen although he acted so 'fool-fool' at times.

GB defended Parson Allen: 'Him is more sensible than 'im looks. It is so Englishmen look idiotic, but yet no nation is smart like them. Parson Allen is so good-'earted that it don't matter if 'im don't 'ave sense.'

Ruby declaimed that slavery was long abolished, hence she did not intend making herself a chattel to heartless white foreigners who had been so cruel to her people in the past and still were.

In total agreement, GB added that white people were very ungrateful to blacks and liked to see black people suffer.

Ruby's expressions were then faithfully memorized by GB for reproduction to Mrs Allen as soon as was convenient.

'Miss A,' she confided, ' 'ouse enemy is the worst kind. You cannot trust some of us black people. It does not matter what you do for us, all you will get is hate. I know 'ow you is kind to Ruby and yet she never has anyt'ing good to say behind your back.'

GB thereupon recited all that Ruby confided in her, adding lies to make Mrs Allen more upset.

Her employers' behaviour soon made Ruby's position untenable. GB was the first to hear of Ruby's decision to quit the job before she was fired.

'Me don't blame you,' she said sympathetically. 'You put up with too much from them. God will 'elp you to get a better job. Anyone knowing that you work 'ere for so long will employ you, because if you can endure it 'ere, you can bear anyt'ing else.'

34

Encouraging Ruby to go, GB flattered the trusting girl: 'You is very intelligent, young and good-looking. You can make a nice home for any ambitious man who has money and want few pickneys. If you don't 'ave the luck to get married, you can still 'elp to people the world. We the older ones will soon die and the world will always need young people to carry on. Trust in God and don't worry. God will send you a good man and me will pray for you. Don't bury yourself in this damned place. Me is not going to stay 'ere long. We only want to get some'ing out of them.'

Ruby's resignation was a triumph for GB, who at once endeavoured to silently slander her predecessor by doing far more than Ruby did.

To the last moment GB frustrated Ruby's plan. Out of vengeance rather than dishonesty, Ruby had stolen a jewel-box containing Mrs Allen's valuable gold chain. She also took a treasured pendant in the form of a compass belonging to Parson Allen. These she hid in Panty's room to be taken at the moment of her departure. However, GB was with her all the time, giving her consolation up to the last minute, so that Ruby left without taking the articles she had stolen.

A few days later, Panty found the box which he took un-opened to GB. She never asked him where he got it. She took it like a sacrament from his hand telling him:

'Don't say a word about this to nobody. What the left side of your mouth knows, don't let the right side know.'

Then, as the boy was going, GB said partly to herself and partly to him: 'A person who walks with head in the air may see stars, but will never find money. It is good to walk with the head down: stars will always be up yonder, but money and good t'ings never on the ground for long.'

Another day passed before Panty found the beautiful pen-dant. It was such a handsome plaything that he decided to keep his mouth shut. Not even GB would know about this.

He must have had it for more than a week before Mrs Allen missed the items and raised the alarm. Suspicion fell on Panty and a search revealed that he had the pendant. He disclosed where he had got it, but no one believed him. He was branded as a thief and Mrs Allen was ready to throw him out. Mr Allen's sympathy prevailed in Panty's favour although he agreed that the boy should be punished.

With a show of self-righteousness and indignation, GB collared Panty and hammered him with her open hand. The heavy blows were accompanied with advice and condemnation.

'Let this be the first and the last. Never steal anyt'ing that is not useful to you. You will get into serious trouble if you love useless t'ings. You is a damned t'ief.'

She hit him hard and long, and when he screamed she hit him again to shut up. The Allens must have heard the cries of the maltreated urchin but, of course, thought it was his justified reward.

After satisfying herself that she had avenged the Allens, GB cursed the boy into his room and went to her own where she searched for the box with the gold chain stolen from the Allens. She fingered it tenderly as if it were a petalled thing. She placed it around her neck for a moment, then returned it to the box.

'If me give it to them, they'll think I am a thief. The best t'ing is for me to keep it for me might never hold gold in my hand again. Parson should have treasures in 'eaven. Neither 'im nor his wife should 'ave gold and such t'ings on earth. Gold was made for sinners, not for saints. Me is holding on to this chain and me will pray that God recompense Mrs Allen for it. Me not giving it back. Me must protect my good name and hide it away where nobody will find it.'

The next day GB helped Mrs Allen search the whole rectory as well as Panty's room for the missing chain. All through the detailed search she comforted and consoled Mrs Allen, assuring her at intervals that she did not believe that Panty had stolen it. Perhaps the item had been temporarily mislaid, she said, promising to continue her unending vigilance until the chain was found.

She undertook to wrestle with God, who she believed would in due time reveal the location of the missing thing. Mrs Allen was forced to admit that GB's faith was the only bright spot in the circumstances.

'Have faith, Mrs A, God will give you more than a gold chain. Me believe that this is just a test for you, but you will find it in the end.'

Mrs Allen abandoned the search, physically tired but spiritually stimulated by GB's assurances.

The Allen family esteemed her to the extent that Parson Allen seriously suggested that she would be better employed bringing salvation to her own people in Swine Lane. He thought she was a kind of unrecognized prophetess, and a living and wonderful example of practical Christianity.

Demurely GB rejected the suggestion, saying that she loved the Allen family too much to leave their employment. She declared that she felt much better working for them than she would working with her own people: 'My people would never show me so much kindness and love as you do. You don't treat me as a servant but as a friend. That would never 'appen if I was working for people of mi own colour.'

In due course, an arrangement was completed whereby GB had freedom to visit Swine Lane as frequently as she liked. Naïve Parson Allen imagined he was indirectly subsidizing an energetic Jamaican missionary and expected a rich harvest of souls, saved by GB from the slums of hell.

In the meantime, GB prosecuted her Drop Pan activities more vigorously than formerly.

One day she met stork-legged Ivy Wattey, nicknamed 'Benky-foot' and one of the most ancient and colourful denizens of Swine Lane. Decrepit and destitute, Ivy complained: 'Oh, GB, I can't win not'ing at all and I can't stop, although I am starving. Sometimes me 'ungry till mi belly roll thunder and instead of buying food me take the last penny to buy a number, all in vain. GB, me beg you to do somet'ing for me.'

GB advised her to go to church and listen to the numbers of the hymns, add them up and divide them and buy the resulting number in the Drop Pan game: 'God works in a mysterious way.'

Ivy confessed that she had no church clothes. One of the reasons why she wanted to win money in the game was so that she could purchase a dress to go to church and worship God: 'Me t'inks God would understan' me needs and grant me a few pounds in the game, but auw . . . !'

GB insisted that church-going was necessary. She said that God was not going to travel to Swine Lane. Those who wanted Him must seek Him at His house. If God went to all the different places, there would be no need for churches. She encouraged Ivy to rend her heart and not her garments, advising that God was not particular about the clothes one wore to church, but only wanted the person to be present in His house, even if merely to take a nap. God, said GB, liked to receive visits from His children.

The hunger-sunken eyes of the haggard Ivy Wattey fell in desperation to the ground. She promised to make redoubled effort to attend church, if indeed that could help her to win in the Drop Pan lottery.

'If God doesn't see you visit 'is 'ouse after too long, He just forgets you and gives His blessings to those present at His place.'

This was the only missionary work GB ever did.

Her visitors to the rectory from the slums were numerous. This caused Parson Allen to glorify God, and himself take some credit for the evangelic work which he imagined GB was doing. Little did he know that all comers were on missions connected with lottery or some other illegal matter.

The rectory grounds had special advantages in that they were relatively safe from police-raids, hence many lottery buyers used them as a sanctuary. GB enterprisingly assumed the agency for distribution of tickets of still another popular Chinese lottery known as Peaka Peow. It proved quite profitable, so later, in collusion with some rascals and spivs and robbers, she became a secret pawnbroker or rather the arch-receiver of stolen goods in the area. Her room was a depository also for thousands of pounds' worth of narcotics, chiefly the noxious weed known as ganja or Indian hemp. At any moment, if the police should call, there was enough evidence to earn GB a few life-sentences, running consecutively. The law would have perhaps discovered that it was quite inadequate to provide fitting punishment for the masquerading missionary GB.

Keeping her Drop Pan papers between her Bible leaves for luck, she could frequently be seen poring over the Holy Book, much to the delight of Parson Allen. At church GB continued to be a sedulous note-taker, or rather number-taker, by which she flattered the unsuspecting Parson Allen.

In his sermons from time to time, Mr Allen made references to the humble, unrecognized saint in his congregation who indeed was spiritual leaven in the community-loaf.

Many vain persons erroneously believed that Mr Allen's tribute referred to them. Secretly they imagined that their little, rather insignificant acts of charity or service had come to the notice of the clergyman.

But GB knew for sure that she indeed was the 'saint' nominated from the pulpit. She accepted the tribute without uneasiness of mind, saying to herself:

'A man of God is always right. God must reveal it all to him. Who am I to contradict?'

6

Swine Laners developed a peculiar concept of God. He was patient when asked favours, but swift with vengeance, ever-ready to hurl fire and brimstone at sinners in the same manner as terrorists throw plastic bombs at their foes. In heaven, He luxuriates on a great Golden Throne holding in His hand a pencil longer than the tallest telegraph pole. Ceaselessly, He records the wickedness of man in His massive tome. He keeps no eraser for those times when He forgives. What is written is written.

Although Jesus continuously makes merciful intercessions on behalf of sinners, God takes little notice of Him, but there have been times when God postponed His vengeance, in order to give His Son an occasional victory. Swine Laners had an incapacitating dread rather than a holy fear for this elephant-memoried God who sometimes waited passively to punish sinners after death. Although they believed that He had omniscient plans for all men, yet He could be coerced by man's perseverance to make frequent alterations to His original intentions. Prayer was a reliable way to weary Him into acquiescence. Swine Laners created their God in their own image, adding ubiquity and power.

Their peculiar deity, delighted to see repentant sinners biting the dust in sackcloth and ashes, was constantly devising devious ways of bedevilling man's earthly life in order to test man's love for Him. His spontaneous wrath could be appeased by bribery, cajolery, adulations as well as through self-sacrifice or intelligent self-service.

The means through which Swine Laners sought to mitigate the perennially smouldering wrath of God was to offer gifts at the annual Harvest Thanksgiving Service. The festivities included religious celebrations on Sunday and a secular concert on the Monday. It was a semi-mortal sin to attend one and not the other.

Harvest offerings were the charity to cover the multitude of Swine Laners' sins. Stealing gifts for the Harvest was neither uncommon nor considered sacrilegious. Rather, it was regarded an act of unselfish devotion to risk prison for the benefit of the Church.

There were those who placed special significance on the trivial gifts, remembering Jesus's tribute to the widow's mite. They imagined that the largest vaults of the celestial treasury were depositories for small coins which God needed in great abundance for distribution to the poor. It was quite in vain that various impecunious clergymen attempted to correct this misunderstanding.

In connection with the Harvest, the church distributed small sealed collection-tins, labelled in red 'God's Treasury' and bearing serious warnings of the unfortunate consequences of tampering with them. The fact that money could be put in these tins freely, but should never be withdrawn, earned them the pseudonym 'Marriage Boxes'. Swine Laners had sobriquets for almost everything.

A few God-dreading but destitute persons made their own collection-tins, which bore no threatening warnings and hence could be broken into for the same reason that caused King David to eat the sacred shewbread in classic times. When extraction was found necessary, they would quote the scriptures in order to excuse their embezzlement: 'He that giveth to the poor lendeth to the Lord.' They reasoned, therefore, that it was not amiss to borrow from God directly and, in any case, the home-made tins were not inviolable as the official ones were.

Sixty-seven-year-old Mother Crocks, alias Mother Young-

Gal, traditionally collected money to produce for the Harvest what she called 'God's Corncake', but which her enemies nicknamed 'Dog's Corncake'. The money left over after purchasing the ingredients for this item was kept by Mother Crocks as payment for her labour. She insisted that God was not like a capitalist, wanting people to work for nothing.

The pastry she produced resembled wax, felt like cork, tasted like chalk, but had the unmistakable odour of boot-polish. In this 'consecrated cake', Mother Crocks placed a high concentration of baking-soda and salt, flour, and orange-peel, but she counted each separate currant and added sugar with strict economy. In spite of her experience and care, sundry foreign matter found its way into the concoction. Once, accidentally, a bad egg was broken into the compound. Finding it impossible to dump the mixture, Mother Crocks philosophized that the cake would be like creation, an alloy of good and bad. Furthermore, she said that the customers would profit because they would never be expecting chicken in a cake. Unless fatal results occurred, Mother Crocks expected her customers' ready forgiveness, seeing that it was for God and the Church that she laboured. Christians were expected to mortify the body for the benefits of the soul. She sold cuts of her sweetmeats at unreasonable prices, but again, since it was in the name of the Church, she imagined that the unfair charges were in order.

Another important character in this farce was a plump, ladle-bottomed, grey-haired woman, Mother Jove, alias Mother Cow-breast. Her short tufts of white hair resembling a crown of thorns, she was the local authority on brewing ginger beer. That she made for harvest was from a special recipe apparently containing gunpowder, vitriol and pepper. In bottles, it exploded volcanically, and one taste of it set the mouth on fire. She called this witch-brew 'Long Remembrance'.

On Harvest Sunday, the church was a mecca to which sinners brought gifts, a temple they helped to decorate from floor to ceiling. A number of them brought trifles in their

43

hands, but huge headloads and heartfuls of sorrow. Un-inhibitedly, they related their cares to each other.

'Me 'ope Massa God look down and sees what me give His church this year. Last year, me give two dozen eggs and one hundredweight of fufu yams. Yet, God never stop mongoose from eating all mi chickens! Rain spoilt all the balance of the yams and in spite of mi very 'ard work, me nearly starve,' a man complained. 'Me trying again now, but any more bad luck and God won't get one damned t'ing and it won't be my fault.'

'Shhh ... hush! You is in God's house. Don't talk like that or God will burn up the church with us all, or strike you dead and me deaf. Move from beside me, quick!'

'Make me talk, man! God can't bother to listen to all our li'l conversations and even if 'im hear, He can't deny the truth. God won't kill anybody for speaking the truth, 'im is not like man.'

In the midst of the bustle and lively conversations, another giver arrived, confronted the altar, genuflected reverentially, made the sign of the cross, bowed and moved her lips in prayer for prosperity. This newly-arrived, wiry, slim little woman approached an acquaintance, 'Snakey boney' Violet, who was stringing peppers around a column.

'This 'arvest is a real blessing for some people,' she said. 'They get more than God out of it. It saved Mary Jane from trouble. Two of 'er goats strayed into a neighbour's garden and eat down the whole crop. Mary Jane claimed that the goats belong to the church. The man 'ad to bear the losses because 'im couldn't sue God.'

'What 'appen to the goats then? Is she bringing them to church?'

'No. It's what me want to tell you now. Mary Jane cook them last Thursday night and sell for one shilling a plate. People buy it good and plenty because Mary Jane told them that the money is for the Harvest. Yet yesterday me see 'er hidin' coming from a store with a big parcel under 'er arm!'

44

GB usually gave service; as a stonebreaker, her wares were not acceptable at Harvest time.

The afternoon service for children was an important session of the Harvest festivities. Children of different races and stations carried gifts in fancy baskets to the altar whilst the happy, admiring congregation sang:

> All things bright and beautiful,
> All creatures great and small,
> All things wise and wonderful,
> The Lord God made them all.
>
> The rich man in his castle,
> The poor man at his gate,
> God made them, high or lowly,
> And ordered their estate.

Following this, the clergyman gave an address stressing the good things everyone received from the generous Father in heaven.

'All you little children should be ever thankful to your kind Father in heaven for your daily food, the homes, the loving parents, the pretty clothes and many, many other blessings you enjoy from the Almighty,' he assured solemnly.

Nearly all the things he mentioned were lacking to the Swine Lane children, hence they thought that as he was only a visiting clergyman, he was ignorant of what God had allotted to them.

During the tedious address, the poverty-ridden elder folks slept. They accepted with passivity the words of the hymn that God had ordered their estate. It was a cruel thing to do it seemed, but they were powerless against God. Now Parson was saying that God had given good things—all they had received, was wants.

On the Monday night, the church-hall was divided into three sections for the big concert. In front was a stage veiled

45

by a thin brown calico screen, in the centre was the auditorium for over two hundred people and at the back were refreshment stalls.

For the concert, Mrs Allen had specially written and directed a play in which her eight-year-old daughter Paula was billed for the star-role as angel. Panty played the 'devil', a role which Mrs Allen thought appropriate to his talent and background.

Provision was made on the programme for two impromptu items to warm things up, so to speak. The announcement was hardly made before a ten-year-old, lanky, potbellied boy whose knees bulged like a pair of footballs beneath his tight, short trousers, was catapulted by his ambitious mother from his seat to show his ability.

Smartly, the boy ascended the stage, bowed energetically, saluted, clicked his heels, opened his mouth like the whale which swallowed Jonah and, forgetting what he was to say, placed his little hand before his big mouth. The impatient audience jeered as the boy shamefacedly withdrew in disgrace.

His frenzied, disappointed, shame-crazed mother came halfway to meet him. Hitting him a box and grabbing him in his collar she led him outside to the whipping-post. No sooner they were outside the building than she shouted: 'Take off the shoes and give them to me now, you stupid, foolish brute. If it was to tell a lie you would not close up your plate-mouth which looks like the behind of a donkey. Come 'ome with me let me murder you,' she invited with enthusiasm.

Although loud voices called: 'Item, Concert! Concert!' no other child volunteered.

The curtain rose on the first scene, showing two small boys sleeping on a rough wooden bed in a shack. From dreamland appeared the devil, circling the bed and whispering to the sleepers:

'Don't go to church. Don't throw your money in the collection-plate when you go. It's a racket. You need the money to buy cakes. The Church has no mouth to feed.

46

Don't respect anybody because they are no better than you.'

Punctuating his advice with fiendish guffaws, he jumped and skipped joyously, then addressing the audience said:

'When they awake, these children will do exactly what I command. I love children. They never want to rule me as their parents do. My father's house is full of them.'

Pirouetting like a *danseur-noble*, the devil hopped gleefully off stage as the curtain was drawn.

The next scene presented two boys playing marbles in the street when a dispute arose in which neither would submit. At long last, one of the ragged urchins, looking a scarecrow, proposed a settlement. Before he could finish his suggestions, the devil thunderbolted into the midst of them.

Putting a friendly arm around each boy's shoulder he asked:

'Have a knife or anything pointed?'

Both boys shook their heads regretfully.

'Pity, pity it is! You should join the Boy Scout movement. They issue knives and teach boys to be prepared.'

Taking the boys into his confidence, the devil continued as they all sat on the ground: 'When the nations have quarrels, they use guns, swords, bombs and bayonets. You are growing up in a civilized world and must learn to fight. One of you might become a political leader, so you must begin from now to learn hate and violence. You must follow wise example.'

The boys, in the meantime, had quite forgotten their contention. One boy remarked that next time he would know what to do. Hereupon the charming devil admonished: 'There may never be a next time. Never, never put off till tomorrow what can be done today and never give up your rights. In the world we live in, everybody is right. All the Churches are right. If they gave up their rights, there would only be one Church.'

Dragging them both to their feet, the devil bumped their heads together, thus starting a fight. When the battle was at its peak, he slipped stealthily away only to return shortly with a collection of broken bottles, stones, brickbats, nails and knives with which he littered a corner of the 'battlefield'.

'Help yourself, gentlemen. Learn to use the things at your feet.'

The impassioned fighters, stimulated by having an impartial witness, fought with unusual violence although they knew not what they were fighting for.

Delightedly, the devil urged: 'Have courage! Never give up! Fight like a lion. Don't mind that cut at your eye. The world loves a good fighter.'

As the boys fought madly on, the devil exhorted: 'There is a justice in the world which protects the weak against the strong. It generally comes into effect after the weak dies fighting.'

Skipping like a happy schoolgirl and laughing weirdly, the devil addressed the audience: 'There is one thing I don't like, it is disorder. I am a law-abiding citizen. I was born in the law courts and my father behind all the laws of man.'

Rushing offstage madly, he returned in a few moments leading a comically fat, short, stupid-looking policeman with a bushy moustache.

'Officer,' he pleaded in his falsetto voice, 'please read the riot act and shoot these two trouble-makers. Rid the world of two young criminals so that it might be a better place to live in.'

'Lemme speak to them,' suggested the officer, obviously drunk. 'Stop it, boys! Pack it up! Gee out of it!'

Becoming irate, shaking his fists, the devil screamed: 'The government expects you to do your duty. Shoot them! What you think government gives you a gun for? Shoot! Fire! Shoot I say! The neighbours want peace and quiet. They pay taxes.'

Slightly aware that the sound of a gun could not increase the peace of the environs, the policeman nevertheless obeyed the devil's command. Luckily, being drunk he did not aim straight. The sudden explosion sent the boys into each other's embrace and when a few frightened people rushed to the spot and saw the boys hugging each other, they set upon the policeman, cursing him for terrorizing the innocent lads. In the meanwhile the devil assisted the policeman in arresting the boys.

Addressing the audience, he said: 'Well, I've done my good deed for today. I'll get another star in my crown for assisting the law. My lawyer friends will be very pleased with me. I provide them with work.'

The curtain went down just as the scene was getting confused. The last scene presented two very neatly dressed white boys, walking and talking harmoniously. Everything about them showed that they were from well-off families. In their nicely pressed blue-serge trousers, white shirts, black stockings and shining shoes, they were vastly different from the children appearing in the previous scenes.

Behind them, the devil came running. He dropped a coin deliberately to attract their attention and, picking it up himself, asked, 'Which of you dropped this money?'

Both boys claimed it at once. The devil suggested that they fight to settle ownership: 'Your parents must have already told you that money is always worth fighting for. You seemed to be well-trained children.'

The battle was just about to commence when the angel, Paula, floated in, resplendent in her seraphic white-and-silver costume with folded wings. Her appearance caused a great stir and spontaneous cheers from the audience. Simultaneously on arriving, she smote the devil with her wand.

'Go away! Don't tempt these children. Leave them alone, you devil!'

Young Satan explained glibly that he was teaching them physical exercises to fit them for an active life. He also wanted to impress them with the value of money, he said.

The angel retorted that she was the protector and adviser of children. Good children from decent homes were not left to the devices of the devil, but each had a guardian angel.

The angel was nimble with her wand, which must have had

a scorpion touch to make the devil scream and squirm with such agony. As he crashed from the stage, the air was filled with melodious music from children's voices paying tribute to the guardian angel.

The curtain fell and the audience rose up in a riot of applause with all the violence of their tropical emotions.

Sue Browley, who was next to GB, commented: 'Your li'l boy is a real devil. You 'ave to watch 'im close. Me always believe that the devil is not a very black man and now me prove it!'

GB was somewhat peeved: 'If there is the devil in 'im, it comes from his father side. But all the same he will grow it out and be a great gentleman someday. He might become a parson for all we know.'

'Some parsons are devils, you know, GB!'

The hall was filled with praises for Miss Paula the angel. Everyone praised the Allens for having such a perfect little lady, a real angel.

While refreshments were being served, an improvised orchestra supplied a weird music. Several couples started jigging, gyrating, advancing and retreating. Some of the fat-padded women moved about like animated jelly-balls.

7

GB and Sue were scrambling through Drop Pan charts at the rectory when Panty surprised them.

Handing GB a pound note, he explained that he found it on the street.

GB's face lighted with joy, but she looked slantingly at Sue at the same time, as she asked Panty:

'Parson knows about it?'

'No, granda!'

'Very good. Sensible boy! Now shut your mouth, tell nobody! Understan'? Remind me not to beat you if you do somet'ing wrong tomorrow.'

Sue watched as a famished bird of prey looks on inaccessible quarry. She wished it were possible to deprive GB of the money.

Noting her uneasiness, GB said to her: 'Good when you train pickney properly. If me didn't train 'im he would perhaps run like a fool to give the money to Parson and that would be the end of it!'

Now GB mildly reprimanded Panty: 'Next time when you find money, don't give me in the presence of strangers. Call me aside or wait till me is alone.'

Panty nodded: 'Yes, mam.'

The envy which was curdling Sue's blood found a means of expression at last when she said peevishly: 'Me is no stranger! It is quite all right in my presence. Don't let 'im feel that me is a stranger, GB.'

'Me don't mean all like you. Me is just training the pickney, for me want 'im to be a gentleman with good manners and kulcha!'

Seeking further approbation, Panty related that on finding the money he sought for the loser, unsuccessfully. This caused GB to lose her patience.

'Go outside!' she commanded drastically. 'You're a damned li'l fool to t'ink Massa God was going to make you so lucky to find two t'ings the same day. You must learn to be satisfied. If the Lord sees that you is unreasonable, He will never let you find valuables again. If ever you find the owner first, then don't bother to look for the money. If you find the money first, then find your home right away, and don't bother look for the owner.'

Frustrated, Panty withdrew, while Sue commented: 'Me don't 'ave a blasted luck! Me never find money yet from me was born. If you give me somet'ing out of the money, I'd buy number seven.'

'Not a bit of that! Me is not touching the money at all! That would be spoiling the boy's luck. By right, me must keep it for a few days to hear if anyone claims it. The boy is sure going to chat his damned mout' off.'

That two cunning men cannot share penny-farthing was being proven aptly in the subtle game taking place between GB and Sue, who now volunteered:

'Me will 'elp, GB. Me know you'd like to find the owner and ease your mind. You feel you is in trouble now!'

'Me used to trouble from me born. You don't bother to 'elp find the owner. You is always willing to 'elp me down, never up!'

GB looked vexed and spoke rather brusquely. Sue observed meekly: 'You know me don't mean any 'arm, GB. Me is your bes' friend; it is my duty to 'elp you in any trouble at all. Count on me.'

There was a moment's silence then GB said: 'This might be a good "rake" indeed. Let's buy number twelve. I'll give you one penny to buy it for yourself, and if you win you give me back!'

'Sure!' Sue acknowledged gratefully. 'Me t'ank you very much!'

GB now began to confess that she indeed possessed a kind heart, would like to help her friends, but could not afford it. 'These English employers still believe in slavery. Plenty 'ard work and very low wages. If God only 'elps me to win a few pounds in the Drop Pan game, I'd retire and open a business of my own!'

'Me wish you luck, GB, for 'tis long time you battering in this world.' Sue was really sincere in this wish because, like a jackal, she was hoping for the portion of the booty refused by lion GB. Sue's envy for GB increased every time she visited her, and now she was upset at GB's latest good fortune. With a sad heart, but a happy countenance, she left GB's company. On her way from the rectory, she met Parson Allen, to whom she curtsied, saying: 'Howdi, my sweet minister.'

The naïve Parson Allen acknowledged the exuberant greeting with a polite bow, making the mistake of pausing for a chat. In recognition of the honour done her thus, Sue was eager to be entertaining and interesting. She felt obliged to report something important. At first she thought of mentioning the pound which Panty gave to GB, but on second thoughts she changed her mind, just because she had received one penny already.

'Minister,' she said, 'me 'ope you know that all the people loves you very, very much. That's what myself and GB was just talking about. We called your veneral name few moments ago and now I sees you. You're going to live long, Parson.'

'Very kind of you to say that. Thank you very much!'

Parson Allen was moving, but Sue detained him by saying: 'Yes, Parson, I meant Reverent Sor, the people seys you is better than Parson Moston. They didn't like him, although

53

he was a Jamaican-born whiteman. They used obeah, black magic, to kill the poor man.'

'Oh, what are you saying! Dear me! dear me!'

'Is the truth, Parson. You don't know, but many of your church members believe in and practise necromancy. They formed a committee and pay an obeahman to set duppy on 'im!'

Wishing to disentangle himself from this embarrassment, Parson Allen made a second attempt to go, but Sue followed.

'Yes, Parson, Reverent Sor! People were vexed because Parson Moston told them that Jesus the good shepherd didn't come to save goats and monkeys like them. He was no man of God. Besides, 'e was very rich, but a meaner man God never made.'

Parson Allen was unable to hide his boredom. 'Well,' he said, 'I must go now. Excuse me!'

Like a barnacle, Sue stuck to him, quickening her steps and her speech at the same time: 'Yessor. It was a shame to see 'ow the poor man suffered before 'im died. He bawled like a goat, mongoose, monkey and all kinds of animals. It was a johncrow-bird that came to live in the rectory which caused his death. The bald-'ead bird jumped upon the dining-table to eat with Moston. Parson got into a temper and hit the bird and from that moment 'im was no more use to 'imself. GB can tell you all about it, because she was on the committee!'

Having given this last information, Sue was willing to release Parson Allen. She would never imagine that she had indirectly increased the Parson's esteem for GB: he felt that her association with the committee of superstitious people was in an attempt to enlighten them.

GB had never mentioned anything about superstition to the Allens. True enough, she asked Mrs Allen about dreams, but Mrs Allen imagined that GB sought heavenly guidance through this medium. GB was in such good grace and favour with the Allens that everything she did enhanced her prestige. Exploiting her employers' good will, GB formed an apparently affectionate attachment with Miss Paula, to whom she devoted nearly as much time as the child's mother. GB suspected that something clandestine took place between Panty and Paula, but she pretended total ignorance of the matter.

Vividly, GB remembered being intimate with boys when she was less than seven years, so when she became aware of Panty and Paula getting together, GB took a very sympathetic view. She made herself feel that it was her Christian duty not to deny the children the pleasurable experiences:

'Pickneys should enjoy themselves, for when they gets older like me, they won't 'ave any fun in life. It will be all work and no play!'

With feminine intuition, Paula sensed GB's strongly indicated connivance and took full advantage.

GB was now luckier than ever in the Drop Pan lottery and with all the other fortunate circumstances added to her life, she inferred that God was very pleased with her. In her prosperity she sang:

'He has put down the mighty from their seats and exalted the humble and meek.'

Her constant advice to Sue and all others was to 'have faith in God' who would help them to conquer all adversities.

GB had many items of stolen property, clothes and shoes which were useless to her personally, but she hoarded everything greedily, deceiving herself that her loot was a blessing from heaven. She pretended not to know that the wicked shall prosper for a time.

Exulting in soliloquy on one occasion, she said: 'De good Lawd never allow the crow to eat grass. The fattest carcass is not too good for the vulture when God is ready. God give everybody meat in due season.'

8

GB accidentally bruised her ankle against a wooden box projecting from underneath her bed. The wound became progres-
sively worse in spite of several applications of ear-wax mixed
with tobacco-ash, GB's panacea. An amateur alchemist, GB
made a poultice of stale bread, castor oil and sulphur, but
this also failed to heal the expanding sore. When prayer did
not show the desired result, she was forced to seek proper
medical attention.

The doctor, a young Englishman, advised exclusion of
starch and sugar from her diet, a recommendation which
instantly kindled GB's anger: 'Then, docta, you expect me
to eat so-so fat? Me can tell you that not a t'ing wrong with
mi inside, because mi bowels move reg'lar. It is my ankle
giving me trouble. It is not foot and mouth disease me 'ave.
Not'ing is wrong with mi mouth or mi belly, only mi foot.'

'That condition is caused by——'

GB interrupted to tell the doctor how she had received the
damage to her ankle. The doctor again tried to tell her why
the wound was slow to respond to treatment. She was a diabetic,
he said, and begged her to follow the instructions regarding
diet.

GB remained dumbstruck for some moments, then she asked
cynically: 'Tell me, docta, where was you all the while? Me
would 'ave been so glad to know you when me 'ad to suck
salt to stop worm from coming up from my belly to mi throat
to see what's 'appening why them starving. That was the time
for diet, because me didn't 'ave any food. But now me is

57

getting good nourishing food, you is telling me to cut out all the t'ings me like. Consider your mind again, docta; it isn't right and fair to me!'

'I'm trying to help you to enjoy years of happy eating! You'll soon be all right if you take my advice.'

'Me 'ope so! It is very 'ard to restrict eating when me don't have to buy food. Me know long time that if me eat till mi sick, me will 'ave to fast to get better, but me moderate miself becausen mi don't want to miss one day of good eating.'

Good-humouredly, the doctor explained his recommendation to GB who after much argument and opposition reluctantly promised to co-operate.

As soon as she was alone, GB stressed her distrust for the new-fangled medical ideas: 'Me never 'ear that food kill anybody yet, unless poisoned. Many ton-loads of people die from starvation, but never from bellyfull! That young docta is green, don't know one t'ing. Because mi foot swell, 'im t'ink that if me stop eat the swelling will go down. A docta like that can't mix salts for a puppy-dog.'

Pretending to have medical knowledge superior to that of the doctor, GB decided to disregard his advice. To convince herself of the logic of her action, she soliloquized:

'Cow, horse, dog and all the animals eat night and day and not one of them ever 'ave diabetes. They don't 'ave no docta to find fancy name for when they feel bad or to tell them to stop eat. Diabetes is for rich people. Those rich, white people that eat too much fancy t'ings—'tis them that God punish with disease to make them stop eat. But poor me can't 'ave those 'igh-tone sickness. We poor people can only 'ave yaws, malaria, consumption, worms and such t'ings, but the big name disease is for the upper class. My grandmother was hundred and was eating up to the last day. She died with food in her mout'.'

For the next few days, GB lived a normal life and was just convincing herself that she had won a victory by not taking

58

the doctor's advice, when suddenly she collapsed and had to be hospitalized.

As soon as she was conscious, she prayed sincerely, promising God never to disobey a doctor's orders again. Responding rapidly to treatment, she soon became a nuisance and, eventually, a source of humour to the hospital staff. She complained that she was fit enough to have many of the things forbidden in her diet. She said that she could understand that restrictions are necessary for a sick person, but she was feeling too well to suffer any curtailment. She accused the doctor and nurses of conspiring to starve her to death because she was poor and black. However, the nurses treated her with kindness beyond her merit. Perhaps it was because they regarded GB as a sorceress with particular ability to make correct Drop Pan forecasts. On account of her advice, many patients and members of the staff bought and won in the Drop Pan game.

Shortly after leaving hospital, GB heard that Parson Allen was to be transferred to Kingston, the capital city of Jamaica. Sue Browley strongly advised GB to follow the Allens, but GB would not hear of it. She said that she knew nothing good about the capital. It was full of rogues and parasites in human form. Drop Pan game was never honestly played there, and the people did not like strangers.

'T'ink of Panty, GB. Kingston would be good for 'im.'

GB agreed with Sue, but informed her that that had already been settled. Panty would be going along with the Allens. She said that Parson Allen loved Panty as he would his own son:

'Me could not stand in the boy's way of progress. Parson is going to edicate 'im, and with 'is light-colour skin, that boy is going far in life, I tell you, Sue. Light-skin people much luckier than blacks.'

'That's true t'ing you talk, GB. Light skin lucky both with black and white people. They get jobs quicker than black people and they don't 'ave to wait as long for promotion and big pay.'

59

GB again stressed her desire to see Panty get on in life to make her feel proud of him. She told Sue that it was for Panty she was saving her money in order to prevent him from encountering the sufferings she had passed through. She prayed ceaselessly for him.

Sue left the rectory on that occasion with mixed feelings, sorry that GB was not going to Kingston, but glad that she was not losing her old friend and collaborator. Poverty had made her selfish and intriguing, envious and jealous of GB, but still there was a strong sisterly feeling for the scheming, toiling GB.

Parson Allen readily agreed with GB that she should remain to continue her supposed missionary work amongst her people. He strongly recommended her to his successor as a conscientious, dedicated, devout Christian worker. Arrangements were settled for GB to continue her tenure at the rectory, where the new incumbent could profit from her experience.

At the time of the Allens' departure, GB was almost too disconsolate to say good-bye. Hot, regretful tears burned her cheeks when she kissed Miss Paula farewell. Sanctimoniously, she blessed the departing family, promising to remember them in her prayers.

From her stock and store of illegal things, GB chose suitable items as gifts for the Allens, trusting that their imminent departure from the community would prevent embarrassing identification of any of the items.

GB's heart skipped a beat when Parson Allen promised to show to everybody the gift he received from her. Neither Parson Allen nor GB herself imagined the true value of the set of gold cuff-links and studs which GB had acquired from a hard-up thief.

The Allens praised her generosity and unselfish sacrifice. GB took the opportunity of exhorting Panty to obedience and good behaviour as he was going to be a fine gentleman.

9

Parson Allen's thirty-two-year-old successor, John Jacob Wallis, arrived with his pretty twenty-nine-year-old wife Doris at the rectory to commit themselves irretrievably into GB's web. The soft-spoken, medium-height Englishman was extremely sociable, lacking the hauteur characteristic of his class and typical of his nation. Childless, the Wallises possessed every other blessing to make them happy.

At first sight GB loved Mr Wallis with the same kind of affection a cat holds for a mouse or a spider for a fly. Mr Wallis gave her two pounds, which assured GB that he was a true man of God.

Sue's impression was that God would punish Parson Wallis for marrying such a beautiful woman: 'A parson's wife should never be so pretty, it will prevent him from keeping his mind on God's work. Parson Allen married the right type of woman.'

GB started gossip: 'Me hear that she don't want any pickney, she don't want to spoil her shape. They are very rich and well-to-do people from the best families in England. Parson is very godly although 'im look like a sport boy. He put somet'ing in my hand as him arrive.'

Sue regretted that it wasn't she who was working for this rich and kind couple: 'You always lucky to work with kind people!' As GB did not comment, Sue continued: 'Me t'ink that Parson should make his wife 'ave a pickney. It will do them good.'

'Perhaps Parson sleep too much at nights, or maybe don't knows his bed-duty. Some of these 'ighly educated, rich white men fool as duck when in bed with a woman.'

'Ahow you know all that, GB?'

'Someone told me so,' GB protested with virtuous innocence.

Consequently, the two friends penetrated deep into the private lives of the strangers, suggesting a number of things which would help the Wallises produce a family. GB promised to administer aphrodisiacs in Parson's food, which would be sure to result in twins. She was keen for Mrs Wallis to have children to occupy some of her time, lest she become a problem to manage in the house.

Shortly after the Wallises' arrival, there began a new social era and there was a noticeable popular curiosity directed to the church. Doris Wallis became a church 'pin-up' girl for all the young men, whilst her husband was a social thunderbolt.

Enemies quickly mushroomed amongst the snobs. Mrs Wallis's sincere smile was soon given evil meaning. In ignorance of the Wallises' background, some of the neo-socialites scandalized them as obviously low-class English peasants. They declared that the real high-class English were nice to nobody, could not be sincerely affable, genial and human to ordinary humble people, especially if such people were black. English people of quality did not fling their monies around to make a show, but decently piled their riches in bank vaults. They did not put Christian ethics higher than social mannerisms. The Wallises, therefore, were definitely not blue-blood English. The English members of the church described them as either Irish or Scottish.

The informality of Parson Wallis's manner and dress—he wore neither symbolic phylactery nor the orthodox 'dog-collar' —was volubly criticized by the modern Pharisees in his congregation.

It was considered tantamount to a confession of his own depravity to have admitted from the pulpit that he was an ordinary sinner equally in need of the prayers of his congregation as they were of his.

In due course, the white- or fair-shade members of the church volunteered hints to make the Wallises less approachable and more sophisticated. The clergyman and his wife, however, proved to be as independent in their minds as they were in their means.

GB, a virtual elder sister of Satan, became an important figure in the Wallis household and at the same time had the best chance ever to prosecute her illegal affairs.

Mrs Wallis gave her several garments for distribution to the needy in the slums. GB sold the worse ones, keeping the others for herself, and although she now had no necessity to gamble, the habit was too obsessing to discard. Figuratively, she had caught a lion which wouldn't let her go.

In Swine Lane she was a respected buyer of stolen goods and every thief loved, admired and esteemed her.

From Swine Lane, GB hurried back to the rectory where someone inquiring for her had been directed. On arrival, GB met a shapely young lady, beautifully begowned in a dark-maroon suit trimmed with fine white-lace edgings. GB admired the very attractive woman from head to toe, fixing her adoring gaze on the stranger's dress at first, then examining the exquisite white-felt hat with the veil to match the dress. The woman's handbag, smart pumps and gloves all blended in a veritable symphony and told GB that she was obviously in the presence of someone of importance and wealth.

Beaming a flattering smile, GB asked: ' 'Ow is the nice lady? Me wonder what she bring for me.' The visitor's charm and glamour accentuated GB's inferiority complex.

As the stranger spoke, GB advanced closer, her heart rumbling like a boiling kettle. Shading her eyes, GB's mouth went agape involuntarily and no words could express her surprise.

In a voice of delicately sweet assurance, the visitor with a disarming smile, said: 'Yes, GB. It is your own daughter Kate.'

63

Regaining speech after a few seconds, GB exclaimed:

'Oh me lawd God! Kate! Katey Marks! Make me look good!'

Now assured of the identity, GB continued her scrutiny in consternation.

Kate prepared herself for a demonstration like that which the prodigal's father gave his home-coming son. She stood still, the gates of her heart flung wide open as she awaited the kiss of welcome, forgiveness and love in expression of the eternally flickering spirit of kinship which all the wars cannot extinguish in the human breast. Kate could not move as she stood before her mother and her judge outside the outroom in which GB lived. With quivering lips, and trembling with emotion, GB puckered her brow, loosened her jaw, narrowed her eyes and, going through a series of meaningless antics, exclaimed:

'Katey Marks, tell me somet'ing? Ahow you mean to leave me with your bastard pickney all the long while withouten support? Where in 'ell did you expect me to get money to feed and clothes it? You ought to know that me is as destitute as church-mouse! Answer me now?'

GB's facial expression was hard and pitiless, her voice a rapier. Obstructing Kate's attempt to explain, she unleashed a barrage of questions: Who was the child's father? Why did Kate go with a man who was ashamed of her or she of him? How much did the man pay her . . . ?

Parading her own imagined virtues, GB said: 'Me is a woman that never go with a man whose name me couldn't call. Me never in any confusion at any time because me only had one man at a time. Me 'ad krakter and me valued the only saleable t'ing Massa God gave me.'

Although GB could never recall the number of men with whom she had had intimate contact, she considered herself a paragon of feminine virtue because, as she said, she only had 'one at a time'.

She claimed that she was amongst the most decent of her

set and perhaps in the wider community, for according to her, she was very careful, otherwise she would have had a number of half-naked bastard pickneys without fathers to support them.

'Me used mi 'ead more often than me used mi 'eart and other parts.'

Kate was abashed, shocked, frozen but penitent. Her blood was a Stygian fluid, or it may have been lead that her heart pumped. Suddenly, the scene wobbled before her tear-filled eyes as she found herself asking to be taken inside.

Leading her in, GB repeated the question: 'Who is the father?'

Kate staggered into the room, flinging herself down on the nearest seat.

'Where is the child?' she asked wearily. 'I'd love to see him!' She sighed wistfully with some exhaustion.

With manifest hostility, GB thundered: 'Don't you t'ink me should get answer to my questions before me tell you anyt'ing? How come you now just get suddenly interested in the boy?'

Kate shifted in the chair she sat in, kicked off her shoes, then rose up and threw herself across the bed. Like a victorious pugilist GB hovered above her victim, ready to strike again. Kate was sobbing. GB therefore filled the silence by saying that she hoped the boy would not grow to be like his worthless father.

Kate tossed restively, making well punctuated groans. GB seemed to enjoy torturing her daughter and so continued to say many evil things: 'Me was certain of your father when you was born. He was a worthless brute in the end, but everybody know that 'im did look like a good man when 'im befriended me. It was a mistake on my part, because 'im was not in my class, me could get much better than 'im.'

Kate's hands moved to block her ears, but she seemed to be still hearing GB's unkind comments. When at last Kate spoke, her voice splintered like the rupture of a fragile thing:

'For Christ's sake stop it—NOW! Stop it! Finish!' She was hysterical. 'I can't stand it any more. I am going now.'

As Kate struggled to her feet, GB assumed the defensive. Touching Kate's arm, she declared: 'You can't treat your own mother like that. You know that me don't mean anything. Me is just acting as any good mother must. Me is very glad to see you, but only that me want to know who is the boy's pa.'

GB's modified attitude encouraged Kate to tell everything. She knew the boy's father without a doubt, he being the first man she knew intimately and the only one up to the time she conceived. It was not she who was ashamed of the man. He was well respected and very important in the community, so his name had to be kept from dishonour. He was a gentleman.

'What 'im name?' GB's voice was filled with the smoke of burning impatience. 'Tell me the man's name!'

'The Reverend John Oswald Pendance.'

GB exclaimed: 'You mean the Reverend Pendance from Mount Joy church!'

Before Kate could comment further, she continued: 'That damned old 'ypocrite! When that man preached on the Baptist pulpit, 'im rake up all 'ell in sinners' hearts. No wonder 'im used to organize those big mass weddings, saying that 'im stamping out illegitimacy. He used to stamp it in before 'im stamp it out. I suppose it is the funeral that you come to attend now. The old brute gone straight to hell.'

Kate recaptured for GB the first Friday night after Christian Endeavour meeting when Pendance forced her. In subsequent meetings they were sweethearts and when she became pregnant, Parson arranged for her to marry his yard-boy to keep her on the premises. Her refusal vexed him and he threatened to give her trouble if she called his name. He told her that no judge in Jamaica would believe her word against his. She would go to prison if she made a fool of herself.

Pendance it was who sent her away to work in Kingston

soon after the birth of the child, promising to see that it was given help, as he was the Chairman of the Poor Relief Committee and President of the Save the Children Fund.

Kate emphasized: 'He told me not even to write about the child to anyone, not even you.'

GB volunteered the comment: 'And the brute never gave the pickney a single penny. Well, that man! He should have been wearing his trousers back to front instead of his collar. His 'ead was so big me always wonder 'ow 'im get in down through that collar, but that man was really smart.'

Kate continued, to disclose that Pendance wanted her to get rid of the unborn baby, but she was afraid to drink the mixture he recommended: 'He then advised me to fall without damaging myself badly.'

After a long silence, GB spoke as if arising from a dream: 'You know what! This might be a good "rake" in the Drop Pan game. Me is going to buy number three. It is the number for dead rogue. Me soon come back; rest yourself a few moments.'

Kate dozed in GB's absence. She was refreshed on her mother's return to tell her with effervescent joy about her own progress and that of Panty. Kate listened entranced to every mention of Panty's name.

Her maternal love was considerably excited as GB told about Panty's intellectual achievements and his ambition, ending by saying he was very nice-looking and would be a great man like his father: 'All we must do now is to give him a good chance to become a big shot, then we claim 'im.'

'I'd love to see him,' Kate beamed wistfully. 'Whatever money I can save is all for him.'

GB assured her that Parson Allen had fully adopted him and treated him like a son: 'The Parson don't know a t'ing about colour prejudice. He is a true man of God, a true-hearted Englishman.'

Kate blessed the good Parson and his whole nation: 'English people are like that,' she stressed with conviction.

67

GB prophesied that Panty would be a world leader, having been reared in decent surroundings and not like the slum children. Moreover, she relied also on his light complexion to influence his fortune favourably in a shade-conscious world.

'White people will always 'elp that boy. We blacks not 'elping anybody, not even ourselves.'

Kate opened chapter two of her story. She said that on going to Kingston she worked as a domestic servant in the home of friends of Parson Pendance. They were black Jamaicans of the middle class.

The account she gave of their brutal treatment of her nearly caused GB to cry. Kate admitted that she was contemplating suicide when Russ Paul found her a job in a rum bar and became her intimate friend from then.

Her ascent in life began from that point. She sold rum from stock, bought supplies wholesale to replace what she sold and kept the profit. In other words, she bought goods and sold in competition with her employers on their premises. They did not find out, because the business was very good anyway.

After saving sufficient money, she combined with her boy friend Russ in a secret partnership. Russ, a married man, always on average bad terms with his wife, was also a civil servant and thus could not do business publicly.

To GB, Kate described Russ as very handsome and digni- fied, well-built and but a few years her senior. He had light complexion, beautiful semi-straight black hair and was very highly educated:

'He has no children with the wife and that is the chief dissatisfaction between them. He discovered that his wife lost a few babies for different men before marriage to him. He thinks that I am a lady compared to her. He doesn't know that I have an illegitimate child, and I don't want him any the wiser.'

GB congratulated Kate on all points, but in spite of her knowing now the reason for Kate's previous silence, she still suggested that Kate could have sent a few pounds anonymously.

Kate undertook to compensate for the past. At this point, she made a running commentary on the attractive red-tiled bungalow of which she was owner-occupier in Kingston. There was a fairly large mortgage on the house, but it was being steadily paid. The furnishings were elaborate and beautiful.

Kate regretted that Russ was a heavy drinker and a reckless gambler, otherwise he was the most true-hearted man in the whole of Jamaica: 'I could never think of being unfaithful to him, for he is so faithful and kind.'

GB agreed that drinking was a serious fault, but gambling was almost a virtue. It was like investing into a bank and only needed perseverance. From her own experiences, she could state that God helped gamblers who showed patience.

Kate described the domestic servant in her employ. She said that she treated the girl very kindly, paid her reasonably and made her quite happy. The girl was very appreciative and respected Kate, who hoped that whatever good she did in the world would be inherited by her beloved son.

GB said that she knew that a girl child was the best investment for a woman. She was proud and glad to be Kate's mother.

Now Sue Browley arrived. Bowing with deference to GB's glamorous guest, Sue showed some diffidence about joining the company.

Looking askance and smiling proudly, GB asked: 'Sue, don't you know the lady?'

Sue gazed sheepishly into Kate's face, fearing to offend the important lady by staring too directly. She then shook her head, but nevertheless hazarded a guess that the stranger was an American tourist.

Kate enjoyed Sue's perplexity for a moment before revealing her identity.

In utter amazement Sue observed: 'Well mi God, what a pretty lady you turn out to be! Is true old people says that when a pickney is ugly, it will grow to be good-looking. You look so lovely, me could never believe that you is GB's daughter.'

Sue filled the moments with adulatory tributes to Kate, recalling the favourable omens she had noted in Kate's childhood. She said that she could have prophesied that Kate would be a great lady.

The conversation turned inevitably to Drop Pan, when Sue informed GB that number three was the winning number. Kate attempted to congratulate GB for winning, but GB winked at her to keep quiet.

As GB did not show much enthusiasm about the information, Sue imagined that, for once, she had been more lucky than GB. She promised to give GB one shilling out of the fifteen shillings she had won.

Kate looked at her mother with a feeling of pity for GB's rapacity, concluding that whilst breaking stones, GB's heart had become lapidified.

Sue was unusually radiant when she left the company and as soon as she was gone, Kate continued to beg GB to come to live in Kingston.

GB adamantly refused, saying that she wanted to die where she was born and that she was quite happy where she was: 'When God bless you, it is foolish to remove from the spot. It is like running away from the rain of blessings to shelter in drought.'

IO

With excitement, self-righteousness, curiosity and the unnecessary malice some people cherish for those who can no more
offend, GB accompanied Kate to Parson Pendance's funeral.

Strangely enough, although he had been the first to violate
Kate against her will, in their subsequent intimacies, Pendance
had obviously touched her where a woman's love is manu-
factured. Since then, she had feared him, was disgusted by his
heartless hypocrisy, sickened by his philandering, but deep in
her heart she passionately loved this unlovable man. That was
why she was willing to abandon her own child in order to
protect the social reputation of the father. Poor, humble and
poorly educated, she still carried in her bosom true love.

The death of Pendance made Kate realize the depth of her
secret love for him, but now, at the funeral, she'd hurt his
memory if she showed the grief she then knew.

The funeral was an amorphous public picnic. The large
crowd at the obsequies could have well been attending a circus.
The difference was that in this particular case, few were
interested in the clown who was being paraded through the
streets on top of a horse-drawn hearse, demonstrating to all
that no clown ever sees the audience at his last performance.

For Pendance, this final act was his finest and most sincere,
yet he would not have delighted to hear the appreciative
cheers or laughter as he rode in state to the grave.

At this fiesta-funeral, subsidiary attractions included a fash-
ion show, a flower show, a motorcar- and bicycle-rally, friendly
get-togethers and sundry entertainment. Since funerals are

the only diversions certain people can afford and the only social gathering with a welcome for them, the ghoulish throng found Pendance's funeral a rare banquet.

The highly polished mahogany casket with shining brass fittings bearing the last remains of the human enigma Pendance earned the envious praises of the mourners.

The funeral procession, headed by religious leaders of many denominations, included people from every social strata. Shining motorcars followed by pedal-cyclists and pedestrians, wearing apparel of every imaginable colour, formed a snaky line, the head of which was indifferent to the tail. People in the extreme back discussed matters which had no relation to funerals.

At the church and again at the grave, clergymen became eloquent with oratorical clichés. The deceased was described by his colleagues as the epitome of Christian virtue, a friend of the poor, a loving father of the fatherless and a devoted disciple of the Lord Jesus Christ. Some of the eulogies were obviously reserved for the fraternal use of parsons.

Appropriate hymns were sung and prayers were offered imploring heaven to welcome the newcomer amongst the congregations of saints.

With a mischievous restiveness, GB elbowed Kate all during the proceedings and once whispered in the grief-deafened ear of her daughter, 'If all these parsons are like Pendance, 'eaven will be full of li'l bastard angels when they go up.'

There was some genuine sadness in the crowd, but at the same time, some young men who envied Pendance when he was alive suggested that venereal disease was what brought Pendance's end so suddenly. Somewhere in the large crowd, indefatigable insurance salesmen were using Pendance's death to influence possible clients. One was saying that it was insurance money which paid for the elaborate funeral. It was because the widow had no expense that she bore her bereavement so stoically, they said: 'He was worth more to his family than when alive.' 'Many times when you hear relatives weeping at funerals it was not grief for the dead but the burden of funeral expenses thrown upon them,' said one, adding, ' Life without a good insurance policy is not worth living, and to die without a paid-up insurance policy is the same as departing this life without hope of salvation, and it is a sure way of sending one's family to hell and leaving them no loving memory.'

Spectators played a game of counting the number of cars and otherwise estimating the dead man's popularity.

' He was a good and great man, why so many people come from all parts of the island to his funeral. Many now in this town, boasting about their marriage, would never 'ave 'ad a wedding but for Parson Pendance. He was really 'elpful in that way! '

GB eventually gave spontaneous expressions of sorrow at Pendance's demise. She said: ' Me is very, very sorry 'im dead without leaving some'um for Panty. We all would benefit from that. It is a pity you didn't get 'im to sign a paper,' she told Kate. ' I believe 'im leave a good piece of money, poor soul! '

There was one man at the funeral whose grief was greater than that of other mourners. To his grief, a feeling of guilt was added. He was a rough but good-hearted young man named Gusta Philly, a barber by trade, but known to some of his intimates as a laughing savage. Gusta was the proud father of a very attractive girl of fifteen years by one of his many sweethearts. He was making every effort to turn this girl into a lady. Everyone spoke well of her and Gusta received many praises for his care of her. He was absolutely certain of her pudicity and saw to it that she attended church regularly. He specially asked Parson Pendance to take interest in the girl to help to see that she became a lady.

It transpired that Pendance, not feeling very well, called Gusta to the Mission House for tonsorial service. Shortly before leaving for Parson's house, Gusta heard terribly bad news about his daughter Belle. The girl's mother confided her suspicions to him that Belle was pregnant.

In a state of great agitation, Gusta arrived to keep his

73

appointment with Parson Pendance. His excitement was the keener because he had not been given the full details concerning Belle.

He expected to give Parson a quick haircut and shave, then return to investigate the matter which caused him untold perplexity.

He soaped the Parson's face with unsteady hand, spreading the foam over and over from ear to ear. Parson at once sensed that something was wrong with Gusta, but he did not investigate. Gusta took the long, sharp razor and, stropping it furiously, he bit his lips in wild passion. Cutting off someone's head would be the easiest thing for him then. As he scraped the Parson's jaw and chin his hands trembled with rage and in a confessional voice he said timidly:

'Pawson, I have somet'ing very private to say to you. You are a man of God and I don't want to drag you into such t'ings.'

'Don't be afraid to tell me your personal problems,' Parson said assuringly, 'I'll pray for you. Confession is good for the soul. We have no sorrow which God cannot cure!'

'Pawson, me is not going to wait on God to cure this one. Me want quick vengeance and me want to do it mi own satisfaction. I don't care if they 'ang me afterwards. I am prepared for the gallows!'

'Oh, Gusta, don't speak like that, please!'

Making a few more quick strokes with his razor on the Parson's face, Gusta continued to speak: 'Blood must flow like water. I'm going to swipe off somebody's 'ead as there is God in 'eaven, Pawson!'

'Please tell me what makes you so upset,' Parson asked as soon as he had an opportunity to speak. 'You're not yourself today. You're always so jolly and quiet! You must fight the devil. Never follow him!'

Holding the Parson's chin in his thick, heavy hand, Gusta said: 'You're the first person I'm telling this and when I take action you alone will know why!'

He rested Pendance's head more comfortably on the back

74

of the high chair, held his chin firmly and made another scrape with the razor. In this position Parson Pendance could now only listen, without a chance of making comments.

At the mention of Belle's name by Gusta, Parson Pendance's blood froze instantly. He felt as if he were already on the scaffold waiting for the axe to fall.

Gusta continued shaving the Parson and compounding his threats, then suddenly he noticed that Parson had gone pale.

'Me know 'ow you must feel, Pawson. It is a disappointment for us all. I know that you too would like to see the girl become a lady. But you can take it from me, that the man is not going free this time. I shall cut his throat without the slightest hesitation. I shall have no mercy. One swipe with this razor!'

In his rage Gusta was giving Pendance an unusually close shave and Pendance winced with each touch of the cold steel on his face.

During the agonized moments, Parson Pendance once touched his head to feel if it was still on his body. Cold sweat oozed out of him profusely, like pimples of ice on his face; his suffering was almost beyond mortal endurance.

When Gusta let his client go for a moment Parson Pendance nearly fell face forward to the ground. Gusta caught him in time, but discovered that his client was unconscious. Pendance had fainted. Knowing that he was not in the best of health then, Gusta did not imagine that his threats had precipitated Pendance's condition at that moment.

With the help of others in the house, Parson was taken to bed and the doctor summoned.

At Pendance's funeral Gusta felt that Parson must have been shocked about the news regarding Belle, why his heart failed.

Pendance had in truth died from a misunderstanding which no doctor could diagnose. He did not know that Gusta Philly had no suspicions of him and would have disbelieved, had he been told, that Pendance was the father of Belle's unborn baby. Pendance had committed suicide with the sharp instrument of a guilty conscience, the most obdurate of executioners.

After the funeral, GB and Kate's reconciliation was further sweetened, GB's maternal affection reaching its height when Kate offered her a few pounds before leaving. Kate now hoped for a similar reconciliation with her son Panty at some future date. She went back to Kingston, joy swelling in tidal waves in her breast.

A few weeks after Pendance's death, GB attended his memorial service, where she volunteered to be a collector for the memorial fund for him: 'At last Massa God open a way for the li'l boy to get somet'ing through his father!'

After many weeks of coercing all and sundry to subscribe to the worthy cause, GB collected a substantial sum of which she gave a fraction to the responsible committee, receiving their praises for her great help. For a long time, the committee could reach no decision as to the form the memorial should take. Various members made suggestions for their own profit. A budding artist suggested a portrait of the dead man, a realtor suggested land as a playfield for children. Eventually, after numerous quarrels, someone donated a plot of land on which a crèche should be erected in memory of a man who was said to love all children. When the building was completed, it bore a marble plaque written thus: 'To the glory of God and in loving memory of the Rev. John Oswald Pendance, philanthropist and champion of the cause of the poor. His work in helping to improve family life was invaluable, his efforts to bring succour to needy children were God-guided. This building is a humble tribute to his memory and an invitation for others to follow his own good example. Suffer the little children to come unto me and forbid them not, for of such is the kingdom of heaven.'

At the opening of the building, many people of importance once more testified to the goodness of the man in whose memory the building had been raised. Two parsons swore to follow Pendance's example. They said that they knew it would be hard to do of their own strength, but they would ask God to help them follow the footsteps of their deceased brother who was a credit and a blessing to his race.

GB in her usual rough and ready humour said to herself: 'Father forgive them for they know not what they say.'

However, GB was proud for Panty's sake that Pendance was so well honoured: 'The li'l boy will be glad to know 'im father was such a great man.'

As a man who neglected his own child, Pendance became in death the means by which many children were helped.

II

A famished fox is less cunning but more scrupulous than a woman in love—with money.

GB had plastered the walls of her room with religious mottoes: 'Christ is head of this house'; 'They that wait upon the Lord . . .'; 'God is Love'; 'The Lord is my strength' were but a few of the inscriptions on the cards on the walls. On the walls of her heart, however, were written: 'Money is the source of life, my hope and salvation'; 'Blessed are the rich'; 'They that wait on the Lord shall receive money'.

GB did not leave her financial transactions to the Lord. She only needed God's help in acquiring wealth but felt personally competent to keep and care for what she received.

In her peregrination in Swine Lane one day, GB met an interesting returnee, Billy Toms, whom she had known before he travelled to South America. Bill, in his late sixties, possessed the bulge of prosperity in his stomach, a few grey hairs and very heavy greying eyebrows. Although the day was very hot, Bill wore a heavy suit. On his jacket lapel was a large gold pin, a golden chain ran across his waistcoat horizontally, and in his short thick hands he carried a metal-tipped walking-stick. Six-footer Bill carried much adipose. He had a pleasant face, rather youngish, a cheerful disposition and was not disposed to work too hard, always trying to be careful about his cardiac malady.

GB buttonholed him enterprisingly: 'Make me kiss you, Massa Bill,' she greeted exuberantly. 'You dunno 'ow glad me is to see you again. It is only few weeks back you came to mind. You look very rich and prosperous. Money show all over you.'

With his broad, gushing smile, Bill embraced GB: 'Gal, you look as fit as a fiddle.'

In ready banter, GB admitted that she could yet play a few tunes. In the conversation ensuing, Bill told her that he had come to die where he was born. He said that he wanted to help to build up Swine Lane. He was going to build a nice home on his land there.

'And then you'll send for your wife?'

'I have neither wife nor kids,' confessed Bill without regret. 'I had damned good time for my money and now I can die single right here.'

'Few more people like you and Swine Lane would be a paradise.'

'I like Swine Lane,' said Bill; 'I travel to many countries where many people live in better houses, but are not as good as the worst wretch in Swine Lane here.'

'Me so glad to hear that you love Swine Lane. Not'ing would let me give up this place. I live at the rectory, but me belong 'ere!'

'Beatrice, believe me! If I die anywhere else, I'd walk straight back to Swine Lane where my heart has always been.'

'You leave your 'eart 'ere and come back to find it, well, well!'

In further conversation Bill inquired about Kate. 'She's just like me,' GB said rashly: 'God 'as 'elped 'er wondafully, Massa Bill!' With this introduction, GB related an interesting success story in which Kate was heroine and she herself the inspirer. Bill was very impressed and, before they parted, GB offered to darn his socks, sew his buttons or mend anything he might have. She promised to visit him and invited him to call at the rectory whenever he had time. She said she wanted to introduce him to the Parson.

In the subsequent weeks, Bill received regular supplies of food from the rectory. GB baked, fried and cooked, taking to him the best of her efforts. In due course, GB was herself directing the building of the house on Bill's land. He had only wanted a little cottage, but GB made a shop-premises with living-quarters at the back. Bill was glad to leave everything in her capable hands, and when the structure was finished, he occupied the back rooms, leaving the shop vacant for GB to use as she pleased.

At an opportune time, GB approached Parson Wallis and acquainted him with her intention to open a shop in the slum area. According to her, Jesus gave bread to the hungry and she, being His follower, would like to sell bread cheap to the poor.

A delighted Parson Wallis commended GB for the thought, offered every assistance to enable her to serve her own people.

'T'anks very much, sar,' said GB. 'As you and the missis will soon be going abroad, me decide to devote mi full time to the people.'

Prior to leaving on their holiday, the Wallises gave GB generous financial help to start a business which they imagined had eleemosynary potentialities. They also donated furniture and garments to be given to needy people in the slums. Parson Wallis made a special gift of fifty copies of the New Testament for free distribution by GB.

Pretending desperation, GB then visited Bill and between sobs told him that the Wallises were going on holiday and she was forced to leave the rectory. Bill was surprised to learn that GB imagined she had a problem.

'You have nothing to worry about. You can come and live in the shop anytime you like. You're safe here because at this time of my life, I'm only interested in platonic love.'

GB did not know the meaning of the word, but nevertheless she was gratified to hear that Bill was interested in some kind of love.

'Play-tonic love may be jus' the t'ing for us both. Me need tonic badly for years now. There is no tonic which is not good for a woman, "play"-tonic or serious tonic. Me don't like tonic from doctor, it is always bitter, never sweet!'

Much as Bill shared GB's views completely, he could hold

81

out no promise. However, he would try weakly what he once did bi-weekly or oftener.

The day following the Wallises' departure, GB moved into Bill Toms's premises, sleeping in the shop for the first night only. Thereafter, she shared Bill's bed.

In a few weeks, Bill was spending his money to stock the shop. The business fascinated him and he praised GB for her vision. As soon as the trade began to show progress, GB began dropping hints about marriage.

'We is the two most respected people in the whole of Swine Lane,' she pointed out. 'People look up to us.'

'I agree. We must treat them all well.'

'Yes, but we must do more than that!'

'Like what? If we give them a square deal and oblige them any time they ask favour, we will have done all we are expected to do.'

'You don't know these people. They expect more than your best. They will say all manner of evil t'ings against us. . . .'

'But why? In any case, we don't have to bother with what they say,' Bill shrugged. 'We don't depend on them for any-t'ing. I'm getting a pension already. I 'ave my savings, my house, my land and I couldn't care less what they want to say about me. I will be kind to everyone.'

'Kindness is good, but because they respect you and me, we must set a good example in other ways. Many of them come 'ere and call me Mrs Toms. They t'ink we is already married.'

'Good! That's fine. We haven't got to do anything if they think that!'

'But suppose they find out that we is not?'

'Well!'

On many occasions GB tried to interest Bill in getting married, suggesting that it would make him more secured and enhance his good name. Bill was completely indifferent. Some-times, under severe pressure from GB, he relented to promise to give the matter consideration, but he perpetually procrastinated.

In the meantime, all his possessions were under GB's complete control. The wedding ring was all she lacked, but she had as much authority as any wife could have.

Bill, because of his ailing heart, was glad to be rid of many of the heavier responsibilities. He continually told GB that he wanted to take things easy for the rest of his life. He had worked hard for many years and now he had returned home to enjoy his remaining years peacefully. He did not see where marriage would increase his peaceful existence. He claimed that heaven remained paradise because there was no marriage up there. Marriage, he said, was for people who doubted each other's love and wanted to chain each other for fear of their friendship breaking.

He assured GB of his abiding loyalty.

During the first week in the shop, GB advertised her intention of conducting a Drop Pan lottery. The idea was epoch-making, in that she was the first native woman to attempt to be a Drop Pan banker. It was also unique for Drop Pan tickets and Bibles to be sold over the same counter.

GB decorated her shop with the religious mottoes taken from her former bedroom. An additional card displayed very prominently read, 'In God I trust. I don't trust customers.'

Owner and managing director of the business, Bill Toms, was relegated to the role of GB's clerk and assistant. In return, she played an attentive housewife, catering for his smallest need. Already, she was wearing a large gold ring on her marriage-finger and suggesting to all that she be called 'Mrs T'.

GB started the Drop Pan lottery quite fairly. Everyone was satisfied, praising her and saying that they were proud to see their own 'colour' doing such a wonderful thing. GB's early reputation for honesty subsequently encumbered her when she was ready to cheat.

The shop was just marking time. GB complained of the lack of support from her own people. It was strange that they all preferred to purchase from the Chinese grocers. In the mean-time, GB expanded her gambling activities, being a sub-agent for illegal lotteries.

On her way home one day from an illegal mission, GB was carrying a basket containing supplies of forbidden lottery-tickets and a parcel of high-smelling fish which she had bought cheaply, as they were 'off'.

Like an electioneering politician, GB greeted everyone with gushing, insincere exuberance, secretly gloating over her apparent popularity and allowing herself to be deceived by flatterers seeking 'rakes' in the Drop Pan game.

Wishing to show that her success had not gone to her head, GB paused to converse with everyone who gave her a chance smile. Whilst she was engaged in a protracted conversation, she rested her basket behind her on a piazza. Enjoying a series of jokes, she did not notice that a mongrel was rooting through her basket. Another dog, passing, came to share the booty with his fellow. The two dogs began to fight for the basket and GB, frightened, joined the tug of war. Soon her papers were scattered. Passersby who thought the scene comic stopped to watch. The friend to whom she had just been talking was much too amused to assist.

When GB eventually won a pyrrhic victory over the dogs, the bottom was torn from her thrash basket and all her papers were littering the street. The loud laughter of amused onlookers brought a policeman, who reprimanded some of them for mocking a poor woman in distress. With exemplary chivalry, he stooped to help.

'Asayeh! What you doing with these papers, lady?'

'Them don't belongs to me, Massa Police. Don't worry your-self about them. Me don't want them.'

'Whose are they?'

'Officer, me is too upset to answer you now. T'anks for 'elping.'

'You help me now. Tell me about these tickets.'

'Is the two dogs 'ad them last, sah.'

'Where did the dogs get them?'

84

'Ask them! Lemme tell you the godstruth, sah. Me find the papers and didn't know is you lose them, or me would carry them to the police station.'

'You're very lucky to find so many. Take me to where you find them.'

'Officer, as there is a God in heaven, me is not lying to you. Hold the basket and me will come back, but now me 'ave to run 'ome for me leave a pot on the fire and there's nobody to look after it. Officer, as a man of the law, you should tell the govament to protect decent citizens from stray dogs on the streets. Read Phillippians 3 verse 2.'

The officer invited GB to the station. She obeyed under protest, walking very slowly. Her seeming friends followed, happy and curious. GB was greatly alarmed at their obvious lack of sympathy as some of them loudly mocked her on her way to the 'crucifixion'.

'This will be a "rake" for next week,' someone said in her hearing to taunt her. GB tried very hard to cry and at last forced unrepentant tears as she said pleadingly, 'Massa Corpie, Mr Officer, please don't let me fret without a cause. Tell me if anyt'ing wrong with the papers!'

'That's for the judge to decide.'

'Oh! So the judge knows about this too.'

GB was implying that the judge was a customer of the illegal trade, but apparently the policeman did not take the innuendo. Now GB remembered her illegal store at home. She was worried too about Bill Toms's heart. He must be saved from the shock of fright at all cost. GB had already secretly bought a white gown in anticipation of her marriage to Bill. She had chosen white because she had heard that this was the privilege of virgin brides. In her convenient interpretation, GB imagined a virgin to be a woman who had had no physical love for a long time.

As they walked, GB, trying to make friends with her adversary, asked the policeman: 'You t'ink its going rain, officer? Me 'ave all mi few pieces of clothes on the line outside.'

'Perhaps you won't need them for a long time.'

The policeman's portentous reply gave GB a jolt which silenced her for some moments. Like a trapped fox, GB was investigating every possible avenue of escaping the snare, so now she observed: 'You are such a very fine-looking young man! Mi daughter in Kingston would make a nice match for you. She 'as a nice 'ouse and everyt'ing. I'd not mind to 'ave a son-in-law like you at all,' she said with her lips, but in her heart she murmured, 'Ugly brute!'

'Oh you 'ave a rich relative to pay in case of a fine! Very good for you!'

GB was now forced to explain that her daughter was not rich, but just struggling to make ends meet. Nearing the station, GB made a desperate attempt to improve her unfortunate position: 'Officer,' she said, 'me would tell you where me get the tickets, but me don't want to get the others in trouble, if there is really any trouble in it. If you want to forget the whole matter, me would give you somet'ing worthwhile. You won't regret it, sah.'

'Give it to the judge and I must warn you that I may charge you for attempted bribery. That's a serious offence.'

'Oh mi gawd, oh! Officer, you must realize that me is a very foolish woman. Me 'ead is not good at all. Me is just fit for the doctor, but is the money beating me. Right now me 'ave a pain in mi stomach and mi 'ead, every minute of the day me want to wee-wee. My bladder is very weak.'

'Then let's hurry to the station, to save any embarrassment.'

On reaching the station, GB faked a faint. She asked for brandy, but they gave her water and eventually tortuously wrung a statement from her before granting her bail.

GB returned to find the shop closed. Sue was waiting with great excitement. As a friendly service, Sue had rushed the news of GB's arrest to Bill. The sensational manner in which she dramatized the facts and the terrible fears she built up in Bill proved too great a strain for his ailing heart. When GB arrived, Bill had already been taken to hospital in a serious condition. Sue told GB all the kind actions she had done in her absence. She had helped Bill, taken up GB's clothes and helped to close the shop.

Trusting no friend, GB asked at once for the shop key, which Sue produced. Then GB rushed to the hospital, but was told that she could not see Bill.

He died during the night, leaving GB in the depths of a grief she had never before experienced. She wept bitterly for a long period and refused to be comforted by Sue or anyone else. In her crushing distress, she soliloquized between sobs:

'Now me will never get a chance to marry again! Poor me bitch! Me is not born to marry. Look 'ow near me go to it and fail! Oh God! Such a good, kind man 'e was. If 'im was not so stubborn, me could be Mrs T now, instead of the damned GB. Me tired of the name.'

Eventually GB found consolation in the inheritance automatically falling to her. In spite of this, however, she still regretted: 'Look 'ow many men in Swine Lane without a damned t'ing and who would be glad to die, yet they remain alive although they have not'ing but sickness in mind and body. Poor Bill work all 'is life to save up li'l money and now come time for us to enjoy it 'e is dead! Little most 'im would die withouten 'aving someone to enjoy it. If me didn't hold on to 'im, govament would get everyt'ing and the poor man's labour would be all in vain!'

She also expressed sorrow that death had robbed Bill of the opportunity of sharing her trouble. Indeed GB's grief was now a many-prickled thing.

12

A compulsive urge obsessed GB to abscond to Kingston. Kate's rejected invitation now at last had appeal, but GB could not run away leaving her property unprotected.

Destitute of means to solve her problem, she resorted to prayer, reminding Jesus that He Himself, having once run foul of the law, understood her care. She invoked God's most wrathful vengeance on the policeman. Nine times every morning she read Psalm 109, an act supposed to be able to compel God to use his thunderbolts. Dogs were the subject of daily execrations.

'Dogs may be man's best friend, but woman's worse enemy. Anyt'ing good for man is bad for woman.'

Sundays were boom-time for GB's business. People wanting items which they forgot to purchase at the Chinese groceries flocked to GB. Heedless of the law regulating closing on Sundays, GB opened her shop, only taking the precaution of asking customers to close the door behind them.

She constantly reminded customers of the great sacrifice she was making on their behalf, causing her to neglect churchgoing in order to serve them.

During the week, GB encouraged certain customers to gamble in the shop for articles which she sold.

The Sunday following her arrest, she attended church at a sacrifice of her usual Sunday trade. She expected God to note this and reward her by saving her from prison and ultimately her soul from hell. She took Holy Communion to boost the spirit.

After the service, she met an old friend of hers, who came to offer sympathy and consolation. Letitia Buckle, a pragmatic, talkative woman, as meagre as a crow and nicknamed 'Spider-leg' alias 'Meddlesome Matty', was not half as interested in GB as she pretended. Her jaws, denied of the required exercise from chewing food, were forced to chew other people's problems, which Letitia digested with obvious relish. She could be classified as omnivorous, there being nothing which she did not put her teeth into. Rebukes and curses did not prevent her from interfering with whatever did not concern her. GB embraced this owl-eyed, funnel-nosed witch, whose person made an eloquent appeal for human pity.

Cawing like an infuriated bird, Letitia said: ''Tis a damned shame 'ow that fish-mouth policeman ill 'buse you, GB, but you trust Massa God, even if you go to prison. God will give His angels charge over thee. Saints and disciples died in prison, so it is no disgrace if you too die there.'

Letitia's intended comfort increased GB's dismay, causing her to sigh: 'God is not going to make me go to prison. The same God who delivered Daniel will not forsake me.'

'You can't be sure. Big Massa God's ways passeth 'uman understanding. Look 'ow Jesus beg Him for help when He was in trouble and God never even budge! Furthermore, you must remember that policemen go to school to learn lies and you don't 'ave that kind of training. You can only tell foolish lies! Court 'ouse justice is not for poor people. You can win a case and be worse off than if you did lose.'

GB now introduced a bright idea: 'Tesia,' she said, 'you know all about court 'ouse and law. Come and give evidence for me. You will know 'ow to convince the judge!'

'Me!' Letitia winced. 'All me know is that me hear people talk that the policeman would not ease you up!'

'Listen, T. In court two wrongs equal one right. If two of us tells the same lies, the one policeman telling the truth can't win. Justice must be in favour of the majority.'

Letitia remarked that some judges could see lies in people's faces; these judges studied black arts and could not be trusted. Moreover, she asked, what would be the position if the policeman brought many witnesses who had seen the incident? GB assured her that she would call still more witnesses who had not seen the incident. She would get the biggest majority to influence the decision in her favour.

'Listen T! Me don't want waste money paying a lawyer when I can 'elp a good friend. A lawyer would talk as if 'im was eye-witness. You can do the same and you 'ave more sense than some of the pettifoggin' lawyers with rubber heads, lead tongues and quick fingers.'

To Letitia the flattery tasted like wine: 'Is not you alone that tell me that me smart. Lawyering would be mi calling if me was a man and didn't love de Lord.'

Letitia now inquired what profit she would make from perjuring herself. After a few moments of lively bargaining, Letitia agreed to accept an old dress after the case and small gifts of bread and sugar in advance.

'The judge,' said GB, 'is a Englishman, don't know a damned t'ing about Drop Pan. He's not going to probe because 'im will not want everybody to know that 'im is ignorant. Me know all about English people. They all is too proud to ask questions because they want everybody to think that they know everyt'ing.'

As a safeguard, however, Letitia suggested that GB should consult the obeahman to get supernatural assistance in her defence. God gave wisdom to obeahmen that they could help the poor with necromancy, said Letitia.

GB thought it would not be necessary, as the case would be quite easy. Letitia recalled the celebrated case during which the policeman became crazy, the judge committed suicide and the lawyer vanished without trace. She said she knew the obeahman responsible for this rough justice and she could get him to command a cheap ghost to disrupt things in court.

Returning home, GB received a visit from Sue, who had kept scarce since she killed Bill Toms with excitement.

She said she was pleased to see how cheerful GB was through-out all the tribulations and she said that it was a pity that Parson Allen was not present to see GB's faith and to give her some help.

For a few moments GB, looking the picture of misery, sat with her jaw resting in her palm and taking very little notice of Sue.

Apparently inspired by perversity, Sue continued: 'It is troubles like these that you need the 'elp of a man of God. If you too distressed to write Parson Allen, me would do it for you!'

Sue saw where her own reputation would be enhanced if her friend's sins were given wide publicity.

Plunged into a flaming temper at Sue's wicked suggestion, GB exploded: 'Me don't want you to write a goddamned t'ing. Me don't steal not'ing nor cut out 'orse tongue!'

'Don't misunderstand me, GB. You know that court 'ouse is the devil's cathedral. What they call justice there is what we poorer classes call fib.'

Fear and temper enervated GB, causing her temperature to fall suddenly, so that she trembled although she sweated: 'Ga-ga-ga-God wi-will ta-take care of me. Me is in good ha-hands!'

Prophetess of gloom, Sue pointed out that when once a person or thing was committed to divine hands, it was not easy to recover it.

GB receded into thoughtful silence, which was cruelly broken by Sue's wondering aloud: 'Me often wonder what 'appened to poor Quashie. Prison must 'ave mashed 'im up. Ever hear anyt'ing about 'im, GB?'

Exasperation fused GB's eyelids and prised her jaws apart so that her thoughts rushed out of her mouth without hindrance.

'Sue, what the HELL you come to bother me for! Why didn't you keep your behind in your shack and leave me with mi troubles!'

Sue immediately endeavoured to placate her friend by revealing that she had come to put GB on her guard. She said that she had noticed a very suspicious man scrutinizing GB's place and she thought he might be a detective wanting to cause more trouble. She now advised GB that if she had anything risky, she'd better hand it over to her for safe keeping in case of a police raid.

Sue's suggestion commended itself urgently to GB, who at once agreed to hand over a small parcel of Indian hemp she was holding for someone. Sue was not satisfied. She wanted to be in possession of the Drop Pan charts and mystery documents which caused GB to win so often. Reluctantly, GB entrusted everything to her.

At dusk, Sue was hurrying home with her dangerous burden. She had just been thinking that the falling of one is the rising of another. She contemplated selling the ganja for a fair sum when GB had gone to prison. Just as she raised her head from the parcel, she was face to face with the suspicious man she had described to GB. She shifted out of his way, quickened her pace and was almost running when the man asked her to stop.

'Go away, brute!' Sue yelled breathlessly. 'Me is not your type.'

She was making her way like a clipper when another stranger approached from the opposite direction. In panic she threw away the ganja parcel. The stranger turned out to be an indifferent passerby, but Sue did not look back to recover her parcel.

The man behind retrieved the parcel and called out to her saying: 'Lady, you lose something!'

'Yes, me know,' replied Sue, 'it was to a good man that me lose it, if you want to know.'

Like Atalanta she sped on, but the man was a modern Melanion. Catching up with her, he handed her the parcel and disclosed that he was a friend of GB.

Sue was greatly relieved and as she walked in the company of the stranger, she gave him a lot of information. The man advised her to be careful with the dangerous materials she carried and he left her. Sue invited him to call again.

Later that night the police raided Sue and found ganja and other illegal materials in her possession. She was arrested and refused bail.

13

The icy breath of the dragon-tongued law causes forensic ague in every defendant. Man, from time immemorial, fears man's justice. Trained lawyers live in confusion about laws and, indeed the most successful advocates are those who can with greatest facility exploit latent discrepancies of the law.

In the dock, GB shook like a leaf in a storm, a cloud begloomed her face, her wild eyes flashed lightning, fog gathered in her throat, thunder rumbled in her stomach.

Asked whether she was guilty or not, GB replied that she preferred to have the case first heard before giving her own verdict.

'Guilty or not guilty? Please answer,' a voice of severity boomed, relentless and imperious.

Immediately a spark of bravado lighted in GB as she replied: ' Me is not a fool! If me say me is guilty, me would be telling lie on myself. If me say me not guilty, you won't believe me. So try the case and find out for yourself. The Massa judge will decide! '

Again the question was put to GB and she was asked to refrain from wasting the court's time.

GB replied that the policeman was guilty of assaulting her. She said the charges against him were not yet read.

Patiently, the process of the court was detailed to her. When she agreed that she understood, the question was again put.

Haltingly, hesitatingly, reluctantly, she pleaded guilty but insane. She said that if she must admit guilt, then it was a sure sign that she was not mentally normal.

Following another tedious explanation from the court, she pleaded not guilty.

All she had so far done was to convince the judge that she was unreliable as a witness and fairly hostile. Justice had already vacated the courtroom to make room for prejudice, its mortal enemy.

Asked her occupation, GB said that she was a stonebreaker, forgetting that she had described herself as a businesswoman in her signed statement.

'Do you sell stones in your shop?'

'No, sah. Me sell bread cheap to 'elp the poor.'

'You break stones and sell bread! The devil had the same idea once.'

'Stonebreaking is my profession, sah. Bread-selling is just to 'elp the poor people.'

Pretending destitution and ignorance was her line of defence.

'Did you have Drop Pan and Peaka Peow lottery tickets in your possession?'

No answer.

'Do you know that these tickets are illegal?'

No answer.

'Do you understand the question?'

'Well to tell you the godstruth, mi 'onour sah, me is a very clean, neat and tidy woman. Me hate to see pieces of papers flying about the streets, that is the reason why me picked up these papers. Since me open the li'l shop, me notice that children came with dirty 'ands to buy eatables. Me teach them sanitation by using the papers me picked up, to wrap t'ings.'

'These bits of paper are too small to wrap bread!'

'True, sah, but me use them to wrap sweets.'

'Do you buy or sell Peaka Peow or Drop Pan?'

'Me is too poor to gamble, mi 'onour, please. Me did not know that these papers mean trouble until the policeman told me so. In the same way if me did pick up a pound note, the policeman would t'ink is me make it. You can't follow police-men. . . .'

'Are you a stonebreaker or a shopkeeper? Which?'

'The honest truth is that me is a church-worker.'

'How do you make your living then?'

'Up to now I don't make none, but me try to sell bibles. As you know, sah, this book is not so pop'lar since the comic books come in. The people prefer to read joke books, with pictchas of naked people. People find fun in other people's nakedness.'

'I put it to you that you both sell, buy, and otherwise dis-tribute illegal lottery tickets.'

'Who tell you such a t'ing. Bring the person before my face! It is a damned lie, sah!'

'Please respect the court! You are warned! Now answer the question and don't make a nuisance of yourself. What do you know about the Drop Pan game?'

'Me 'ear that it 'as thirty-six numbers which stands for many things.' GB stopped as if that were indeed all she knew.

'Carry on, please tell us all you know.'

'People buys numbers for any amount. A winning number bought for one penny, pays two shillings. Everyday the "Banker" announce what number 'im is under. Like if 'im says 'im is under number ten, which means cemetery, people get a clue to buy the numbers connected with the cemetery and so on. Me know, too, that many govament people, particularly policemen, buys tickets daily. They win more often than most of us. They get good rakes because if they lose, they cause trouble!'

'You said policemen won oftener than "most of us". Are you now admitting that you buy Drop Pan tickets?'

'No, sah!'

'What are "rakes" in Drop Pan jargon?'

'Clues which the banker gives buyers sometimes.'

'You know a great deal about the game! Do you still insist that you never bought tickets?'

'To tell the godstruth, sah, long ago, long, long ago, before me was a church-worker, me used to buy tickets once in a while. But me was too poor to buy reg'lar and now since me is a follower of Christ, me don't bother much with worldly t'ings and the devil's business.'

'Your circumstances have now improved to the point where you do not need to buy Drop Pan—is that what you are saying? In other words, you are asking the court to believe that if you now buy Drop Pan, it is not out of need!'

'Me is still very, very poor, sah. Me too 'onest to get rich as you!'

'Then do you still buy the lottery?'

'Verry, verry, very seldom! Me can't even remember myself. That's the godstruth, sah. Me might as well say me don't buy.'

'How often do you buy, daily, weekly, monthly or . . . ?'

No answer.

'What about Peaka Peow? Do you buy that?'

'Massa, me is begging you to take time with me. Me is still suffering from the rough treatment of the policeman. The wicked man beat me in mi 'ead with his fist.'

'One more question: Do you know that the games are not lawful?'

'Me don't see not'ing wrong with the games if it's played fair. Paying tax is a greater burden to poor people than buying Drop Pan in which they can win somet'ing. The hundreds of people who buy it daily from all class, colour and creed show that they don't t'ink not'ing wrong with the game, sah.'

Eventually, after prolonged argument, GB admitted in a rather oblique way that she knew that the game was illegal.

Old cadger Letitia, a chronic sciatica sufferer, came with accentuated misery to excite the credulity of the law. She went into the witness box, standing in which she resembled a plucked chicken. She said that she was standing in the square on the date in question when GB arrived with a basket of fish. She glimpsed the policeman put something in GB's basket. GB asked him what he was doing, but instead of answering, he attacked her. Letitia further said that she knew GB to be a devout Christian, who knew nothing about Drop Pan and other lotteries. She said she heard the policeman ask GB for money. She also said that she volunteered to give evidence, because she hated to see injustice done to the poor.

At the conclusion of the hearing, GB was fined twenty pounds with the alternative of a three-month prison term. Letitia, adjudged guilty of perjury, was sent to prison for twenty-one days with no alternative. On hearing her sentence passed, she burst into tears as she confessed: 'Is GB forced me to give evidence. Me was trying to do good for me frien'!' As she was being taken from the courtroom, she gave a true, but too late, account of what took place between herself and GB.

Without apparent emotion, GB decided to take the prison term rather than pay the fine. At first she appealed, but later withdrew saying that God would give justice in His own time. Her most pressing desire now was to contact her friend Sue Browley to commit to her her business affairs during the interim. Sue was being led into the court just as GB was being taken away. They met at the door, but neither word nor sign of recognition passed between them. GB's misfortune was a current which electrified anyone coming into contact with it. GB did experience a twinge of sadistic joy to see Sue in trouble. She didn't have to guess Sue's fate.

Lucky GB spent a mere hour in the cell, before her daughter mysteriously arrived to pay the fine. Instead of being grateful, GB rebuked Kate for wasting so much money.

'Prison is no disgrace,' she said. 'Many of the present big-shots graduate from inside it. Life in Swine Lane can't be as good as prison life. In prison people don't know unemployment or starvation.

'But you're free now, GB! Think of it! You can come with me to Kingston!'

'Me is not leaving my birthplace. The only freedom me want is freedom to make money. A 'appy slave is better than a miserable pauperized freeman. Money is freedom. Freedom cannot buy money.'

Eventually, under pressure, she compromised, consenting to go to Kingston after she had wound up her many unsettled business affairs.

Already, GB had been thinking of regaining the twenty-pound fine which Kate paid on her behalf. It was her intention to organize a raffle, from which by fair or foul means she would make a clear profit of twenty pounds or more. In her own words, 'If a thief steals from another, God laughs!'

GB did not indicate to Kate the full extent of her fortune. No one knew how much money GB possessed. Her net inheritance from Bill Toms was a secret.

Kate returned to Kingston with the expectation that GB would join her, as promised.

For many months previously, GB had been collecting rent from a group of maniacs, followers of a semi-religious cult, the 'Pocamania' (Little Madness) sect, who kept their nightly orgiastics in the backyard of her premises.

This group brought considerable nightly revenue to GB's shop when, with their booming drums, they summoned their poverty-crazed, sin-conscious adherents. By the light of lanterns, like human tongues of fire, the cultists danced to hymns, accompanied by the rhythmic beats of their drums. Like vermin under insecticidal attack, these frenzied people wiggled, jumped, pranced, screamed and yelled and prayed in a language incomprehensible to themselves in a ceremony they called 'trooping', with the ultimate aim of self-exhaustion. The gibberish they shouted they called 'unknown tongue', and their strange behaviour they described as being 'in the spirit'. Frequently a number of them fell to the ground where they remained in something like semi-*rigor mortis*, their coma lasting sometimes until morning. While some were obviously possessed with 'dancing' devils, others were the victims of infirm minds agitated by abiding penury. Many of them claimed the gift of prophecy during this state, but none of them, in their prescience, saw anything but catastrophic events bringing suffering, destruction and death to those whom they must secretly envy.

GB's interest in these fanatics increased as she observed their unselfish generosity to their organization. In due course, she joined the superstitious band, becoming one of its chief hot-gospellers and gaining special respect as owner of the premises. Her scathing denunciation of wickedness, and her dramatic, colourfully violent blood-and-thunder prayers, found much favour with the cultists. In fiery language, GB constantly demanded heavenly vengeance on the law courts, policemen and dogs:

'Oh merciful father God, please send all oppressors of Thy poor people to burn in 'ell for ever. Scatter the bowels of these ravaging wolves who persecute poor people in law courts and make man know that Thy law must prevail. All this we ask in the holy name of Thy dear son, our Saviour who suffered at the hands of wicked judges. Amen.'

In concert, a number of petty criminals shouted spontaneous choruses of amens, allelujahs and glory be's.

GB's income increased a hundredfold, making it unnecessary for her to gamble. 'Religious' work turned out to be indeed a gold-mine. With her characteristic resourcefulness, she soon developed the arts of blessing people, telling fortunes, giving bush baths and 'sabotages'—her malapropism for massages.

Forgetting her promise to go to Kate, GB supervised the erection of a long, large thatched hut, which the faithful believers built by co-operative effort, as a cathedral of their odd sect. They gave ten per cent. of all they owned to GB.

Replying to a letter from Kate demanding her advent to Kingston, GB quoted the Scriptures to say it was not meet to take the children's bread and cast it to the dogs. She said that she had been called to serve the people. She reminded Kate of the story of Jonah, who was running away from the Lord's call. GB had convinced herself that she was really doing something of value. The fact that she prospered gave her the impression that God was in favour of her deeds.

14

While Parson Allen educated Panty in reward for the boy's services, Mrs Allen claimed that it was patently wrong to lift the lad above the state to which God had called him.

Mr Allen fought his wife on principle, saying that as an Englishman he had a duty to perform to the less fortunate. 'The world will always be indebted to England for what we have done and are doing for the backward peoples,' he said. 'Some of these people claim that we enslaved their ancestors, but if we did not take them away from their primitive savage conditions, they would still be cannibals now.'

He was sure that England had done more than any other nation to help human progress and he obligated himself to follow the traditions of his nation.

The Allens' daughter Paula was now boarded at a select girls' school where her only interest was adolescent glamour. Possessing all the requisites for social success, she imagined the future to be ripening fruit extending downwards for her to pluck with her soft white hands and touch with her rosy lips.

When Parson Allen wished that Paula would take as much interest in her lessons as Panty did, Mrs Allen was offended at the odious comparison.

Despite his wife's opposition, Parson Allen found great satisfaction and fulfilment teaching Panty. It pleased him to think that he was such a good teacher. Mrs Allen insisted that a classical education was unsuitable for the boy in this modern age. Gardening would be far more useful, and she pointed out that gardening was a very high profession, seeing that God himself was the first gardener.

Fighting to keep the boy backward and down, Mrs Allen never realized how much she indirectly incited Panty's ambition the more she tried to handicap him.

To be like his superiors became Panty's dominating obsession, so he tried in deed and word to ape Parson Allen. Panty was often jeered at and criticized for trying to be a 'black Englishman', but he felt that he was being deliberately persecuted on account of his humble antecedents. He rapidly became socially super-sensitive, developing much intolerance for his grandmother, whom he regarded as a social stumbling-block in his way.

It was like a bomb crashing through the umbrella of his self-esteem when he overheard Mrs Allen secretly instructing Paula, who had just returned on holiday, 'You are a white girl and you have special responsibilities, being an English parson's daughter. You must be careful with all coloured people, particularly the boy Panty. Coloured people cannot be trusted; they are all alike. This boy must be kept in his place. That is important.'

Paula disclosed that he was always very respectful to her. Mrs Allen then said: 'Let that be always so. My dear, you're innocent, inexperienced, you know nothing about the world yet. It is my duty to put you on guard. I want to be always proud of you as I am now.'

Believing that social mannerisms were all that Paula needed to know and were all her delicately pure ear could stand, Mrs Allen continued to lecture about the art of being charming: 'We English are famous for our charm. Hatred of a person is no reason for being discourteous to him. Politeness is a social weapon and if rightly used can do what most violent rudeness could not accomplish. Be graceful and gracious and the rude will fear you.'

Panty now proved that eavesdroppers never hear good of

themselves and from that moment he was suspicious of all display of politeness. Mrs Allen's charming smile he considered the epitome of fraud.

Paula's childish indiscretion with him had left no scars on her personality. She was an emblematic human apple-pie, with the right amount of flavour in terms of modesty and dignity, to tempt the senses of the epicure. Panty's inferiority she took for granted, so much so that she was quite indifferent about the secret he had for her.

No sooner had Panty passed his examination than Mrs Allen began a serious campaign to be rid of him. Pretending to be seeking his welfare, Mrs Allen found him a temporary job in a local office. She wrote many letters attesting to and highlighting his virtues and recommending him to employers, because she wanted to get rid of him.

His success and elevation was most painful to her, yet she smiled most charmingly on all his comings and goings. She made several applications on his behalf, seeking to send him as far as possible from the rectory.

Naïve Mr Allen was pleased with the new interest Mrs Allen took in Panty. He thanked God for changing his wife's heart for the better and personally felt triumph for having brought Panty from the gutter up to social recognition.

Panty was eighteen when appointed to the Collectorate in Montego Bay, a distance Mrs Allen considered far enough from Kingston to relieve her immediate concern.

Montego Bay was the last place that Panty wished to go, it being utterly impossible for him to be his natural self in that locality, owing to his fear that his past might be discovered. He qualified for the dislike of his colleagues on his first day at office. He was envied for imagined wealth, and everyone made jokes at his hauteur.

Jamaica has loose parochial divisions but well-defined social boundaries, but Panty found that he himself was a one-man social class. In a strange way, he caused an unusual unity amongst the office staff, who because they detested him forgot

hatred of each other in order to favour him with their combined abomination.

For Panty, everything was in short supply especially clothes.
His affected gait, likened to a cat's walking on hot bricks, was
caused by the tightness of the second-hand pair of shoes given
by Parson Allen. It was advantageous to him, therefore, that he
was slighted by his colleagues, thereby depriving them of the
chance of discovering his circumstances.

Assiduously, he sought to be recognized by people who could
help him, using politeness as a trap to ensnare any important
person who visited the office for service.

Mr Jason Mitchell, a rich planter and sugar manufacturer,
a direct descendant of English slave-owners, was very favourably impressed with Panty's attention. Mitchell, a man in his
late fifties, with silver hair and bushy white moustache,
developed rather condescending paternal feelings for coloured
native Jamaicans whose adoration he desired in order to
maintain the tradition of white superiority.

Jason Mitchell sincerely felt that coloured people were
perpetually indebted to him on account of an ancient bene-
faction his ancestors conferred on runaway slaves. In the days
of slavery it was the accepted custom to brand with a hot iron
or amputate a limb of a runaway male slave or anyone who
wandered in search of sex-fulfilment. Jason Mitchell's grand-
father, however, was too sympathetic to indulge in such
atrocities against his slaves. He simply had them castrated for
their delinquency, thereby putting an end to their emotional
wanderlust but not impairing their capacity for work. Mitchell
always told his friends of this kindness of his forebear and he
himself regretted that freedom and civilization had prevented
the continuity of this simple and effective treatment for
workers on his estate. He argued with logic that many
besetting social problems would be non-existent if the practice
still obtained. There would be no illegitimacy problem,
unemployment would be considerably reduced, over-population

unknown and crimes of rape and carnal abuse would disappear.

Jason Mitchell was so charmed with Panty's sycophancy that he wrote his brother-in-law the Collector General in praise of Panty's intelligence and astuteness. Panty's prestige was considerably boosted by similar actions from others of the Mitchells' social clan.

Ideal civil servant Panty received promotion in a manner mysterious to his workmates, whose jealousy and hate redoubled because of the preference given him. They imagined that it was granted because of Panty's family connections.

Whilst Panty sat at his desk close to the public counter, a short, rough man in greasy clothes came to pay for a motor-vehicle licence. This man's uncombed hair was discoloured with dirt, his face resembled something unfinished by its maker, and his nose had the appearance of a large onion dipped in pitch. He commanded Panty in a very coarse voice: 'Len' me your pen, brother!'

Panty kept his head bowed over the documents before him. The man waited a little then reissued his command somewhat louder than before.

Finding that Panty took no heed, the man added:

'Is you me talking to boy! You yella-skin people always damned fresh when you in a li'l govament job. You don't 'treat black people good. We all is equal now and before long, black people is goin' rule this said country.'

His tirade having produced no result, he became irate and shouted: 'Yella boy, look at me! My name it Ragoo! Ask anybody about me. Me don't owe anybody not'ing on my two trucks or mi motor-car. Me is a big man in this town. You is just a pauperized govament clerk. If you don't 'ave money try to 'ave manners.'

Panty dared not now look up into the face of his former Swine Lane crony. Turning away his face from Ragoo, he left the office. Another clerk gave Ragoo an approving smile and attended to him. Ragoo commented: 'People like that should not be serving the public. Me is going to see the aut'orities about that boy. 'E will soon be kicking taxpayers.'

A few days later, an aged decrepit woman, bending at right angles to a supporting staff she carried to help her locomotion, came to beg alms. Someone in the office, knowing the woman to be a cantankerous Xantippe, mischievously directed her to Panty, telling her that he was the most wealthy person in the office.

Emaciated by a life of licentious dissipation, the prune-faced, feather-weight human remnant crawled painfully in front of Panty's window groaning to attract his attention:

'Mi dear son, give your poor mother a penny to buy bread. Me is dying for 'ungry. You look like a very nice young massa. Me is pleased to see such a nice person working with govament.'

Stealthily Panty threw her a quick glance to make sure that it was no one he knew and then he returned his undivided attention to his work. With her stick, the woman impatiently knocked on the counter menacingly, repeating her request a little louder than before.

Indignantly, Panty addressed her: 'You come to beg, you should not be so rude to your superiors. I am not your son. Now go away!'

The woman humbly apologized: 'Don't get vexed. All nice young people is my sons and daughters. Me feel proud of my race to 'ave such cultured and kind-hearted young people.'

Panty categorically informed her that he had nothing to give her and that she had better importune some other 'son'.

The old virago's passion erupted like a sudden burst of thunder and as she cursed, a clerk in the office brought her a donation, simultaneously winking to incite her to jibe Panty.

'T'ank you, mi sweet young massa. I see you comes from a good family, not like this ugly mulatto bastard son of a bitch 'ere, as mean as a constipated louse. Him couldn't be my son because me is a respectable married woman. When yella-skin people wort'less, they is worse than pure black negra!'

This was but a mild preamble to a vituperative harangue sparkling with gems of slander.

Panty retreated and as soon as he left, his colleagues laughed and encouraged the woman. She was just leaving when Panty returned to be told by her: 'You face resemble when ramgoat 'ave hiccup. Look at your mouth 'ow it twist and resemble young baby's backside. Govament use to pick and choose first time, but now them take anybody in office.'

When the woman was eventually driven from the office, she positioned herself at a neighbouring piazza where she plastered with verbal mud the reputation of the 'yella fellow' in the office.

Noting the satisfaction his colleagues received from his embarrassment, Panty sought a transfer. For months, he heard nothing about his request. The matter became urgent when the domestic servant at the rectory informed him that he was the father of her expected child. He threatened her with prosecution and the illiterate girl fled in terror back to her mother in the country.

Panty sought help of Mr Jason Mitchell and in a few days obtained marching-orders. Then, he remarked to a workmate tauntingly:

'You will be glad now that I'm going.'

'We don't think you that important,' came the scathing reply.

Panty retorted: 'It is because I am petty why I think you would be interested. You all have never been interested in anything but the petty.'

It was his apt farewell summary of his office colleagues and he was unfortunately correct.

15

In order to accommodate her rapidly growing flock, GB enlarged the hut. She saved no soul, but she saved money. The faith-healing business was booming, GB blaming all failures on the patients' disbelief.

'As me touch you,' she councilled, 'you must tell yourself that you feel better, even if you feel worse. That is faith!'

For chronic maladies which death alone could cure, GB prescribed pungent-smelling weeds for use in hot baths and as drink. Claiming to be under the constant direction of heaven, she advised her followers to wear white robes at meetings. Jesus and his disciples wore gowns, she said, and it was necessary for Christians to be easily recognizable amongst sinners. She also pointed out that the main reason why ministers of religion wore their collars backwards was because no one would distinguish them as Christians if they dressed otherwise: 'Their action is the same as for other peoples. 'Tis the clothes that make the difference. We must follow Jesus example with our clothes.'

GB informed her followers that they could purchase suitable gown materials at her shop. GB's charism was always for her own profit.

GB's strange supernatural powers grew daily; each morning she found herself with new talent. Already, she claimed ability to communicate with the dead, prophesy the future and confer prosperity or cause failure. One of her gifts was the ability to compose spontaneous verses for hymns, using old tunes. A popular one of her poems was:

Me git me edication at the cross,
Me git me edication at the cross;
Me was never sent to college
To git a bit of knowledge,
But me git me edication at the cross!

She also discovered that 'all flesh was grass', thereby concluding that all grass was flesh, hence the power of weeds to
cure human ills. She sold a variety of ordinary bushes which,
she said, possessed special nourishment.

Advice on family problems was the one thing GB gave free.
But she profited from the service, in that she received during
these operations information which was used as prophecy later.

When a grief-stricken young mother, abandoned by her
lover following the death of their child, sought advice from
GB, she was told: 'You mus' 'ave faith. But faith without
works is dead. Get a nice strong young man and let 'im do the
work while you have the faith that you will conceive. Then
you'll 'ave another pickney and another man to look after you.
God 'elps those who 'elps themselves. Don't wait too long. Go
look for a good man at once. Tonight!'

From an unemployed young man who constantly loitered
on the premises GB received voluntary help in closing her shop
at nights. GB used the young man's service constantly without
ever once offering a reward. She always praised his kindness
and advised him to look to God for compensation.

When her shop was burgled, GB's finger of suspicion pointed at this young man. However, she did not report the matter
to the police, lest they should come to investigate her premises.
Moreover, it was impossible to give an accurate account of her
losses. The one thing GB wanted now was vengeance upon
the thief:

'Me is not praying to Jesus about this matter, Jesus is too
merciful and forgiving. Me going to ask Massa God 'imself to
send fire and grimestone on the wicked rascal and break his
blasted neck. Stealing is the wors' sin on earth.'

On the meeting-night following the incident, GB prophesied sudden, violent death in the community. The thief
might have heard it and become scared. Two days after her
warning, GB was urgently approached by a desperate woman.

The distraught maiden begged her to go at once to speak to
her paramour, who was drunk and threatening to hang himself. The young woman reminded GB of the many kindnesses
that this boy Jonathan had done at her shop. GB understood
the position at once and inwardly beamed with sadistic delight.
She concluded that Jonathan wanted to kill himself in order
to escape the violent death she had prophesied. With keen interest she inquired from the young woman: 'You is sure 'im
is going to 'ang 'imself?'

'Positive! Sure, GB! You is the only person who can save
'im, that's why me come to you. Do, GB, 'elp me please! Me
love 'im.'

'Me 'ave to go to prayer-meeting,' GB excused, 'Me don't
'ave the time to go to 'im. Furthermore, me know that this
was to 'appen. Me saw it in a vision and me already gave out
the warning of sudden death. Me can't stop it. God's will must
be done. Sins must be punished and if there is no sudden death
as me said there will be, people won't believe in my warnings
again. Let 'im 'ang 'imself, if that is God's will. We will 'elp
you to cut 'im down from the tree and me will personally see
that 'im get a good, decent, Christian burial.'

With a scream like the wail of a mortally wounded beast,
the woman ran away from GB's pitiless presence.

At the prayer-meeting GB repeated her warnings with
greater authority and accuracy. She invoked the mercy of God
on the soul of the prospective deceased in the manner of a
judge passing the death sentence, with the conclusion: 'God
have mercy on the soul.'

The following morning, a large crowd of excited spectators
who regarded death as an object of curiosity invaded the dead
man's yard after the news of Jonathan's suicide had spread.
They had cut him down from the tree and brought him home.

Here was death in its stark horror. The agonies, fears, frustrations and perplexities were yet alive on the dead man's face. Out of his bulging wild eyes came a look of rebuke on those who came to amuse themselves staring at him. Out of his mouth his stiff projecting tongue preached an eloquent sermon on life. He was dumbly saying to a deaf world: 'You used my own hands to kill me after trying to starve me to death.'

The crowd kept coming and going during the whole day, and at night, out of respect for the dead, a traditional 'wake' was held. This indeed was a veritable Walpurgis night when witches, ghouls, fanatics and drunkards met for a revel with the devil. They drank gallons of rum and buckets of coffee, ate pounds of 'corned' pork and bunches of boiled green bananas. They played cards, dominoes and draughts and told folklore stories until midnight, when GB presided over the religious part of the gala function. She raised a hymn and all the people joined in to bawl out hymns until the morning, when some guests expressed regrets that ceremonies of the kind were not more frequent.

For weeks afterwards, GB referred to the suicide to prove her gift of prophecy.

Hunters are sometimes eventually trapped by their quarry. People hunting in the economic jungle in search of the centaur called Success are vulnerable to the prey they seek. Success is a killer—with arachnoid ingenuity.

Successful GB daily looked into the faces of sovereigns, forgetting that on the reverse of the coin was the effigy of an animal which, unknown to her, had firmly attached its paws to her vitals.

Without warning, she was stricken. Anaemia was amongst her several maladies. Within two days of her illness, her daughter Kate, like a ministering angel, appeared. GB soon improved. Kate again urged her to come to live in Kingston.

GB refused to go. She owned too many things to leave. Members of her organization took care of various domestic animals for her; her investment in the community was too considerable for her to leave at short notice.

GB had a formidable objection against sudden removal. She rightly claimed to be a very important member of the community and that it would be unbecoming to spirit herself away without giving her friends a chance to fête her as valedictory. She said: 'As soon as they 'ear that me is leaving, they will do everyt'ing to show their love. Me know mi own people, it is only when one is dead or going away that they show love. My people is very kind 'earted. If you saw what they gave Parson Allen when 'im was going away! They will do much better for me, because me is their own colour. We black people love one another. Pity we is so poor. No matter 'ow we hate each other, in our 'eart of 'earts, we love each other.'

In due course, GB advertised her regrettable intention to leave the community. Well-wishers volubly expressed sorrow. Everyone said GB would be sadly missed and that she was irreplaceable. GB made no secret that she was expecting a tangible show of her people's affection.

Her chief lieutenant, Brother Mospin, a rogue, alias Brother Mongoose, took great interest in GB's welfare, or farewell. He told her that in his humble way he desired to continue the good work she had initiated. To this end, he wanted to purchase the premises. He undertook the organizing of a valedictory ceremony for her.

Simon Mospin, tall, hunch-backed and bandy-legged, usually carried his head facing downwards, avoiding his own reflection in everyone's eyes. He was a mystery character, no one knew where he came from, although his enemies claimed that he was a native of the mythical 'Ugly Island', the imaginary habitat of ogres. His face supported the unkind legend.

His head was long and flat, whilst his large square teeth resembled pieces of a jig-saw puzzle. He drizzled when he spoke, and the spray was said not to be sweet-smelling. A drug addict, Mospin was a secret accessory to several crimes, but nevertheless preached righteousness.

GB told him that she would accept £700 cash for her property, but after long bargaining she agreed to reduce the price by thirty shillings, because Mospin was going to organize her farewell function.

'Me don't want any gift. Me prefer the cash money. Money can never rotten and me can always buy what me like with it!'

Mospin agreed: 'Leave everyt'ing to me. You is more than a mother to all the people. They'll do anyt'ing for you, they all love and respec' you, GB. Me is not going to take coppers from a soul, only silver and paper money me want from them!'

'Good!' GB beamed a delighted smile. 'Me is so glad that is you in charge. Me trust you and you 'ave plenty sense.'

'GB! Me is going to make you yourself surprised. It will be one of the biggest functions in this town. We all is going to unite as one, to make you feel good!'

'Whatever money you collect, put it in a beeg envelope and just give it to me at the function. Me will show you my gratitude in a good way. You won't regret what you do for me!'

Mospin launched a collecting campaign and was soon extorting contributions on a very comprehensive scale. He described GB as a modern saint and benefactress of her race. He used every means at his disposal, including patriotism, race-prejudice and blackmail to gather funds.

In the meantime, GB spent a considerable time composing and polishing a flowery speech of thanks. Every day, on hearing the reports about the fund-raising effort, she sweetened what she intended to say.

Sincere and frequent prayers went from her heart, requesting God to increase the generosity of the people to make them give abundantly.

Mospin had made a small deposit at the time when they settled the purchase agreement. After he began collecting for the send-off, he paid two substantial instalments to GB on account of the purchase money. GB saw no relation between these payments and her send-off money. She concentrated all her thoughts on what she expected to get and the high expectation blinded her.

For the great farewell occasion, the hut was beautifully decorated with flowers and banners. The table for the guest of honour and chairman was covered with white and carried a vase of gorgeous blooms. An improvised shed for refreshments stood nearby. Pots bubbled with spicy cookings on open fires. Mospin had punctiliously prepared everything for the great night. Cultists dressed in flowing white robes and turbans jammed the hut.

GB was as happy as a prize-winning schoolgirl on graduation-day. She sang bright, happy hymns and danced as she moved from one place to another.

According to what Mospin told her, she anticipated a substantial sum of money. So sure was she of the windfall, that she had given a small goat to add to the night's feast. Doubly assured of the generosity and good will of all, her heart went out to them in gratitude.

Great applause greeted GB's arrival in her white robe and paper crown designed by Mospin. She carried a large bible in which were two sheets of paper with notes of her thanksgiving speech. No sooner was she seated in the chair of honour, than Mospin raised his right hand heavenward, beckoning silence. He announced a hymn which he described as GB's own composition. The whole audience joined lustily in the singing. They were all in picnic spirit. GB sat coy and demure with an affectedly saintly look on her face. Her heart was turgid with pride and expectation. It was indeed, the moment of a lifetime. No one in Swine Lane had ever received this honour.

The hymn ended, Mospin thundered: 'Let's pray. Oh Gawd, we cum in Thy presence to 'onour our beloved sister, leader and frien', GB, who needs no introduction to Thee. Tonight, if we fail to show 'er our true love, we beg You, Fadder Gawd, to make 'er 'eart undastand, that it is not the gift we give, but the spirit in our 'earts that counts most. We know, dear Fadder, that only You alone can repay GB fer what she 'as done. Amen.'

Shouts of Hallelujah and God bless-es exploded through the hut spontaneously.

GB glanced sideways at Mospin suspiciously, but his bulbous eyes were still tightly closed, he continued another prayer:

'Oh dear Lode, Thou has given us wisdom to arrange dis function, we beg You to make us all satisfied with what You have provided and most of all, me beg that You will make GB use our gifts to remember her many friends. Amen!'

The united voices of the congregation blended with amens, with finality.

Mospin then began a speech in which he extolled the cardinal virtues of GB, which, he said, were too numerous to mention. GB was bored at the tortuous adulatory speech and longed to hear her own voice as well as to receive the money. Mospin, however, continued to stress GB's disregard and unconcern for money. He said that had she been a lover of money, she could have been very rich.

Loud and lively cheers interrupted him, but GB's suspicions mounted and her throat was sanded by a burning thirst of disappointment.

The back of her hope was broken by the last straw when Mospin said: 'If we gave 'er money, we all know she would give it to charity. We know GB's kindness. She told me that she didn't want money, all she wanted was to be sure of our love and so we give 'er our 'earts.'

GB's face became grave and her lips moved involuntarily as she whispered: 'Lying bastard. Damn lying stinker! T'ief! Crooked brute!'

The audience cheered Mospin's remarks, many nodding approvingly to GB, which caused her to assume a sardonic smile.

Every word of praise and flattery wounded GB. Tears of bitter disappointment began to cloud her eyes, fusing the whole scene into a block of ice. At this moment, Mospin glanced at his victim and with a clean smile on his broad face, he said: 'Friends look 'ow sad GB is to leave us. We all feel sad to lose 'er. We is just putting the best outside when we smile on this sad occasion.'

This was a signal for weeping amongst members of the audience. GB herself sweated as her eyes could not shed the tears in sufficient volume to fit the occasion.

Amidst sustained cheers, Mospin spoke of the food to be consumed. He gave GB full credit for the goat she had given, making the number of goats killed for the feast three. 'Me know my people don't like cold food, and me is not going to keep you long, because already we all can smell the sweet odour of the curry. GB won't mind if we 'urry the presentation ceremony.'

From beneath the folds of his robe, Mospin produced an official envelope. A faint gleam of hope flickered in GB's gloomy heart. 'This must be a li'l money,' she muttered to herself. The shadow of a smile flashed on her face as Mospin said: 'GB never expected this, but it will show our appreciation in a strong way.'

From the envelope, he withdrew two sheets of foolscap paper and began reading a nonsensical address.

'Don't worry friends. Me is not going to read the whole t'ing. It is too long. GB will 'ave time to read and ponder it, so me will only read the first and last paragraphs.'

Thereupon, he garbled a few muffled sentences: 'We the friends and true admirers would 'ave liked to do more for you dear GB, but our plans was "castrated" by circumstances. However, it is my 'onour and privilege to present you with dis paper as a certificate from the people.'

He then handed GB the envelope with the address which she pulled from his hand rather brusquely. Mospin told the people that there was a cheque to follow, but GB would receive it the next day. He said that he had told her about it already and she said it was quite all right as the money didn't matter really. There were other gifts too. Mospin made sure that the people were impressed with the number of things given to GB.

'Friends,' he said, 'me 'ave yet another su'prise for our dear GB. She will never forget us!'

Mospin now beckoned to Bullyman, his accessory in crime, who brought a beautifully wrapped parcel. Mospin handed it to GB amidst riotous cheers.

GB used all her strength to prevent herself from bursting into tears. She remembered nothing about her sedulously prepared speech. At the moment, her thoughts were too vile for utterance and her heart seemed to be pumping mud to her head. The audience was greatly impressed by the grave look on her face which they mistook for grief of parting.

Many expressed praises for Mospin, describing him as a great leader and organizer, a true Jamaican.

GB flinched when called upon to speak. She rose mechanically, opened her mouth, but her voice was gone.

Gallantly, Mospin intervened:

'Our dear GB is too sad to speak. She is overwhelmed with the love we shows 'er. God bless 'er. Let's sing 'er favourite song.'

The singing ended, a man rose amidst the confusion of voices and shouted: 'Brodders and sisters all, Brodder Mospin 'as made a motion and me want to move a commotion.'

There was silence in deference to the speaker, who spouted praise for Mospin. He praised Mospin's honesty and good sense and wished him long life so that he might ever be useful to his people. No one knew that he was Mospin's paid henchman. The speaker was loudly applauded. Encouraged by the approbation, he expressed thanks for those who prepared the food and said that without them the proceedings would not have been enjoyable. When he sat down, someone asked for an exhibition of the mementoes. One parcel contained a small mahogany tray, reminding GB, apparently, of the tray that she used as a stonebreaker. In the other parcel was a large blue and white enamel-ware chamber-pot.

GB's heart was already too sad to be further affected by this new ridicule. As the crowd cheered and joked, she sat aloof, too disappointed to think.

Mospin asked the audience to join in singing the doxology, then he offered a prayer and by the time he was finished, several members of the audience had already stampeded to the refreshment counter in order to get first service. For the cultists, all the sadness of farewell was now ended. They chatted happily as they rushed for the food and drink.

'That's why me believe in pooling and partnership,' said one. 'When you pool things together you get back more than you put in. Me subscribe one shilling only and me is bound to eat about three shillings' worth of food, and drink till me get drunk tonight.'

'We should 'ave celebrations like this more often. De las' time me get satisfactory enjoyment with free food and drink was at a funeral.'

Occasional references were made to GB. Some said that she was very rich. They said it was nice of her to refuse money as Mospin had said. She's a genuine Christian.

It was believed by a few that GB was in prayer and silent contemplation seeking divine guidance. Some said that she had been fasting the whole day.

All that time, GB was cursing them, wishing the food would choke them to death.

'Me give mi nice goat to the gluttonous bastards,' she regretted. 'Me 'ope it stand up at their throats and kill them with indigestion. Those wicked brutes give me up to flowers and me not dead yet. Mospin is an ungrateful, thieving rascal. Me 'ope 'im end up on the gallows. Never will I trust any one of my people again, 'specially if them claim to be Christians.'

16

Panty, returning to Kingston to board with the Allens, was unaware of the domestic controversy he caused. Mrs Allen's prejudice towards him was undiminished, although disguised by a thicker coating of politeness. Parson's attitude was, as usual, fatherly. He called Panty 'Son' often enough and confessed to Mrs Allen that the boy belonged to the lower branches of family.

Wishfully thinking that he was totally accepted by the Allens, Panty dispatched secret love letters to Paula to which he received no replies.

Panty's presence at the dining-table was responsible for Mrs Allen's indigestion and frequently upset stomach, which sometimes necessitated her premature withdrawal. Seldom was Panty given a chance to speak, except Mr Allen addressed him directly. Paula skilfully avoided looking at him and often excused herself from the table following her mother. But the mere sitting at table with them blinded Panty to these slights. He saw himself getting into the hearts of all the Allens and was quite willing to exercise the necessary patience, which would ultimately make him a bona fide member of the family.

One day, however, Mrs Allen broke under the tension which Panty's presence caused. Becoming overwrought, she lost her usual self-control and demanded of her husband:

'When are we getting rid of our guest? We have done quite enough for him already. Heaven didn't ask as much. It is not necessary to be stuck with him for life.'

She was weeping hysterically, as if there were a death in the family.

'He's thoroughly a nice boy,' Mr Allen defended. 'It is good for us to show that our family does not practise race discrimination. We will get much respect and it costs us nothing. He pays for his board and lodge to help the family income and he's no trouble to any of us.'

Mrs Allen exploded: 'Say what you like. I know my feelings are right. The boy has too much ambition. Ambitious coloured people are the most dangerous of all human beings.'

Mr Allen argued that if a social wall were erected, it would challenge the boy's ambitious spirit. Then he'd want to make a really long jump: 'If we raise no barrier, there is nothing for him to scale, nothing will happen. He will keep in his place, for there will be no line to cross. His social ambition, as far as we are concerned, will die a natural death, can't you see?'

'But, darling,' Mrs Allen pleaded, 'if we just get rid of him now once and for all, there'll be no problem to solve. We will just live our own ordinary simple lives. But as long as he is here, I must have a protecting wall. God does not desire that we encage ourselves with a lion in order to prove our Christian bravery.'

'Not all walls are protective, my dear. Some walls restrict only their builders. Any wall to check the human spirit in any way is not protective, but dangerous. I believe that if we did not make these racial barriers, the coloured people would not be any nuisance to us. Let people be free and each race will live within its own boundary. Man's spirit is like steam: compress it and it explodes; leave it free, it dissipates into the air.'

'Maybe I'm thick in the head, but I've made up my mind now: as long as he is here, I'm going to stop sleeping in your bedroom.'

Nothing was settled when the Allens finished their argument.

That evening at dinner, Mrs Allen was most charming to Panty, inquiring what sort of a day he had had, although she did not listen to his reply. She paid undivided attention to Paula, who related interesting happenings at the Commercial School she was attending. Panty was glad of Mrs Allen's apparent interest in him.

Seeing a look of pleasure in Panty's face, Mrs Allen ingeniously sought to embarrass him. In a queer way, she did not think that coloured people had a right to be happy. To her, they were less detestable when they were sad. Grief befitted their dark faces. When they were happy, they were troublesome and fractious, she thought. In her own sociological survey, she had discovered that all the happy-go-lucky ones were irresponsible, subject to swift and violent changes of mood. They would be this moment jumping up for joy, and the next would be plunged in savage temper. The sadder ones were more predictable. To make Panty sad, she asked him about GB, smiling graciously at his obvious perplexity. Panty lied that he had written to her recently and was awaiting a reply. He also disclosed that on the last occasion he was in contact with her, she was well. That at least was true, the occasion being when he left her with the Allens for Kingston.

Parson Allen suggested that maybe GB was busy with her missionary work. This gave Mrs Allen another opportunity for an innuendo: 'I don't see why she should kill herself working for those slum people. She has done enough already. They are the type who never know when enough is done for them. Sometimes I feel sorry for them, knowing that slum life permanently damages the human spirit. People from the slums can never be properly adjusted to a good life. They cannot stand on their own!'

It was now Panty's turn to have indigestion and stomach upset. Paula stole a glance at him by moving her eyes without turning her head. Panty caught her eyes and mistook the sympathy in them for affection.

From behind the glass wall of prejudice erected by Mrs Allen, Panty saw the family magnified several times larger than life. Success for him was to be as 'big' as he thought they were. Conscious of Mrs Allen's dislike for him, he assumed the vain task of trying to win her esteem. His devotion to this quite unnecessary undertaking was a feat of tolerance and self-effacement. He never showed any resentment to Mrs Allen; instead, he was always too polite to her. He had exceeded the seventy times seven pardons recommended in the New Testament. Mrs Allen herself, on occasion, was moved by his almost grovelling co-operation and spontaneous gratitude. A few times, she honestly wished she could be kinder to him. But unfortunately, she could not undo the damage done her by acquired ignorance. She could not even stop herself from handing down to her daughter the lamentable inheritance of ill-will, the heirloom from her illiterate parents.

Panty's politeness to her had an ulterior motive. He wanted to win the mother in order to win the daughter. Paula's eloquent glance that day haunted him and gave him strange urgent ideas. In the glance, he saw a message of tenderness which needed quick answer.

Night found him restively tossing in his bed fighting the imbecilic urge to visit the woman he supposed loved him. His stockinged feet got out of bed and he obediently followed them in the direction of Paula's room. He was quite sure she desired intimacy. He had read it in her eyes. He was confident of success, if only he reached her room without any mishap. Caution! Stealthily, he inched his way. He turned the girl's door-knob very slowly, without a sound. It was an assurance to him to find the door was not locked with a key. He inferred that Paula expected him. He was successfully in the room now. Cautiously he closed the door, making no sound. The greatest part of the risk was accomplished. He remonstrated with himself for being such a sensitive fool, when he could have been having an affair with the lovely girl. He knew now, he thought, the reason why she did not reply to his letters. It was because she wanted him to come in person. He thought himself very dull for not understanding the position long before. But now, here he was, ready for the big chance to make up for the past. He would apologize to her tenderly and she would forgive him. All this was passing through his mind while passion surged through his body like a river in spate. This was a moment when lust strangled reason. In the darkness, he approached the bed whereon slept the delightful object of his passion, perhaps in the nude, he thought. He slipped his hand underneath the sheet, moving it like a feather over the sleeper's body. Would she wake up and scream in fright! No, he told himself. Certain of her co-operation, he gently awakened the sleeper, at the same time moving his hand to the vital spot. And now he received a shock which would have sent an older man to the grave. His father Parson Pendance would surely not have survived it. The dim bedroom light was suddenly turned on: Panty blinked as he found himself looking into the face of Mrs Allen.

Mrs Allen controlled herself because she did not want to awaken her 'angel' daughter to the revolting reality. In a subdued voice, but one full of unmistakable contempt, she ordered the intruder out.

By signs, Panty mimed that he was a somnambulist, but his ridiculous acting was meaningless to the irate Mrs Allen. In a whisper which nearly burst Panty's eardrums, she commanded: 'Get out, you infernal gutter-rat. Leave the house tonight! I knew that you slum niggers couldn't be trusted.'

When Panty recovered his reasoning, he was on his way from the rectory. Luckily for him, his personal effects were few.

Throughout the incident, Paula pretended to be asleep, watching through the bars of her eyelashes as from a prison cell. She made no stir, although it was difficult to repress laughter. This joke could be postponed without losing its risibility.

Mrs Allen, glad that Paula's delicacy had been unassailed, imagined that the girl knew nothing of the occurrence. She was also glad to be rid of Panty so conclusively and, in a way, triumphantly.

Because she thought the incident too disgusting, she made

no report to her husband. The following morning she appeared to share her husband's ignorance regarding Panty's mysterious departure. Paula herself seemed mystified.

Shame, guilt, perplexity, all blotted out everything else from Panty's mind, except the terrible words 'gutter-rat' which he imagined written on his forehead in red.

He spent the rest of the hours before morning in a notorious gamblers' den, a veritable headquarters of shady, underworld characters. It seemed the only place he felt fit to go, the only company he considered appropriate for a gutter-rat.

17

In Kate's comfortable three-bedroomed bungalow in a quiet residential area in St Andrew, GB quickly adjusted herself to luxurious living. With a maid to serve her, GB crowned herself undisputed head of the household, a position formerly she had reserved for Jesus. A living epitome of the proverbial truth which says that the earth trembles when a servant becomes master, GB was exacting and ridiculously fastidious, behaving more like a grand duchess than a Swine Lane expatriate.

To the maid, she gave conflicting orders, expecting both to be obeyed, but if either was, she would still cavil.

GB copied the habits of her former employers except, of course, their benevolence. Breakfast in bed was a frequent request, but it took a long time for her to learn to handle the cup and saucer without spilling the tea on the bed and harming herself. GB now found the two gifts from her Swine Lane friends very useful. She had torn up the address on the same night, knowing that it was pure flapdoodle.

In puerile ostentation, GB tantalized her maid Lucia by frequently calling the girl's attention to expensive dresses she owned:

'All my clothes cost a lot of money. Me never buy cheap t'ings. Me don't allow maids to wash these. Most maids can only wash the rags they're accustomed to wear.'

GB now pretended to be an authority on domestic etiquette, merely to make Lucia feel stupid. GB the former 'slave' became GB the slave-owner. Lucia, once a happy girl of nineteen who used to sing whilst working, became a morose, timid, wretched wreck only a few weeks after GB's arrival. She longed to leave the torture, but could not, because she was helping to support her ailing mother and her own illegitimate child whose father had absconded.

GB spent much of her time in telling about her luxurious antecedents, making an effort to conceal her low origin and fill in the obvious cracks in her personality. Not infrequently, she made deleterious comments about slum people. She took pains to convince Lucia of her inefficiency and laziness: 'Me can do everyt'ing better than you fer miself. Me is trained in 'ouse management. When me was a young gal like you, me 'ad to get special training. My parents paid fer mi edication.' GB claimed to be a B.A., but never explained that the abbreviation meant 'Born Again'. In her case, she could aptly have added B.D., to indicate she was born again in the blood of the devil.

Although it was not her own money, GB begrudged Lucia's wages, suggesting that Kate reduce it. One Friday evening she confiscated the girl's wages, covertly accusing her of the theft of a pair of scissors which GB herself had mislaid. Lucia rightly refused to search, lest finding the missing article bring suspicion on her. GB accused Lucia of insubordination and in a fit of temper told Lucia many unpleasant things. GB eventually recovered the scissors where she had put them and, without apologizing, paid Lucia saying: 'You must glad me find it or you'd be in trouble!'

Lucia's patience was exhausted and throwing caution to the wind, she replied: 'A ugly old bitch like you should never 'ire servant because you is not a good servant yourself. You don't come from anywhere otherwise you would act better. You must 'ave come from the slums yourself, you is just a hurry-come-up mackerel.'

GB, a former prophetess, was astonished at Lucy's ability to recapture the past. In passion and horror, she dismissed the girl, of course without paying the wages due in lieu of notice.

As was the custom in the locality, GB made a flower garden. She hoped it would be possible to sell the flowers, as she herself had little use for them. Already, she was doing all the domestic work since Lucia left and she increased her own wages out of the money Kate gave her to run the house.

While gardening, she met her neighbour over the hedge and from then on, GB's social contacts began blooming rapidly.

Comfortable, happy and secure, GB was proud of Kate and grateful to her, until the day when desperation forced Kate to ask her for a loan.

Instead of readily sympathizing with Kate, GB reacted as if attacked by a highwayman: 'Me don't 'ave no money! Me is a poor woman.'

At once she regretted having left Swine Lane, suspecting that her own daughter wanted to extort money from her. GB's indifference and initial unwillingness to assist forced Kate to disclose her personal troubles. Kate's lover Russ was in danger of imminent arrest for embezzlement of Government funds. Four hundred pounds were needed in a hurry to put things right.

'His wife is the cause. She went with her lover, telling Russ that she was going on an excursion arranged by a church society. The wife came back very late in the night from the imaginary trip. In the next morning's papers there was news that the bus carrying the said excursion party had collided with a truck, fallen over a precipice with all its occupants killed or severely injured. Discovering that she had lied to him about the excursion, Russ boxed her and, in revenge, she wrote the authorities that Russ was stealing their money. A friend of Russ, who saw the letter, gave him a tip. He must now get five hundred pounds odd.'

Kate's desire to help him, although genuine, was also increased by the hope that the final break between Russ and his wife would be to her advantage.

GB contracted her lips and squeezed her nostrils as if to avoid some very bad odour. Then she said: 'But is not you send 'im to steal govament's money. These young men are too wild and reckless. Pshew!'

'I must help 'im, GB. He was the first person to help me in Kingston and it is through him that I have anything today. I scrape everything in the bar, but I need four hundred pounds more.'

'Don't worry yourself. If 'im go to prison 'im won't be in any danger. When 'e is gone, the bar will be all yours! Take my motherly advice and never do too much for any man. Even God A'mighty cry when 'im make man. Look after yourself. Pray about it and leave it to God. When you see your neighbour's 'ouse blazing take water to yours.'

'GB, me cannot wait on prayer. The matter is very urgent. If any scandal, I'll be mixed up in it. Maybe it will be a disgrace to Panty when we meet.'

The mention of Panty at once mollified GB. 'Yes, for Panty's sake, you must not get yourself mixed up. But all the same, the man don't do not'ing for you free. Him got your body. You can't take that back. If you give the needy, God will give you more needy people to give to and you become needy yourself.'

In desperation, Kate rashly offered GB generous interest, pledging the house as security. At this suggestion GB showed understanding, although she grumbled, saying that she did not know the man and he had done nothing for her personally, except disturb her rest when he came in late in the nights and sneaked out early in the mornings.

'You're just like me,' GB complimented Kate, 'very soft-'earted. It is only lately me is learning to protect myself in order to avoid dying in poverty. Furthermore, me want to 'ave li'l somet'ing to leave my gran'son. It is no good that me work so 'ard and then allow stranger to get the money and me own blood relation to go without.'

Kate now was in sympathy with GB's position. They were both working for the same purpose—Panty's security.

Under further pressure from Kate, GB agreed to loan three

hundred and seventy pounds provided Kate gave her a written undertaking. Kate would have sold her soul to the devil to help her man.

It was not possible for GB to increase her authority in the house. She had long ago been *de facto* possessor-occupier, Kate being merely the owner. Now in possession of a direct financial interest in the house, GB effected numerous but quite unnecessary economies, reducing the living standard almost to that of the slums. It was a joy and delight for her to live poor in order to die rich.

Waiting for the repayment of the loan was shortening GB's life minute by minute. She fretted and fumed, although she possessed the written document and knew that her capital was accumulating interest. In her anxiety and distress, she turned to the Lord and, in fervent prayer, implored Him to prosper Kate, so that she might pay her debts.

This unselfish prayer did not receive the immediate attention of heaven, hence GB decided to visit the Lord's house and make her appeal from His earthly headquarters. She had not attended church since she came to Kingston. There was nothing she specially needed, no problems to solve until now, so there was not the need for church attendance.

One night, whilst Kate and herself sat in the sitting-room, GB suddenly wondered aloud: 'My mind just ran upon Panty, me wonder what 'appen to 'im!'

Kate's attention was that of a cat hearing the squeak of a mouse. GB continued to speak: 'Of all the pickneys born in Swine Lane, 'im is the very best. Him 'ave good religious blood and me know that 'im is going 'igh up in life. The colour of 'is skin will be a great 'elp, and 'im 'ave plenty of ambition.'

Entranced in a reverie, Kate exclaimed: 'A mother's love is a funny thing, a mother can love even if her child does not know her or she him. Sometimes, that love is stronger than all.'

GB supported: 'Your child will love you. Any pickney would love such a nice mother. You is good-looking, decent, independent, industrious and you 'ave a business which . . .'

GB stopped abruptly, as her voice tapered off. She was obviously inviting Kate's comment on the state of the business. Kate missed the bait, being too engrossed in thoughts of her son.

'Will he forgive me?' she wondered wistfully. 'Will he forget the past?'

Prophetess GB now made a prediction: 'One of these fine days, your boy will come right into this 'ere 'ouse. He will come as soon as 'im know that you 'ave money!'

'I pray for the day. It would be too good to be true!'

'Me would never allow any silly man to stop me from getting in touch with me own pickney!'

Kate again explained that, up to then, Russ was unaware of Panty's existence: 'He told me that his wife was a living graveyard, the number of abortions she had had before their marriage. He thought I was virtuous, he never having met a virgin, and so, I could not disclose that I was already a mother. If he knew, he would leave me.'

'The man is a blasted fool altogether! If 'im want virgins, ten of them in the Bible, five of them is foolish like 'im. Not a t'ing is wrong with 'aving a bastard pickney. Children is necessary to woman, for 'ealth and security and other things, but marriage is only necessary to make a show and to make everybody know that a woman has a licence to sleep with a man. If me did wait till me married to 'ave a pickney, you wouldn't be born yet. Woman can marry at any age and stage, but she can only 'ave pickney when she young. Me believe in making 'ay while the sun shines. Wise people teach me that.'

'I agree . . . but . . .'

GB interrupted: 'You know what I've been t'inking?' Kate paused. GB disclosed her desire to recommence church attendance. She wished to renew acquaintance with the Allens in order to learn of Panty.

Kate offered her enthusiastic encouragement. GB continued: 'Me didn't bother with Church all the while, because me know what the Church wants and me can't take my li'l money to give them. But now me don't 'ave no money, me can go without fear.'

'Not for long, GB. I'll soon pay you,' Kate was obviously annoyed, judging from the tone of her voice.

'Me was not t'inking about what you owes me. Me never even remember that and in any case me know that that's safe, plus the interest that's growing and growing every day!'

GB was very glad to hear the promise of early payment, for although she said that she had forgotten it, she thought constantly of nothing but the debt.

A few days later, Kate paid a substantial part of the loan. GB was so delighted that she rushed to church the following Sunday to offer thanks for the deliverance.

She contacted Parson Allen who was very pleased to see her, thinking that she had but recently arrived in Kingston. He asked her to visit the rectory as soon as she was settled.

To her query about Panty, Parson could give no enlightenment. He did not care to speak much about the subject because he suspected that Panty had fled because of Mrs Allen's persecution and this caused him personal embarrassment.

In a few weeks, GB was virtually back into the bosom of the Allens, at the same time becoming a devoted member of the church.

Parson Allen pushed her into every important church organization. She became a member of the Daughters of the King Society, showing extravagant interest in the section concerned with rehabilitating 'fallen' girls. A sinner of GB's experience found the most succulent gossip at this source and, because of peculiar ability to unearth scandals, she became a veritable patron saint of the many middle-aged and old women, mostly spinsters and widows, who set themselves up as moralists, being deprived of the opportunity to commit the original sin. Rather than being sorry for the unfortunate girls who went astray, these women found much entertainment discussing the plights of the luckless girls, pregnant extra-maritally.

GB soon became high priestess amongst the self-righteous,

pharisaical heirachy who sublimated their longings for physical love by persecuting those who had the opportunity and the daring. They were vixens for whom all grapes beyond their reach were sour.

The chief victims of the 'battle-axe' committee were teenage girls expecting their first illegitimate babies. There were scrutineers whose effective espionage detected a case a few hours after conception. They gave the alarm for the 'Sandhedrin' council to be convened, as a sort of war cabinet, as soon as they had any suspicions. This committee's first duty was to get the suspected girl excommunicated, if she happened to be a communicant. This done, envious, unfulfilled spinsters, or regretful widows were selected to give lectures to the suspect, dealing with the gravity of the sin, of fornication, pretending to be unaware that without this honeyed sin, humanity would have very little pleasure and the human race become extinct. These women gave the impression that the privilege of having children was a middle-class right, reserved, subsequent to marriage. In suitable cases, when the girl named a putative father of her own social class, efforts were made to promote a marriage of convenience, which was said to bring automatic absolution from the sin already committed.

With more than the necessary experience in the various social vices, GB proved a blessing to this psuedo-religious gossip club. The 'sins' of the young girls enabled the ancient eaters of forbidden fruit to forgive their own multitudinous transgression, although there were times when they begrudged the improved facilities for sin which modern society had produced.

In a hurry to build up her prestige, GB now thought the time convenient to distribute some of the large quantity of old dresses which she had been given for the purpose. Realizing how much significance was placed on charity by the church, GB also donated five pounds during a fund-raising drive. The gift made a great impression on Parson Allen, who confirmed all his past respect for GB's self-sacrificing charitability.

GB's prestige grew continuously amongst the church people.

Whatever she was asked to do for the church, was done with great zest. Committee members readily grabbed the glory but left the work to GB to perform; her devotion was everywhere acknowledged.

She had no rival when she was proposed as president of the Society for the Prevention of Cruelty to Animals. GB accepted responsibilities with the same avidity with which she always grabbed money, but now she made a zealous, if comic effort to improve her speech and grammar.

Attending her first meeting of the Society for the Prevention of Cruelty to Animals. GB confessed her abiding love for animals. She incautiously regretted that at the moment she was without a pet, but said she would soon acquire one or more. She referred, of course, to her plan for raising pigs in the backyard, which Kate had already told her was illegal.

To her profound horror, before the meeting ended, sympathizing 'fellow pet-lovers' offered GB a number of dogs, the animal for which she harboured the greatest dislike.

'Oh, me will be very glad to 'ave one only,' she said with a beguiling smile. 'I love a good dog, but I'm so unlucky with dogs!'

The following afternoon a weary messenger brought GB an elephantine Alsatian, as greedy as it was savage. Endowed instinctively with a canine but uncanny judgment, the dog instantly scented the lack of affection in its prospective owner and, without tact, the brute expressed with doggish eloquence its own want of feeling for GB.

It was hate at first sight between GB and Rexi, whose manner could not be mistaken. With dogged tenacity, Rexi made it abundantly clear that he was not remaining in the same compound with GB. The haughtiness of this beast gave GB an inferiority complex, but she was glad of this display of canine forthrightness. She made a half-hearted and insincere attempt to coax and quieten the monster, but only succeeded in increasing its infuriation.

The fatigued messenger fearing the necessity of returning with Rexi, did his best to convince GB that the dog was not so bad and would eventually adjust itself to the new environs. GB told him, 'It will be me who will 'ave to change to please 'im. Maybe me would 'ave to get another 'ouse if 'im don't like this one!'

Rexi's agitation increased momentarily. Every time GB opened her mouth, Rexi interrupted with a blood-thirsty growl.

Hiding her joy, in a regretful tone GB told the messenger to take the dog back to Mrs Jones and tell her how very sorry she was to lose the lovely pet. As the dog was led away, it became calm and quiet, whilst GB raised her hands to heaven in thanksgiving for yet another deliverance.

Mrs Jones was not only profoundly disappointed, but upset to have the problematic Rexi returned to her. This was about the third attempt she had made to be rid of him. She was annoyed with GB for not taking the dog. Mrs Jones, therefore, told everyone that GB was not a lover of pets. She advised that no one should offer GB any more dogs or any kind of pet. GB was ignorant of this kind service Mrs Jones had unintentionally done to her.

GB's multifarious engagements created the necessity for a domestic maid. This time, she wanted a trained domestic scientist. Maud, a superior domestic with light skin, shapely figure and good looks, was sent to GB. At the sight of her in her neat, stylish, pink-cotton dress, GB had a severe attack of inferiority complex. Maud wore shoes, which was quite unusual for a domestic. She spoke good English, and her tone of voice was as refined and gentle as her manner. GB was terribly afraid of her, imagining that Maud may have learned her vocation at a university.

A few years ago GB would have readily addressed her as 'madam', but now GB's welcoming words were: 'Listen, miss what's-you-name. Me didn't go to college, but the money me is paying is good as that of anybody's and therefore, me want

138

the same respect you would give to a white person. Me is the 'ead of this 'ouse and me not desirous of getting anyone to rule me, understan'? You'll find that me is very, very kind and don't give trouble. Me love me own race and like to see them rise, but tell you the truth, me is afraid when them elevate. Me don't have to tell you that most of us only want a li'l independence and prosperity to lose respect for God and man. They get "stocious", if you know what me mean. Although you 'ave better colour than me, colour don't matter. Is me paying you and you must treat me just the same as if you was working for "backra people". You is an intelligent lady, and me don't need to tell you all this, but me must let you know that many big shot people come 'ere from time to time—me don't mix with small fry—and me want you to treat me very "coachius" in front of them.'

'Yes, ma'am.'

'Ah! That's what me mean! That's 'ow me like it! We will get on very well. Me like to see my own people with culcha, come of them is too rough and piece-up; don't know their place, believe them is equal to their betters. We all is God's children, but some 'igher than some!'

In this lecture, GB mentioned nothing about Kate. It took months before Maud understood the true position that Kate was the owner and proprietress who paid all the expenditures. Timidity prevented GB from calling Maud by name for a few weeks. She continually styled her a ' Miss-what's-you-name', although she quite well knew the name was Maud. As if by radiation or remote control, Maud exercised a strong influence over GB. It was now GB who was always on her guard and trying to please. GB praised everything Maud did, whether it pleased her or not; she was continually afraid of being considered a fool. She had the highest regard for Maud's judgment, always trying to win the maid's esteem and approval.

Kate was glad to see the unusual co-operation GB gave the maid. She herself was much impressed with Maud, who she treated more like a younger sister than as a domestic servant. Relations between employer and employed were never better anywhere in Jamaica.

GB kept the Bible as her constant companion. She constantly prayed for wisdom, made every effort to increase her education, while her cunning increased of its own accord.

Once, she was a member of a panel of judges at an elocution contest sponsored by a church organization. The word 'elocution' puzzled her. She asked Maud craftily: 'Even been to a "Qussian" contex?' On further explanation from GB Maud described the procedure, informing GB that she had once been the winner of a prize for selection and delivery.

Being an old midwife, GB thought the word 'delivery' had one connotation, and that was why she asked Maud with demonstrable shock: 'Oh, so you 'ave a pickney! Me is a midwife so me know all about delivery. Me never get no prize, not even when me deliver me own pickney.'

When Maud clarified her meaning, it was GB's turn to disclose how talented a public speaker she was. To demonstrate her skill, GB recited a portion of a Bible verse: 'The race is not for the swif' nor the backle for the strong. . . .' It was also an advice and warning for Maud.

18

It was unusually early for Kate to be home. Throwing herself limply on the sofa in the sitting-room, she did not have the will or strength to put her feet up. With hands for pillow, she gazed through tear-filled eyes on the ceiling which reeled above her semi-conscious gaze. She pursed and bit her lips intermittently. She was in trouble.

GB thought it was a love problem which Kate had to settle, but when she gave a cheerful hint, Kate divulged a story far more grave than GB anticipated.

Kate said that she had been prosecuted for selling rum below the legal proof strength.

GB's logical comment was: 'Me don't see not'ing wrong in that. Everybody put water in rum before they drinks it. Me bet is some damned 'urry-come-up bastard that call 'imself govament man who prosecute you. He must be looking promotion, you bet!'

'This has to happen just at the time I'm trying to get money to finish pay you. I don't know what I'll do if they fine me heavily.'

'Don't worry yourself, my daughter. God will help you to pay me.'

Kate dreaded to ask for an outright loan, she vainly hoped GB would volunteer financial help. After some moments' silence, GB disclosed that she knew the judge's wife and undertook to beg her to influence her husband on Kate's behalf. Encouraged by this favourable prospect, Kate related the happenings which led to her prosecution. GB commented:

'Me is going to read the hundred and ninth psalm for nine mornings and if the govament man who prosecute you don't turn worthless, no God is in 'eaven. Watch out!'

With simmering indignation, Kate described how rudely she was used by the officer, who called her a whore: 'I told him that his mother could not have been a good whore, to have brought the likes of him into the world!'

GB interjected: 'Perhaps, not only 'is mother, but great-great-grandmother down the line were whores. If you know 'is name we can fix 'im.'

'I don't think the son of a bitch has a name!'

'You should pay five shillings to get someone to break his backside for him. Or better, you can put a good obeahman on the job and then he will be no use to whores or virgins. Then he'd know where water walk go to pumpkin guts!'

The women dug deep in their brains to find evil descriptions for the officer and his entire ancestry, including the devil.

GB surmised: 'When ragamuffins dress up in govament clothes, it always make them act foolish. I bet 'im is like the policeman who got me into trouble. Those sort of people is accustomed to 'aving their arse exposed and their "seeds" begging bread and so, when they put on good clothes, they believe they reach 'eaven!'

Discussing the law court, GB described it as a place of truth and right. There, one should tell the truth if one was right. There was no point in telling the truth when in the wrong. She inveighed against lawyers, who she said were glorified vultures, profiting from people's misfortunes. The only way to get justice was to have a friend in court, like the judge. Then one was sure of getting justice.

Kate was greatly disturbed, but GB pointed out that under the first offender's act, Kate was entitled to be leniently treated. She advised Kate to free her mind from fear because the judge's wife would certainly assist. GB promised to take flowers for the judge's wife when she would explain things to her.

Referring to the man who prosecuted her, Kate said: 'Better the bugger's mother had suckled a pig which would have some use to humanity. It was a waste of time to bear pains for that monster.'

Kate wished that the government would be more selective in employing staff. They should get only cultured and educated persons to serve the people. 'Education makes all the difference in people,' she observed. 'I shall always love educated people, they know how to treat others.'

'Yes, edication is a very good t'ing, but is not all of us 'ave the 'ead for it. It makes some of us mad. Me glad that our li'l boy edicated in the right and proper way and 'ave the brains to balance 'imself in life. 'Im is trained to be a gentleman, just like Parson Allen and Parson Pendance.'

19

A saint by day, devil by night, Panty returned often to the
illicit jungle of a club to gamble at all-night sessions with
spivs and poltroons whose sources of income mystified honest
brains. Panty found a special prop there whenever he was low
in spirit and funds. Accepted as a sort of honorary member
of this unholy freemasonry of social bacteria, he was on
intimate terms with the barmaid, who was extremely fond of
him. Although the price of the liquor varied according to the
mood of the barmaid, Panty received drinks free of cost on a
number of occasions.

Above this bar and secret gambling-den were a number of
rooms used by the ladies of the streets who nightly sold plots
of Paradise to transient tenants. These sin-ridden bed-chambers
were known to the 'trade' as the 'Upper Rooms'.

Panty used all the facilities of the 'club' and was very lucky
in the poker games, though not so fortunate at dice.

As an inferiority complex goaded him on to seek social
recognition; he saw sexual promiscuity as one way to be above
somebody. Affairs with married women generally gave satisfaction according to the social position of the wronged
husband. Whilst he was looking down into a wife's face, he felt
a psychological triumph over her husband.

It took him months of sedulous pressure to seduce the very
good-looking mulatto wife of a senior Civil Servant. This young
woman, Mrs Keans, apparently had not married for love, but
for the security her wealthy husband provided. He could have
been her father as far as age was concerned. He was ugly, his

nose resembling a Japanese fan, and his manners were far from attractive, although he was well brought-up and educated. If one saw him standing beside his chic, shapely wife, one would be unchivalrous not to feel a strong desire to rescue beauty from the beast.

Ada Keans was a girl of good education, breeding and charm. Her parents had bankrupted themselves investing in her education and, before they died, sought to regain interest on their capital by stage managing Ada's marriage to Peter Keans, a man of substance.

Panty saw traces of unhappiness in Ada's face on their first meeting at a party where he tried to give the appearance of being the epitome of chivalry. On subsequent occasions they met clandestinely when they exchanged deep confidences and sometimes caresses. Gallantly, Panty allowed her to escape without intimacy.

He never guessed how disappointed Ada was that he never made any attempt to rape her on the second occasion they met. Not that she would have allowed him to succeed, but at least she would be reassured that she was strongly desired by him. Because of the lack of violent effort on Panty's part, Ada complained to herself, quite unjustly, that she was losing her sex-appeal. When she looked into the mirror she saw herself a mere shadow of her well-acknowledged beauty. Instead of seeing her face, she possibly was seeing the reflection of her state of mind. Youth was apparently running out of her veins like a tributary into the vast river of time cascading into the sea of eternity.

Using that feminine psychology which makes a mature woman act like an imbecilic infant in calling attention to herself, Ada sought by devious means to increase Panty's interest in her. She told herself that she merely desired to have him tied around her little finger. She wanted the thrill of having a man ardently chasing her in order to rid her life of boredom.

On one occasion she gave Panty some unmistakable hints,

even going as far as to mention some of the bedroom deficiencies of her ageing husband.

Ada's intuition had deceived her into believing that Panty's failure to 'attack' was occasioned by lack of physical interest. The truth was that because of her background and position he was hesitant to treat her like a common wench afflicted with nymphomania. For a lady of her social status, Panty wanted a convenient place to consummate the affair.

At their latest meeting, Ada made several references to her constant headaches. Between kisses, she confessed that she had to take sleeping pills frequently as her husband never put her to sleep naturally.

Panty immediately placed himself under the obligation to provide Mrs Keans with the physical peace arising from that deep sleep which only one thing in the world can give.

'I shall make you sleep.'

'Will you hypnotize me or something?'

Panty kissed her for answer and in the subsequent long embrace, their passions exploded and the smoke of burning discretion blinded their eyes.

As if suddenly aroused from a nightmare, Ada released herself from Panty's arms, whispering a fusillade of sweet meaningless 'Nos'. In rather apologetic manner and tone, Panty told her about the jungle club, outlining in details all its attractions and privacy.

Ada inquired how he knew so much about such a place. He replied that many decent persons went there to gamble for fun because it was so private. He hinted that she should take a look at the place, but Ada recoiled from the idea. After a pause she confessed:

'I have a secret desire to do something quite scandalous. At times when I'm in church I feel to scream. I suppose 'tis because I never had a chance to be myself.'

A sigh of regret concluded Ada's confession. They parted with a feeling of urgency for the next meeting.

Two days later, Ada phoned Panty and during the conversation told him that her husband would be away for a few days on business. Very casually, she asked about the 'club' he was describing at their last meeting. When their conversation ended, arrangements were made for Ada to visit the club one night during her husband's absence. She would disguise herself appropriately and Panty would be waiting to guide her into the den with as little publicity as possible.

The only thought in Panty's head the whole day was that of the coming tryst with the shapely, beautiful and sweet-mannered Ada. Almost every minute he heard her calling his name with an emotional resonance that excited his passion.

He could not wait for the evening to come for him to rush from work straight to the club to prepare for Ada. He was exactly two and a half hours too early for the appointment, so in order to still the beating of his anxious heart, he joined in a game of poker and thus dissipated the haunting moments of bubbling erotic anticipation.

He was soon convinced that this was indeed his lucky day. He started winning as never before, but whilst his winnings piled up to a sizeable heap, he hardly could estimate the height of the mounting envy and wrath of the losers and onlookers. It appeared that he possessed a secret lodestone flashing magic ray to influence things in his favour. But this, like all successes, was not unmixed. Still more considerable than the money he won was the hate he simultaneously earned from the other gamblers. He sensed it accurately and, at one moment, it was as if he had diligently climbed over the high wall of happiness to pick up a fruit of success in the garden of chance, but having retrieved the golden fruit, was imprisoned by the wall he had scaled.

As the game went on and on, he was so engrossed that he forgot his important date by one minute.

At 8.31 p.m. when it was dark outside, he looked at his wristlet watch and in excitement and horror exclaimed:

'Good God, I have an important date. . . . I have to go. . . .'

Before his words cooled, there was a series of clicks sounding much like morse code. Looking around, Panty saw himself surrounded by a veritable forest of flick knives held in combat position. It seemed as if the men had been commanded by some unseen general to present arms, but their eyes were not filled with passive ceremonial attention. The cold, still alertness in them belonged to death itself.

In anger, voices raised to rebuke Panty with explosive threats. They said that no date with any woman could be more important than money. They made it clear that Panty would not be allowed to leave with the winnings. If he wanted to go to his appointment he would have to leave the money behind.

Panty tried to remain calm and cool, for he knew a false move might lose him his life. His was a beautiful dilemma if ever there was one, with desirable alternatives at either end, but neither could be chosen without danger to the other.

Panty quickly found perhaps the only compromise. Interrupting his winnings for a few moments, he asked a girl attendant to take the key to Ada. As he whispered instructions to the girl, she was very sorry to see a winner in such a dire predicament and was glad to help him in any way.

Receiving the key from the girl, who pointed out a room near the entrance, Ada slipped in, feeling as light as a feather although her heart was leaden. Shaking with fear, she sought to understand the situation, thinking that perhaps Panty had taken this step for security reasons. Nevertheless, she was in a complete vacuum. Her former desire to do something scandalous proved to be a bluff for, now that she was in, her mind wavered, and were it not for a paralysing fear, she would have run back out into the street. The pain in her head increased violently during the first few moments as she contemplated remorsefully how foolish she had been to come. Almost involuntarily, she took a phial from her handbag and swallowed two tablets with water she drew from the tap over the basin. Each moment crawled like a postponed day, her pride rose from the cavern of her heart like a megalomaniac sea monster, consuming her.

She began thinking of her dead parents and the sacrifices they had made to make a lady of her. She thought of her husband's generosity and obvious love towards her, and just as once she had seen her beauty melt in the mirror, now she was seeing the petals of her spirit searing. Soon she was remonstrating bitterly with herself for throwing herself at Panty, who seemed to be so little interested in her. Her prodigal spirit rose, directing her to go back to her lovely home, but something which she could not explain prevented her from following in body. She also wanted to get the earliest chance to tell Panty exactly what she thought of him. She waited.

What had begun as a headache was now the sensation of having a steam locomotive shunting in her cranial tunnel. She felt dizzy, and the whole room seemed spinning in an opposite direction to the earth. The floorings undulated beneath her feet. She was barely able to take a few more pills in an effort to regain her self-command. Her pain was not eased, and as the moments lengthened she became increasingly thirsty for respite. Her pride was shattered.

She took another supply of pills recklessly, kicked off her shoes and threw herself on the bed, which appeared to have risen half-way to meet her falling body.

Panty played without caution, hoping to lose so that he could escape from his captors, but it was his night and nothing could stop him from winning.

When the last man was broke, Panty was released, so to speak. He ordered a round of drinks for everyone, and while they were drinking, he quietly slipped out and rushed to Ada.

Seeing her shapely figure lying on the bed face downwards, Panty took pains not to crash her sleep. Noiselessly, he locked the door, took off his jacket, loosened his tie and, taking off his shoes ever so quietly, stretched himself out beside her in the very dimly-lit room.

Stroking her back tenderly, he pleaded:

'Ada, darling, I'm sorry. I couldn't help it. God knows how I wanted to come to you so long, but those ruffians would not let me.'

Receiving no answer, he thought that it was mere feminine caprice responsible for Ada's indifference, or maybe she was in a deep sleep.

'You've a right to be vexed, but, darling, please forgive me I love you with all my heart. Don't let this incident mar our everlasting love. From now on, I'll cure all your headaches and make you sleep like a top.'

Still receiving no reply, he gently turned her over to awaken her with his kisses. That would make her speak indeed.

He shook her vigorously, whispering her name tenderly but not without excitement. Placing her head in the crook of his arm, he gazed into her half-smiling face; his thoughts began jumping from his brains like tenants fleeing from a burning building.

It was a strangely fortunate period for Panty. Not only was he lucky in gambling, but apparently whatever he said then would come true.

He had promised to cure Ada's headaches and insomnia and, whether he meant it or not, he had succeeded far beyond his own power.

When Panty became fully aware of the situation he was in, he forgot where the door was. Hastily putting on his jacket and shoes, he escaped through the window into the night like a frightened child being pursued by a monster in the dark.

He left behind all the money he had won. He did not pray, for he knew that prayer was powerless to replace life in the dead woman. Instead, he promised God that he would thenceforth forsake the paths of unrighteousness.

Realizing that God is a spirit, Panty had decided that he could best reconcile himself with his Maker by strict observance of the Spirit Licence Law. He recalled hearing Parson Allen say on many occasions that Jesus had come to fulfil the law. He therefore inferred that if he fulfilled the law relating to the sale of spirits and alcoholic beverages, his heaven would be sure and he would win the respect of the world at large. Never again would he visit the dens of vice to purchase cut-price drinks and sex. The jungle club and similar places were out of bounds for ever, he resolved.

Although he was very sad about Ada, he comforted himself somewhat in his belief that her death had brought a favourable change in his life. Perhaps it was fated that she should have died so that he might live more nobly, if not more abundantly.

He deceived himself into believing that it was some kind of conversion which made him desire to forsake his old ways, but in truth it was fear.

Reports regarding Ada's death made it clear that she suffered from amnesia and epilepsy. It was said to be on one of the occasions of her affliction that she had wandered away from home and was rescued by a heroine at the jungle club. The money found in the room where Ada died made the club-hostess very co-operative in endorsing this story.

Her husband's influence and wealth helped to make the report credible to sympathizers, although his social enemies whispered their doubts.

Panty was never associated in any way with the matter. However, he never felt at ease when the police were around and was on the alert even if the word 'police' was mentioned suddenly.

20

With sincere earnestness, GB invoked heaven's wrath on the offending officer and all who concerned him. On second thought, she decided against approaching the judge's wife on Kate's behalf, lest she be recognized as the mother of a dishonest barmaid. GB considered that her reputation demanded that she remain in the background as far as the case was concerned. Kate was not told of this.

It needed great effort for GB to attend the trial; she made no plans for assisting Kate with money. Kate was already in her debt.

In the dock Kate felt assured that GB had made contact with the judge as promised. In a clear confident voice, she pleaded guilty to breach of the Spirit Licence Law. She was ready to co-operate with the judge. She of course expected to be given the opportunity of recounting the happenings to the court. She discovered soon enough that it was not the government man who was indicted for bad behaviour. Twice her attempts to describe the officer's conduct were frustrated, and she was curtly advised not to stray from the facts of the case. She now presumed that the judge must have already made up his mind in her favour and did not care to listen to the unpleasant story in detail. Kate's back was turned to GB, who sat in the extreme rear of the long room. Could she have seen GB's face then, Kate would not have felt as confident of success as she did. GB had done absolutely nothing to help, which was bad enough, but, what was worse, he made Kate believe that the forces of authority were in her favour.

Kate was rudely shocked when the judge, from whom she expected understanding and co-operation, scathingly reprimanded her and imposed a fine of fifty pounds plus costs. She did not expect the case to finish so quickly before she had the chance to give full evidence. The judge described her as an obviously low type, who was very impertinent to superiors. He said that it was patent that she wished to scandalize the Government Official after he honourably resisted her indecent advances.

'The civility of civil servants in this country is one of the most hopeful aspects of our national life. The land is proud of the courteous and painstaking service given by all government servants in all branches of the service. It would improve public manners if more people in other walks of life followed the example of civil servants. I refuse to believe that this trained, cultured officer used obscene and abusive words to you. He had no need to do so, and it is not in the tradition of the service for officials to curse members of the public. I find your evidence totally unreliable.'

Kate was stunned, she summarily lost all respect for justice as administered in the law courts. Justice was indeed blind, and deaf also, but not dumb. She summarized her feelings in a murmur betwixt her teeth: 'The law is the worst criminal in the land.' But grief, alarm and anger did not spoil the kindly beauty of her face. There was a peculiar quality of beauty accentuated by adversity which polished her attractive face. She was alluringly attired in a midnight-blue linen skirt with a white embroidered blouse, sleeveless with low neckline. The tight-fitting skirt was like a speech, short enough to be interesting and long enough to cover the subject. A large white handbag and white pointed-toe, high-heeled shoes completed her ensemble. Her dress gave the judge a totally wrong impression about her.

GB in her ordinary dark nondescript gown, had fled the courtroom during the unhappy climax and, like a dog fresh from the whipping-post, was whimpering softly whilst she awaited Kate. As Kate was somewhat long in coming, GB's fears increased and she found herself involuntarily sneaking down the steps of the courtroom, willing to deny Kate if anyone chanced to associate them. GB found an obscure spot behind a column where she could see, but not be seen easily. She had a great dread, as a modern pharisee, to be seen with a publican though it be her own daughter and benefactress.

With measured steps, happy in heart, coming from his triumphant engagement, the offending officer with his little brown bag approached. He looked very smart in his short white tunic and black-serge trousers. He might have been thinking about the kind remarks made by the judge, for he was wearing a very pleasant smile, as if he were pleased with something.

GB shifted from her hiding place and moved menacingly towards him. She wanted to warn him of his impending doom. When she confronted him, she fell back, frightened as if she had touched live wire; her mouth sprang open with surprise, but she covered it with her trembling hand. She was momentarily speechless and thought that recent events had befuddled her mind. Her reason was in violent disagreement with her eyes.

'Pah . . . Pa . . . Paha . . . pa . . . pa . . . Pan-ty!' GB stammered uncertainly, her heart like a machine-gun firing at random. Her respiratory circulatory and digestive systems all were hit by surprise attack. 'It is not 'im . . . but . . .'

Regally, the officer walked on, not deigning to notice the impudent stranger who dared to accost him with such familiarity in public. She should have known to address him properly at least! GB followed closely behind, scrutinizing and wondering. She could have been mistaken, but yet she could hardly believe that anyone could so resemble Panty and not be Panty himself.

Crawling behind him, GB touched him timidly as soon as they were out of hearing of everybody. 'Massa, me don't mean to be rude . . . bu . . . bu-but . . . !' She was now in a position where she could closely examine his face, so instead of asking him, she affirmed positively: 'It is Panty! Don't it is you, Panty! Me is GB!'

In a voice extending downwards and modulated with rebuke, the officer replied: 'I'm afraid you're mistaken.'

'But even the voice is like Panty's. . . . But if you was Panty, you would remember your granda. Don't you come from Swine Lane?'

'What you want, my good woman? You must be crazy! You should not obstruct a government officer on duty. Go away now!'

'Govament officer mi foot! You can't fool me with your pose! Me know that you is Panty from Swine Lane. Me know you! Up to t'other day me ask Parson Allen . . . for . . . you!'

People were approaching, GB was speaking loudly and the officer desired to escape, for he suspected that GB would soon embrace him. Furthermore, the mention of Parson Allen cut into his heart, so that it bled a gout of blood.

'You're GB, so what?'

'Good! You remember me at last! Me is satisfied now! Me so 'appy to see you me don't know what to do with myself. You really come up well in life. Me is proud of you. Me is not too bad. Me 'ave a few pounds saved up for you.'

GB now held his hand. Panty was too embarrassed to jerk it away from her. Like a trapped crab abandoning a limb in order to escape, Panty allowed GB to hold his hand which, for the time being, he discarded mentally. He hoped sincerely that no one of importance who knew him saw this scene.

GB now whispered, although no one but Panty could hear her: 'Me 'ave something very, very important to tell you.'

'I can't listen now. I must rush back to work. I have an appointment at the office.'

'Well me will tell you part of it quickly as we walk. Me will follow you as far as possible.'

Panty would sooner die than face the risk of social death

which he imagined would result if he were recognized with his relative. 'No!' he said. 'I must hurry. You can't follow me.'

'Well then. Me live at No. 8 Watalow Street in St Andrew. Write it down. It is a nice 'ouse. You will like it. Come and see me very soon so that we can 'ave a chat. It is very important and you will benefit.'

Whilst Panty noted the address, GB said, 'Me must tell you . . .' She was just about telling Panty of his mother when she heard a clapping. Turning around, she saw Kate coming with vengeance. Panty saw her too and, fearing a scene, rushed away. He was glad to be thus rid of GB. Kate, seeing GB talking with the Excise Officer, imagined logically that GB was burning him with her flame-thrower tongue. Kate thought that GB needed her help and she herself wanted to expel some of her venom on the young brute.

'What was the stinker saying to you? You should spit on him or box him.'

'Not'ing. I was talking to 'im!'

'You shouldn't waste your precious breath. That mangy bastard will end on the gallows yet, if he's that lucky.' Looking in Panty's direction, her eyes scorched the earth he walked on.

Kate returned to the shop and GB home. When Kate was alone, she wept bitterly for shame. She vowed never to forgive the Excise Officer. There was no evil she did not wish for him. She particularly lamented the waste of fifty pounds odd now that she was in debt and, besides, needed money to pass to her son at the coming meeting which intuition told her would be soon.

Kate returned early home to join GB in vengeance—prayer for the Excise Officer's destruction. She wanted to read Psalm 109 which was said to be effective in bringing down a curse from heaven.

The love of her son drove her to the depths of passionate hate for the Customs Official who had indirectly deprived her son of the money she wanted to give him. The brutal disrespect which he accorded her was also against her son. Kate was reluctant to imagine the horror her gentleman son would feel at the knowledge that his mother was so badly handled by a ruffian. She would tell him about it, to make him hate the Excise Officer.

Kate was astonished to hear GB talking the language of the forgiving. It was so unlike GB altogether. Forgiveness was for wrongs unintentionally done, not when a person deliberately and unnecessarily wounds another.

GB assured Kate that she was praying about the matter and had put the case in the hand of God. Sincerely, she addressed the Almighty: 'Oh dear God, please don't bother to answer the wicked prayers me ask Thee. Me didn't know it was mi own grandson Panty whom I love and Thou lovest. Please, dear Father, do not destroy this boy, but prosper him and bring 'im into Thy Kingdom. Forgive us all, for we know not what we sometimes ask of Thee. Do, dear Massa God, let 'is mother forgive 'im when she finds out, and make us into one loving 'appy family through the grace of our Lord and Saviour our dear Brother Christ, Amen.'

21

Economic progress enhances social advancement. It is not uncommon, however, that social gain is disadvantageous to economic progress. Social popularity is frequently uneconomical. None knew this better than Panty, who in order to maintain his social standard on the small government salary had been secretly receiving money from the trollop barmaid at the jungle club. Since the Ada incident, however, this source of income was cut off as well as the gains from gambling. Panty had discovered that righteousness didn't pay, at least not as well as crime. He now thought of GB, to whom he made a prospecting visit.

'Come in! Please come right in, my son!' GB beamed delightedly on opening the doors of her house and heart at once. 'Kiss your granda!'

She pressed her cheeks against Panty's, who frowned as if he had come too close to an infectious leper.

Panty now received a series of surprises. First, the manner in which GB invited him to come inside, emphasizing 'Please', was amazing, this word being disliked by Jamaicans of GB's class. The concrete-and-wood bungalow towered above GB's standard. It had a well-kept lawn, the beautiful garden, and the wide veranda attractively painted. Panty's greatest shock was the manner in which the house was furnished, so clean, neat and tidy was everything, the furnishings selected for beauty and comfort.

With the air of a grand duchess or dowager, GB said: 'Doo

please si' down.' She adjusted the cushions for him. 'Make yourself comfitable.'

GB sat beside him on the sofa gazing at him with deep admiration before asking: ''Ow 'ave you been, son? Me is so glad you come. You would not know the many times, me look to see if you is coming.'

'I'm very well, thanks. You have really done very well for yourself!'

'Faith in God, much 'ard work and careful living, my son! Me don't waste the opportunities Massa God give to me. . . . May I . . . well let me get you some tea or . . . coffee?'

'Ye-yes, thanks very much. Tea, please!' Panty tried to be polite beyond his ability to be to people of GB's class. He would not allow this low-bred countrywoman to surpass him in good manners.

Without moving from her seat, GB clapped her hands like a magician about to produce a rabbit from a silk hat. Very ostentatiously and affectedly, she called simultaneously: 'Mude! Mood! Moad; Come yah!'

'Yes, ma'am,' said the girl as she appeared.

Wishing to show off, GB rebuked: 'You're getting deaf. Didn't you 'ear me calling you?'

'That's exactly why I came!'

GB had hoped that by a kind of 'gentleman's agreement' between Maud and herself, the former would not return any embarrassment in the presence of guests. GB now was not so sure that the agreement was still operative, so she ordered tea in less provoking tones.

Panty never took his eyes off the attractive girl. He then made up his mind to visit GB frequently.

GB noted the look on his face and inquired solicitously: 'Are you quite comfitable, son?'

'Oh yes. Sure!'

The maid gone GB made an unpleasant comment about maids generally. She complained how difficult it was to train them properly and this was also profitless, because as soon as they could be of use, they became impertinent, demanded more pay, or left the job. It was essential to keep them low and in darkness.

The tea having been served on the little glass-topped round table, GB graciously granted the maid a holiday for the rest of the evening.

GB wanted to talk to Panty privately, without the possibility of interruption or eavesdropping.

'Who owns this house?'

'Drink your tea. We'll come to that in time.'

Obediently, Panty swallowed a mouthful, impatient to hear what GB had to say.

'What are you going to do with your money?'

Instead of replying immediately, GB sipped her tea leisurely with grace and relish. Subsequently, in her own time, she said: 'I've some very good news for you. And,' she paused, 'some that's not so good!'

'Go on! Tell me all!'

For the next few moments, GB gazed at Panty's handsome face, thinking how unjust was Kate's description of him. He had much of his mother's good looks.

Tactfully, GB began the happy opening chapter of her story: 'There's a home for children in Montego Bay. It was built in honour of a great Jamaican beloved by all that knew 'im.'

Panty wished that GB would omit the obvious irrelevancies and give him the solid meat of the tale, especially about the money. He did not want to hear anything about any children's home in Montego Bay or anywhere else.

GB continued: 'The man was one of the best preachers ever. . . .'

Panty yawned mechanically. 'A good preacher—you say,' he repeated in order to show interest.

Unhurriedly, GB told him about his father, ending by saying, 'You see now! You have good religious blood! Many

161

people owe you through what your father did for them. You're bound to succeed in life. They say that the sins of the father will fall on the children, but me know that God give blessings to the children what their fathers should have got.'

'But my name is Panton Brown! How come?'

With the same tortuous slowness, GB expatiatingly related the second chapter of the story, disclosing why Panty was given her surname instead of his father's.

Panty nodded with interest and surprise. More tea was served; both of them, with aristocratic delicacy, munched biscuits and cakes. Thinking he had heard the worst, Panty did not consider the story quite as bad as he feared. It was good to know of his important father; it would be another string to his social bow, it was a supporting corset to his prestige.

What he wanted to hear now, was of the greatest importance to him—the story of GB's money, how she came by it, what she was going to do with it. It now flashed across his mind that it may have been left by his father. He thought he saw guilt of misappropriation written in GB's face. He was disgusted when GB began another rigmarole introduction which seemed remote to his interest.

At long last, she returned to the vital subject: 'Your mother is a very nice young woman. All that she 'as is all yours—eventually. She 'as been working for you all 'er life, she loves you. But there is a little difficulty. I 'ope it will soon clear up though.'

His heart now hammering against his breast like a hydraulic ram beneath a cataract, Panty asked anxiously: 'Where is she?' He was impatient for news of his impending inheritance.

'She not far away. You introduced yourself to 'er not so long ago.'

'Me!' A look of consternation distorted Panty's face, his

blood was like ductile material being drawn through metal veins.

'This 'ouse is your mother's. It is yours! If you wait, you'll meet her again tonight!'

'Where is she now? I'll go and fetch her.'

'It is a tricky business, son. Your mother knows you very well. She would recognize you at a mile distance.'

'Funny! Then why she's never called to me?'

GB dropped her head in contemplation for a brief while, then resumed her disclosure.

Panty's seat virtually blazed up underneath him. The soft velvet cushion became a mass of thorns, the room an inferno. A great lump blocked his throat so that he could not speak for some moments.

GB observed him quietly, sorrowfully, forgivingly, lovingly as he said: 'It must be the sins of the father falling on the son. If my father had . . .' Panty halted as he remembered what he did to the girl at the Montego Bay rectory who conceived for him. 'Maybe,' he said, 'I've inherited my father's disposition. Parents' disposition is sometimes a sickness which infect the children.'

The relentless accuser Conscience bombarded Panty's weak self-defence.

GB tried to comfort him: 'Your mother will understan'. A mother's love is the strongest of all love. Me is a mother myself. You and your mother must talk t'ings over. All of us will talk t'ings over in a nice family chat. Me know your mother will agree by the help of Massa God.'

Panty kept a watch on the door in order to give himself time to flee in case of his mother's sudden arrival. He would have already gone from the unsafe place, but he needed money from GB.

'I must have been depressed why I treated her so badly. I remember the day: I was broke, just as I am now. We civil servants cannot live on our pay. We have too many social expenses, too many friends to entertain and we have to keep up a standard. Life is very hard for us and that's why we sometimes abuse and get impatient with the public. Horse sweats but long hairs cover it.'

'Cheer up. Me can give you a few pounds. 'Tis 'ard to get money in this country unless you get a fair and 'onest chance to steal it. Most poor people never 'ave the luck to get that chance, and the few who do never get the opportunity of escaping without being caught. Me don't believe that stealing is such a bad t'ing if you can get away with it. Jesus don't despise thieves, for He took one to paradise with 'im. God 'imself must know 'ow 'ard it is to get on in the world and be honest.'

Panty was not listening to her philosophy. As soon as she was finished speaking, he profusely expressed his gratitude for her kind offer of a few pounds.

Leaving him for a short while, GB returned with twenty pounds, which she handed to him, saying: 'Son be t'ankful for small mercies.'

On receipt of the windfall, Panty was anxious to depart before his mother returned home. GB, however, persuaded him to remain longer as she outlined the ways to worldly success. Whilst her mouth boiled like a kettle, Panty was silently recalling the reasons for his over-vigorous defence of the Spirit Licence Law. Having been guilty of so many breaches of it, he was merely trying to reform himself, posing as a defender of the law when he prosecuted Kate, unaware that she was his mother. He was thinking too of the incident which first caused him to make the acquaintance of the vagrants who frequented the jungle club. Had he slept in his bed the night he invaded Paula's room, the rest of his life would have been different and, most probably, Ada Keans would still be alive.

He needed a drink now to clear his brains or confound the muddle, having discovered another shady spot in his mazy life to hide from the prying eyes of the world. He considered that he would now need to be even more aggressive socially.

From then he was tortured on a rack of his own making: one part of him had to be lived up to whilst the other part needed living down, while excruciating tension centred in the middle.

22

The glass globe sun exploded in the sky, scattering splinters of multi-coloured light. The larger particles assembled themselves into millions of galaxies.

Inside Kate's breast the sun of hope exploded and splinters of pain floated around in her head. Noting her distress, GB was afraid to question her, thinking that perhaps it might have been an encounter with Panty.

Kate's despair eventually found voice. 'I'm fed up with life,' she grieved. 'I wish I was dead!' A hot jet of tears squirted from her eyes as, almost sobbing, she concluded: 'My life is wasted in vain.'

GB's gloomy suspicions increased, and she pretended to anticipate trouble of another kind. 'Me know well 'ow this shop business ungrateful. It is trouble! Me 'ad the experience.'

'The shop isn't trouble now! 'Tis something much worse!'

'Jesus! What could that be? Is it? . . .'

'That goddamned man . . .'

'Which man?' GB interrupted hastily, fearing to hear the answer to her query.

'I should never have given him a damned penny. The criminal should have gone to prison, although it is still not late yet.' Love infected with jealousy gets stink in the twinkling of an eye. Kate's emotions were festering at the moment. She told GB the heart-breaking tale of Russ's deception. He was now in the process of getting a divorce and had told her that he couldn't think of marrying her.

GB was relieved that Kate's distress had nothing to do with

Panty. She could now express consolation. 'Me did tell you! Man is the only animal that causes his Maker to repent. God never sorry to make lions and tigers and monkeys but only men. Man and snake is one t'ing, only that snake crawls on its own belly. Trust no damned man, they are all wicked liars. That's why I never married! I kept my eyes wide open all mi life, so that no man could fool me!'

'But GB, how could I not trust Russ, after all the sweet pledges he gave me! If you should hear all that he said since our friendship! I was faithful to him. He told me that I was the only woman ever to make him happy. That ugly, lying, thieving bastard!'

'The prison is still open. Mi dear daughter, you don't need a man. You can support yourself and what you 'ave can't spoil. You is still young and let me tell you that a woman is like a 'ouse where there is always room for a passing lodger. The 'ouse don't 'ave to look for the tenant. Every old shoes 'ave a old socks to match!'

Kate was not comforted. 'From now on, there will be one man in my life and that will be my son. Thank God I still have him!'

GB winced, and in the silence contracted her body to its minimum bulk. Kate continued her self-consolation:

'I have a nice home for him to come. I'll compensate him for everything. I shall be his servant!'

Addressing GB directly, she said: 'You will help me to make him happy. You must speak to him, tell him everything to make him forgive me!'

GB jumped as if she were pierced with a sharp instrument. She made a funny sound. Kate spoke again, feeling assured of GB's unexpressed support.

'If that damned wretch, the Customs boy, did not cause me to lose so much money, my son would be that much better off!'

GB still made no comment, she seemed not to be understanding what Kate was saying. At long last, GB found courage to say: 'Yes, me believe 'e will forgive you, but you too must

forgive your enemies like the Bible say. Me believe that the
Customs boy will regret what 'im done you. Maybe 'im is sorry
already. If you forgive 'im, Massa God will put everyt'ing
right!'

'Never! Even God Himself, with all His mercies, will not
forgive certain sins. I will never, never forget or forgive that
boy! He's a son of a bitch. All the while I keep thinking what
kind of woman produced that. At least I can console myself I
am luckier than such an unfortunate mother who brought a
curse into the world. I won't forgive him, I swear!'

Very prudently GB opined: ''Tis good that God don't answer
every prayer as it reach 'im.'

'He very seldom answers any of mine,' said Kate. 'I fail to
see the goodness in that! One prayer I'd like to be answered
now is for destruction on the Customs man. That would be a
great satisfaction to me!'

Inhaling deeply, GB receded into silence with a sigh. After
a long pause, GB suggested: 'Maybe Massa God is testing you.
He wants you to forgive the Customs man, and then he'll 'elp
you meet your son. Massa God works in strange ways to bring
about 'is plan.'

'God knows the difference between the Customs man and
my son. Don't you compare them! They are not in the same
class.'

GB could have well been sitting on an ant-hill for all the
comfort she experienced at the moment. All the nerve-endings
in her body associated with pain became alive.

'I'm sure that God will bring that Customs man to a bad
end. I'm reading Psalm 109 as you say, and praying. If God
doesn't answer my prayer, He'll answer yours!'

At the end of a weary yawn, GB wished: 'I hope 'im answer
my prayer!'

The clock on the wall chewed the fresh crisp moments
avidly. Each tick was breaking of the frail bones of time, a prey
in the inexorable jaws of the merciless mechanical monster.

GB yawned incessantly, sometimes to prevent giving tongue

to her thoughts. The silence was unbroken for what appeared to be an interminably long time, then GB said daringly:

'I saw 'im the other day,' adding nonchalantly; 'I mean the Customs Officer.'

'I know! I saw you speaking to 'im outside the courthouse!'

'After that I mean. 'E came 'ere!'

'What! He came here! In my house!' Kates eyes bulged with anger as she gesticulated with one hand violently. 'Did he bring a searching warrant! GB, why didn't you scald the beast with boiling water? He had no right in here, you could tell the police that you thought he was a thief.'

GB remaining calm and unruffled said: 'He is very sorry for what 'appened!'

'Sorry indeed! 'Tis too late now: Nothing can wipe from my mind the nasty words that stinker told me, then caused me to lose money and be humiliated by the stupid judge. Let them all go to hell! . . . But what in hell did he come for!'

'Because he is . . .' GB stopped what she was going to say. Kate finished it for her: 'A crow. That's what he is, even if he wears peacock feathers. Jamaica will never be better for having such people in Government service.'

'I think me and 'im is related.'

'You would find a relative like that! Man springs from the lower animals all right, but I don't see why you must trace your relations with the pig family. If I had a relative like that I would keep it secret. I suggest you do the same.'

'You would like the chap if you really got to know 'im.'

During the ensuing moments, GB suffered a peculiar agony in her desire to help one who unwittingly evaded needed assistance. At this moment, truth would mean doom to Kate. Ignorance and lies were now her best allies.

Several times GB opened her mouth to speak the whole truth, but each time, she swallowed the facts again, literally bruising her throat in the operation. At length, she observed sadly: 'Well! Well! Sometimes it's better that we don't know certain t'ings!'

170

Kate paid no heed to GB's apparently irrelevant remarks.

'Don't let me keep you up, GB. You must be tired. Go to sleep!'

'Me is not sleepy, me is just t'inking about life in general.'

'Yes indeed! It is a funny life! Some people get more than they want and others never get the smallest thing they need!'

'If we all got what we wants, we would be very disappointed. We mustn't worry Massa God too much or 'im give us 'ell if we ask for it, just to show us a lesson.'

GB prepared to release an explosion. It was impossible to calculate in advance the damage, but she knew that a calamity would descend in the home that night.

The first cocks began crowing. GB attached a superstitious meaning to the weird wailing of the birds. It was more urgent and frequent than usual, she thought.

Kate's voice splintered the ominous silence: 'Tell me, GB! How come you to be related to the Customs man?'

In a figurative sense, GB now set the gauges, fidgeted with the detonating controls in preparation for an explosive release. 'Well,' she said cautiously, 'all the human race is related. We all descended from the same monkey!'

'But, GB, that doesn't make sense now. I don't want to hear about any other relative but my son. You and I and him are enough for this family.'

'I think you'd love the Customs man as a friend!'

'Why you try to hurt me, GB? What has the Customs man to do with me? I cannot forgive him! I repeat for the last time, definitely. I say that if I'm going to heaven and see him, I'd turn back. The one thing I love about him is his absence.'

The zero-hour was at hand. GB pressed the trigger. 'He's a close relative of . . .' GB paused. Apparently, there was a failure in the complicated mechanism. Something had jammed preventing the fulmination.

'How close! GB, keep your skeleton in the cupboard. Don't bring it out to frighten me!'

'One thing you should know!'

'What?'

'That the Customs Officer is . . .'

'For godsake, GB! Stop talking about the brute,' Kate interrupted; 'Every time you mention him, I get goose-pimples!'

'Well, I won't mention him any more after this. He is Panty, your beloved and only son. That's what I want to tell you!'

The deed was done at last. In Kate's head there was a volcanic blast, putting all her mental forces out of action at once.

GB was much comforted to realize that Kate had only fainted and was not permanently asleep. GB applied oils, ointments and smelling-salts as first aid. With deep feelings of sympathy, she stroked the limp limbs of the unconscious woman, but she could never reach the gaping wound torn in Kate's heart.

'A frail t'ing is man,' GB voiced poignantly. 'The body can be paralysed by a single word of truth. What is man, indeed!'

23

(Old proverb: *'Chicken merry, hawk is near.'*)

Foppishly elegant in his brown tropical suit, white shirt and colourful tie, Panty entered the exotic Swan Club, the exclusive trysting place of economic self-torturers who took illogical delight in paying twice the normal price for drinks.

Panty was willing to spend the twenty pounds he had, if only he found the 'right' social group.

It was a few minutes past six, and the regular, fastidious, fancy clientele of night-lifers had not yet arrived. Two white men sat at a table near the entrance, bathed in the soft red light which pored from dim Chinese lanterns.

To these men, Panty said an exuberant 'Hello'. They both sipped their whiskies and soda instead of returning his cordiality. With a swanky swagger, Panty glided over the thick red carpet on his way to the long bar, where he took a high seat. Surveying the room for possible companions, he ordered a double Scotch. Finishing it with one gulp, he ordered a repeat. The first drink must have opened his eyes, for now he saw a light-shade man, possibly in his forties, sitting in a corner.

The man, dressed in sportswear, wore a neatly clipped moustache, and heavy horn-rimmed glasses magnified his eyes. Beside this man sat a pretty young blonde, plainly dressed in summer clothes. The couple were talking animatedly; the girl frequently smiled, but her companion periodically burst into haughty primitive guffaws, evidently to call attention to himself. With money in his pocket and two whiskies in his head, Panty was socially reckless. The man had given him a friendly wink and Panty, mistaking this for an invitation, approached the couple. The man—Russ Paul—was lighting a big Cuban cigar when Panty slapped him on the shoulder, an action beyond the requirements of the very superficial acquaintance he had with Russ. The frown on Russ's proud face was almost audible. He examined the reaction of his lady companion, but took no notice of Panty.

Russ, fired from the government service, was now a self-appointed civic leader, championing the cause of his oppressed race as chairman of the Coloured People's Integration Society, which vainly sought to promote understanding between coloured folks of various social classes and shades.

It was through this group he made the acquaintance of his present companion, Constance Kenny, a Canadian university student on a fellowship in sociology, doing research in race relationships in Jamaica. Russ had just been painting an attractive picture of the prevailing accord amongst all groups in the multi-racial, piebald community of Jamaica.

'We have solved the race problem here,' he said 'The rest of the world can learn from us. There has never and will never be a race riot here. We all work and play together.'

At this point, he was interrupted by Panty, whose money was obviously burning a hole in his pocket.

'May I join you?'

'Ye-yes, ma-man, su-sure,' smiled Russ ironically, 'if you can't find anywhere else to sit.'

Previous to Panty's interruption, Russ had told Constance that many good white people became spoilt soon after arrival in Jamaica. They came with mistaken ideas about the standards of the predominantly coloured population.

Russ himself was reputed to hate white people publicly, and was also known to despise black people privately. He headed an organization to secure inter-racial unity, but his main interest was to feather his own nest economically and socially. A very controversial demagogue, he loved his race, but loved white foreigners even more.

Panty was standing up to his waist in embarrassment, from which he found difficulty in extracting himself. Encouraged by a charming, sympathetic smile from Constance, he said: 'I happen to know your friend here. He is one of our leaders. He knows me well.'

Russ looked at him angrily and said: 'Ye-yes, I know you. My nostrils ne-ne-never fo-fo-forget anyone!'

High in his own esteem, Russ, a dandy, was like a shopworn article in life's show-window, upon which passersby gazed and wondered why it was not discarded. Russ mistook these alarmed glances for admiration, actually believing he was indeed the chief attraction in the display. Imagining himself adored for his glibness, he was unaware of the secret hate widely held for him because of his inability to keep his mouth shut.

Panty could neither go nor take the silly grin off his face. To mollify his embarrassment, he asked with a touch of irony: 'May I have the pleasure of buying a drink?' To Constance he remarked: 'We Jamaicans love strangers even more than we like the natives!'

Russ answered the innuendo: 'Ye-yes we will 'ave the drink wi-with ple-pleasure,' adding the barbed proviso: 'Order arsenic for yourself, or cyanide if you can get it. That's quicker.'

Giddy with embarrassment, Panty secretly wished a cloak of darkness would envelop him.

Coming to his rescue, Constance made a favourable comment about his tie. The remark was like a tonic to Panty. He asked if she was English. She told him no.

Russ's temper reached boiling-point in the interim. His exclusiveness had been violated. He wanted to give the impression that the girl was his intimate friend, but Constance told Panty the truth about her mission.

'Bu-bu-buzz off now, young man! Have some manners!

Scram! Beat it! Get out! I'm sure I didn't call you here. Now go away!'

Panty informed him that he was not the main attraction in the club at the moment and that as a coloured leader, he ought to be more civil.

'Cheeky bastard!' Russ thundered as he rose, and Panty heard the terrible words simultaneously as he felt a crashing blow on his jaw. He fell bleeding to the ground.

Muttering execrations against Jamaicans' lack of culture, Russ looked for approval from his fair companion. Constance was almost in tears as she screwed up her small mouth in disgust: 'It is a shame. You are very cruel. You should not treat your own countrymen like that. He did no wrong.'

Constance asked if that was the general standard of cordiality in the multi-racial society and declared that in her country, people showed their love for their fellowmen in a different way. She swore that the boy could not have been treated worse in South Africa or Georgia and finished by suggesting: 'Now I know why you don't have race riots here. You're too busy fighting amongst yourselves.'

Crestfallen, Russ defended: 'We coloured people have our social grades and levels. We are not all the same. That boy is too impertinent. He comes from nowhere! Everytime he comes here he makes himself a nuisance and causes people to disrespect our race. The place will soon be losing customers on his account.'

Constance could not see what particular interest Russ had in Panty's conduct: 'Don't you like to see your own fellows enjoying freedom in this country?'

Two bartenders had mercifully taken Panty to the men's room where they gave him first aid and expressed sympathy for him. They affirmed their dislike for Russ, whom they claimed was always causing excitement: 'He never wants to pay his bills, gives no tips and causes a lot of complaints from good customers.'

To palliate his odd behaviour, Russ assured his companion, who had indicated her desire to go, that the matter was not of any serious consequence and even if it were taken to court, nothing would happen because he had good friends in high places.

Russ, whose background was doubtful, was a stalwart protagonist of class-prejudice. He needed rigid class-barriers to protect him from his past with its unpleasant memories.

He bore social stigmas and cicatrices of humiliation from the days when insult was the only welcome he received anywhere. His own black people had crushed him, hammered his bleeding fingers when he had held on to the narrow ledge of ambitious social hope. He had been literally kicked, ridiculed and spat upon by influential people of very low character.

Now it was his turn to crush the ambitious climber, his opportunity to close the door in the face of the caller.

Pointing to the table where the two white men sat, Russ said: 'Those are my two best friends. The elder one with the grey hair is Jack Otter, a Canadian like yourself. The other is my dear friend Al Sinter. He's English only by birth, but Jamaican by heart. He loves our country and its people. I will introduce you before we leave.'

The men caught Russ's eye, but neither of them heeded his friendly nods. They were discussing him.

'A damned upstart,' Al Sinter described him. 'I wouldn't mind much if he dropped dead a couple of times. He's the most impossible nigger I ever met. Don't know what he thinks he is.'

'What does he do really? He is always over-nice to me, so that I always feel that he's going to touch me down for a loan. I reckon he's some kind of spiv or bum. I suppose we could find out from the police. He often escorts white women. There he is with another low-type bird, maybe she's in the 'business'. He's too dishonest to work, so he masquerades as a social leader! I am always polite to him; it is part of the price to live in this paradise island.'

'Don't look now, but he is watching us. We'd better go before he comes here with his new victim. He has a rather adhesive personality. Drink up. Let's go.'

They rose to leave. Russ waved his hand to catch their attention, but they both kept their heads in another direction.

The men gone, Russ explained to his companion that they were obviously tipsy or very busy why they did not rush over to him before going. He said that he felt sure they approved his conduct. They were the nicest persons in the world to meet socially. Jamaica has some of the best white men from all countries. Jack and Al were only two examples. If the world had more people like them, there would be no racial troubles. Colour of skin is quite unimportant to them, they were just jolly good fellows through and through.

Sweetly Constance suggested: 'You must make others say the same of you.'

'I'm different. A coloured man must have class-prejudice or lose the respect of his people. Black people don't readily respect or appreciate other blacks. A coloured man has to be pretentious to gain his people's esteem. He has to show off or his people won't take notice of him. If a coloured man is humble in spirit, his people trample him.'

24

Metaphorically, Kate was killed by an arrow of truth piercing her heart on the night she learned of Panty's identity. Now she was an animated tomb inscribed with despair. With no love and no hope, her life became a progressive malady, a wasting disease, a blight.

She dragged herself mechanically to her bar daily, but lost all care and interest in the returns of the business. Her faculty to calculate was so impaired that she gave extra change to almost every customer. News of her unintended generosity spread, bringing streams of new customers to collect their bonuses after drinking *ad lib*. Very few were honest enough to call her attention to her self-destroying errors, or to return the extra cash she absent-mindedly gave.

Sometimes Kate closed the business to wander aimlessly around the town, unkempt and bedraggled. It was often difficult to remember whether or not she had eaten. The poison gas of sorrow inflated her stomach. Thoughts of suicide were persistent, but either life was not worth taking or she lacked the energy.

One day in town she glimpsed Russ with a very fair girl in a nice new car. He must have seen her too, because he swerved the car violently, nearly causing an accident. He uttered curses about jay-walkers. This incident brought her no pain, her capacity for agony had been already saturated. Men had lost their attraction in her sight. It was woman's worst punishment, she thought, to be born to love men, who were created to cause them such suffering.

To stop Kate's rapid deterioration, GB urged her to leave the island and go anywhere out of her present world of misery. Love and forgiveness could have saved Kate, but hate and bitterness left no room in her heart to compromise with her son. Eventually, GB took matters in her own hands, arranged for the sale of Kate's business and sold the house to herself, then booked Kate's passage for England.

GB apologized when paying Kate for the house, having kept the extent of her wealth a secret all the time.

'Ah, mi daughter,' she sighed, 'me live too long in Swine Lane not to 'ave respect for money. Money is God's RICHEST blessing. It was in Swine Lane that me learned that God 'elps those who 'elps themselves, financially. Once you find the money, God will 'elp you to accomplish anyt'ing with faith!'

Kate had no interest in what GB said. Money or anything else didn't matter. In extenuation of her feelings of guilt as she produced a huge sum of money, GB said that when Massa God gives a blessing He expected us to care for it. God, who has the whole world to help, cannot, she said, spend too much time on one person: 'The bes' gratitude to Massa God is to hold on to whatever money blessing you get from Him or anybody else. God is drastic when we waste His gifts. The Bible says, "Hold on to that which thou hast and let no man take away." Is money they mean.'

The only blessing Kate said she wanted was death.

Always generous with advice, GB now opened her heart to pour out consolation and warning:

'You is blessed to 'ave your misfortune whilst you is young. Now you know not to trust your own mother or son or any man. God 'imself never trust man from the beginning. Him put an angel with sword to watch Adam. Trust Massa God alone and, next to 'im, money. With God in your 'eart and money in your pocket, you'll find peace in 'eaven and happiness in the world. One withouten t'other is no good. God is Three in One and so is money: pounds, shillings and pence. The pence is the Father, the shillings the Son and the pound note the

Spirit. Never boast about money you 'ave lest people will come to borrow it. Give no beggar not'ing, because you don't know if God wants 'im to suffer. Always remember the 'oly Bible which says, " He becometh poor who deals with a slack hand, but the hand of the diligent maketh rich." Love your neighbour as yourself, but never lavish money on yourself, so that your neighbour can't be vexed when you deny help. Property is a slice of life; try and get it anywhere you go. You will succeed because me will always pray for you.'

Kate's baggage was light. Heavy was her broken heart. The day was bright when she left her native land, but none of the silver paint from the sun touched her rusty heart.

The friendlessness she heard of in England would be no new experience to her. In a foreign land amongst strangers of another race, she could fare no worse than she had suffered in her own land amongst her friends and relatives. Unkindness, deceit, snobbery, greed were not English monopolies made in the factories of England. Kate had already known the worst of these human weaknesses amongst the best of the dwellers in the land they call Paradise—Jamaica. Had she been leaving for hell itself, she would have been relieved. Now she was manifestly well-equipped to face loneliness in a strange land, she being beyond the reach of disappointment, having no hope. The unborn tomorrows held no haunting terrors and she was secure from frustration as only the truly desperate can be.

Like the damned in the darkness of hell, there was no new calamity she might expect. That was a form of security which Kate enjoyed, having no peace of mind, no happiness to protect against change and loss.

25

Sole owner of a beautiful, well-furnished home and widely respected for her seeming devotion to the Church, GB, like an octopus attached suckers to every object of security.

Already, she had done much to improve her speech and general demeanour, the maid Maud being unofficial head of GB's finishing school.

In the manner of a vainglorious schoolgirl, GB spent long hours dyeing and straightening her few hoary strands of short wire-hairs. She washed her face frequently with lye and blended herbs to restore youthfulness, and used face-powder as a carpenter used putty, but because of her inexpertness in 'make-up' she often made public appearance in a mask of cadaverous blanchness. Often patchy coating disfigured her face as perspiration mixed with powder to form a kind of batter.

Deviously, she gained places on church and social committees, rushing in where angels would travel with caution. Subsequent to her election to an important church body, Parson Allen assured her that God had chosen her for a wise purpose. Because of her increasing prestige, GB socially discriminated against her betters who esteemed her far beyond her merit.

A few minutes past 2 p.m. while GB was enjoying her constitutional siesta, she was shocked by a heavy hammering on her front gate, interspersed by loud shouts from a husky voice bawling:

'Bah, Bee! Gee Bah! Beatrice! Granny Bah!' Writhing with embarrassment, GB, frightened into consciousness by a nightmare as it were, rushed to investigate the nuisance. Indignant and ashamed, she was greatly afraid of what neighbours might think if they heard the rude assault on her prestige.

To her supreme horror, she beheld Sue Browley who, on seeing her shouted in excessive delight, 'Come out, you old bitch! You is always so lucky to work with nice people.'

Surprised by the ribald greeting, GB sped from her aerie to silence the caller before more embarrassing utterances were made to the hearing of respectable neighbours.

Hardly disguising her annoyance, GB inquired what Sue was doing in Kingston. GB's cadence and manner caused Sue to comment: 'Eh! eh! Mi God oh! you talk like you go to college since you come hup yah. You look very well. Make me kiss you, if Bill Toms did live to see you now, 'im would be proud!'

Sue, who had succeeded GB as domestic servant with the new parson who replaced Rev. Wallis, had visited Kingston in the hope of making GB jealous of her progress. She was unaware of the substantial earthly gains GB had made whilst ostensibly working for heaven. GB, a social flea, had literally bought her own dog of success and was suckling herself fat long ago.

Chattering endlessly, Sue began to lead GB into the house, but GB stopped when they reached the veranda. Sue dipped her voice to say: 'Me don't want to disturb the people 'ere. They seem to treat you very nice.'

GB was glad to inform her that she owned the house and was no employee, but an employer.

A lump of envy rose in Sue's heart as she asked GB to let her go inside and sit.

Sue, in her best dress bore the unmistakable stamp of a country bumpkin. Her cheap straw hat, and high-necked and long-sleeved printed-cotton dress offended GB's sophisticated eye. Ball-of-fat Sue, with distended ballooned breast and bustle-behind jumping like agitated jelly, was out of place in GB's home. As Sue sat, it appeared as if her torso had telescoped into her abdomen.

GB broke her reticence to ask Sue not to sit on the cushion and although she made the request through the corner of her mouth, it was opened wide enough for Sue to see the gold fillings.

'Eh! eh! Good and proppa! Gold teeth and all! Well! Well!' Not knowing what to say, GB asked Sue if she was returning the same day.

Sue, inferring an intended invitation to remain, said that she was not particular to go, if her presence was desired by GB.

She now brought GB up to date on Swine Lane matters and the Drop Pan lottery game, boring GB.

Tactfully inviting Sue to leave, GB disclosed that she expected important friends that evening.

'Good!' said Sue. 'They will get a chance to meet me. Maybe you will tell them 'ow we lived like sisters in Swine Lane and that although you gone up so 'igh, me never forget you.'

GB's eyes dropped to the ground in desperation. Eventually, she asked: 'You didn't tell me why you came here.'

Sue emphasized or rather reiterated that she came to look for GB and nothing else. However, she now inquired about Panty and Kate, asking if the latter was married. GB informed her that marriage was not for everybody, some people are much better without it.

'Quite true, GB. Me could marry many times already. In my whole life, me don't t'ink me ever sleep with more than thirty or forty men, but me never 'ave pickney for none, t'ank God, and me could marry any of them me pleased!'

'Then why you didn't please any of them?'

'You see, they wanted to marry me just as 'ow Bill Toms was anxious to marry you, but me love freedom too much.'

Whilst GB winced under the innuendo, Sue described the wonderful opportunity GB missed by not going to gaol. Sue said that she thoroughly enjoyed her stay. Food was good and plentiful, the work was not hard for a stonebreaker, there were many nice and honest people inside, and the cells were much better than Swine Lane huts. She stressed that GB would have enjoyed it inside the prison and it was truly a pity to have missed the experience.

Heedless of Sue's rumbling commentary, GB regretted: 'I'm very sorry indeed that you've to go back tonight.' Pretending to be annoyed she continued: 'People are always coming to stay 'ere as if the place was a "hostile".' In GB's *lapsus linguae*, hostel and hostile were synonymous.

Sue assured GB that she was not obliged to return with Parson.

'Jesus!' exclaimed GB, informing Sue that she felt a sharp, sudden pain in her head.

'You must expect that at your age, GB. Me is younger than you and me 'ave the same experience many times.'

Protesting that she indeed was the younger, GB recalled that one of the main reasons why she befriended Sue was because she always liked to have the advice of an older woman. She confessed that it was hardships and not age which was responsible for her grey hairs. She said also that it would have been her great pleasure to accommodate Sue for the night, if she didn't expect friends to stay.

'It is all those worry with stranger people, that makes me looker older that me is. When you 'ave to take your 'ard cash to buy food to entertain company, it gives you grey hairs before time.'

However, GB invited Sue to return early next year as the present year had just begun and it was only fair that Sue should have a long time to prepare.

'Don't worry about me, GB. If you want, we can share the same bed. Make your other visitors comfitable. Me is not fussy.'

Sue, not expecting to be discriminated against, refused to take any of the several hints regarding her unwanted presence. GB would have thrown her out bodily, before she commenced to suspect that she was an undesirable guest.

Returning to the Swine Lane scene, Sue told GB how the people spoke well of her, daily. They didn't like Mospin, who robbed them in the shop and could only talk but not preach. He had bought a car, wore his collar backwards and demanded that he be called 'bishop'.

'People would gladly 'ave you back, GB. They love you since you left.'

GB categorically declared that she had no intention to return to Swine Lane and asked Sue not to mention Mospin's name to her: 'That thieving bastard looks like sea-crab with whooping cough.' She commented on the untrustworthiness and disloyalty of her people.

In support of the observation, Sue asked: 'Don't you remember the parable about the monkey?' GB, a fairly well-informed Bible student, could not recall this 'Monkey' parable, hence Sue related:

'A monkey was running down the streets and met a white man who gave 'im a piece of cheese. The animal then met a Chinaman who gave it a cracker. It ran up to a Jamaican from Swine Lane who was eating a piece of sugar cane. The Jamaican hit the monkey in the 'ead and kicked it. The monkey looked up sadly on his attacker and sighed: "Fancy! Look at that, from my own people!".'

Sue had chatted herself to near exhaustion and now complained of hunger, demanding something nice to eat.

GB, now without a regular maid, employed a charwoman once a week. Unfortunately, this woman was not present to take orders from Sue, hence GB reluctantly started to provide the food. She told Sue that there was no yam, mackerel or dried cod, these items having now proved harmful to GB's aristocratic health. Sue commented that too much fancy food was good for nobody. GB, however, declared that strict dieting was essential for her health, but in truth she was merely economizing.

Sue observed that all the big shots who fed on luxury foods died from diseases with long names. She followed GB into the kitchen, passing envious comments on everything. Sue now regretted that she was unlucky to work with poor English people who conserved stale food like jewels. They gave away nothing, but expected poor and foolish black people to support them. According to her, the new parson was more interested in saving money than souls. Every Sunday he preached about church debts, but it was not clear how the church owed so much money since it did not wear clothes or eat food.

Sue was served on the kitchen table usually used by the maid, but she was glad of the intimate informal atmosphere. She ate ravenously, whilst giving a running commentary on what she imagined interested GB.

She suddenly noticed that GB was very downcast, so by way of encouragement said: 'You must not be vexed because me not staying this time. Me will come back for a week.'

GB brightened instantly: 'You really 'ave to hurry back?'

Sue explained that, seeing that GB was not very well, she considered it unwise to remain, lest GB got sick in the night.

After chatting like a demented parrot, Sue requested a pan of 'wash', the Swine Lane name for lemonade or sugar and water mixture. GB briskly responded, then sighed: 'I feel so tired!'

Sue explained that GB's feeling was caused because, 'me is goin' so quick. It is because me come and you glad to see me why you feel bad.'

Sue was still talking volubly to a disinterested GB when they heard the toots of a motor-car horn, at which Sue announced that it was Parson who came for her.

Gladly GB sped her departing guest and at the gate, Sue

promised to advertise GB's success to Swine Laners and extended an open invitation to GB to make a return visit.

Closing the gate with relief, GB muttered haughtily: 'Return to Swine Lane! She must be crazy. My Swine Lane days are over.'

26

Panty wrote to GB expressing his desire to fête her on her birthday. He well knew that GB had no idea of her date of birth. Most Swine Laners never bothered to register births and deaths, and no one forced them to. Omission of this kind made the government's statistics more tidy. It prevented national scandals when there was no record of the near hundred per cent. illegitimacy and ninety-five per cent. under-age pregnancies normal in Swine Lane. Furthermore, women could remain forever young, since there was no certificate to attest their exact age.

In his letter Panty referred to the lack of funds which prevented his showing due appreciation to his grandmother.

GB felt sorry for him, but was nevertheless glad to know he thought of her. She wrote to tell him that her birthday had already passed, but she enclosed a few pounds as a gift.

Reading between the lines of her letter, Panty fancied that his inheritance was not distant. Knowing himself to be GB's sole heir, he felt obliged to prevent her from dying intestate. He learned that his mother had vanished without a trace, this he considered fortunate under the circumstances.

Before paying GB a business visit therefore, Panty contacted funeral directors to apprise himself about undertaking expenses. With ghoulish anticipation he calculated his expected profit. He expected to cry at the appropriate time, for no one would know whether his tears were as a result of his grandmother's demise, or whether they flowed because the bereavement had been delayed. A tombstone, he thought, would be unnecessary for GB.

Like a hired mourner, Panty arrived with sombre countenance and a head-load of spurious consolation.

He nearly died of shock on arriving to see GB looking as strong as overproof white Jamaica rum.

'From your letter, I thought you were poorly!'

GB explained that she wrote thus to test him whether he would come to see her, as she longed to see him.

Having proved his interest in his grandmother, Panty now suggested that she should make a will. GB refused, saying that there were yet many years to consider such a matter.

Hopping with delight, she offered Panty a drink from the assorted liquors and spirits left by Kate. For herself, GB poured a dry sherry, commenting as she smacked her lips like a connoisseur, 'This is luvly stuff.'

Panty finished his drink rather quickly, served another and in the rippling conversation which followed made an apparently disinterested query about the maid Maud. Maud had married and was mother of two nice children.

Wishing aloud, GB said: 'It is time for me to 'ave a great-grandchild.'

Panty did not disclose that she was already so blessed, maybe a couple of times and more.

She asked Panty why he didn't marry.

'No money,' came the inevitable reply.

'Find the lady yet?'

Panty did not reply immediately, so GB added a further query: 'Ai, whatabout Miss Paula? She did love you when you were pickneys. Her father love you very much too, and the mother always speaks well of you.'

Panty took a deep breath while GB incited him, telling him that Paula and himself were ideally matched, seeing that they were children of two parsons and had been in love from childhood. She claimed that their marriage would be a good religious one between two churches, Baptist and Anglican, and she said that she knew for certain that Parson Allen was interested in church unity. She had heard him speak of his wish to abolish all Churches but his own.

Panty thought he would enlighten her by saying that Mrs Allen hated coloured people.

Expressing shock, GB disagreed violently: 'Oh, shame on you to say that about the good lady. She's one of the best white persons in the whole island, a very, very kind and good woman, a real Christian. You would hardly believe she was English! She dunno what they call colour-prejudice. I know 'ow she loves coloured children.'

'Don't believe it.'

'Massa P, you 'ave edicutation, me 'ave only common sense, but yet me can see many t'ings much better than you, especially simple ordinary t'ings that don't need 'rithmetic. Me know that white is hypocrites, but Mrs Allen is not one of them. She treated me much better than would my own colour people. Most white people keep us poor and down so that they can get to 'elp us and make us indebted and respec' them. Mrs Allen is different.'

'Yes, but . . .'

'Massa P, speak from your own experience. I think that you is a coward, but coward man cannot win fair lady. You is no servant no more, you is equal to Parson 'imself, you is edicated like 'im, and you come from a good family. Your father was a parson, your mother a business lady, your grandmother a property-owner, no pauper, and you is a big government servant, plus the fact that you have a light skin. What more could you want?'

Panty expressed reluctance to go back to the rectory. GB volunteered: 'Me can arrange for you and Miss Paula to meet 'ere in this 'ouse.'

She outlined her plan to invite Paula, imagining that from her scheme might eventuate a cherubic offspring, a pinkish fruit from her ragged family tree.

Panty shared hope and happiness. Their meeting was a festival and they drank freely to accentuate their joy.

27

'Oh, Miss Pahoolah! Me is so very glad to see you. Mi dear, you look like something to eat. Come in to your ol' nana, mi beautiful!'

In her pied blue-cotton dress with tight-fitting bodice and wide skirt, Paula was indeed a picture of youthful loveliness. Cordiality radiated from her beautiful face when she greeted GB smilingly. Her delicately sculptured nose, small perky, expressive mouth and buoyant ice-blue eyes blended in a joyous sympathy every time she smiled. She walked with a graceful swing to the eternal strains of the rhapsodic music of youth.

GB enthroned her honoured guest on the sofa, then asked:

'Ow's the dear Parson and the Missis?'

When she was suitably answered, she inquired about Paula's job. Paula described things as very good considering that her employer was a close friend of the family.

'So you is now saving up to get married, I suppose!'

Paula was not thinking in that direction. GB offered refreshment consisting of everything she knew Paula liked: chocolate biscuits, ginger snaps, strong tea with plenty of sugar, and cheese sandwiches. Paula was uninhibited and communicative, as their relationship justified. GB concentrated on the subject of marriage, but Paula treated the subject with levity, saying that it would be years before she gave it serious consideration. She revealed, however, that when she got married she would like a small cottage like GB's with the same kind of front lawn and garden. GB assured her that such a desire would be fulfilled.

Their delightful dialogue was broken by a knock at the door. Grumbling at the unexpected interruption, GB went to see to the caller. Histrionically, she staged a most convincing surprise-act in welcoming Panty in his natty grey suit, his face fresh and cool as a cucumber, except that it was creamed and powdered.

'Come in,' GB invited loudly, 'me 'ave a great surprise for you. You have changed very much since the last time! What brings you 'ere this time?'

Forestalling a reply from Panty, GB continued loudly for Paula to hear: 'You look so much like your father now. It is a pity you didn't take up his profession and be a Baptist parson.'

Panty, led by his grandmother, reached the sitting-room where he pretended to be surprised seeing Paula, who now suffered from a condition resembling sea-sickness. The room rocked in her imagination, the walls swayed like huge waves dashing at random. Under guidance Panty sat beside Paula, whose radiance was now superseded by an aspect of gloom.

Making a great fuss, sycophant GB flattered both her guests, saying that she never expected to have lived to see such a moment: 'Lord, let Thy servant depart in peace, for me eyes see salvation.'

Metaphorically, the ashes of Paula's perplexity quickly covered the flames of the conversation. In vain GB tried to fan the ephemeral sparks. She brought Panty a cup of tea whilst still harping on her pleasant surprise to see him.

Paula gave undivided attention to the polished wooden floor, thinking hard for a way of escape.

GB now interviewed Panty socratically to enable him to give a glowing account of his achievements and prospects. Paula did not listen, although it was all done to impress her.

At a convenient moment, GB, pretending to hear a knock at the door, excused herself from the company. She was gone but a few moments when Panty moved closer to Paula and said meekly:

'I owe you an apology. . . .'

'For?'

Panty could not proceed. He was not certain if she knew the reason for his flight from the rectory. Silence ensued.

Panty spoke again.

'Paula, why can't we be as when we were kids? Don't you remember the lovely times we had?'

Paula kept silent. Panty prodded her, mildly blackmailing.

'Go away from me. I don't know what you're talking about!'

Very lightly, Panty placed his hand on her arm. She jerked and brushed it away summarily.

'Don't touch me. I'll scream! I better be going this minute!'

Quietly, Panty informed her that screaming would not help, they were completely alone and GB was not coming back immediately.

Paula disbelieved and again said she was going.

'You cannot leave now. I must talk with you,' Panty stressed. 'In any case the door is locked and GB has gone with the key.'

Panty's subsequent utterances convinced Paula that she was trapped. The knowledge weakened her.

Panty pleaded with her to be reasonable: 'You cannot now quench the fire you lighted in childhood. What happened then was beautiful and innocent. You made my life a long loneliness till now. You gave me the only happiness I knew as a child, the only hope I have as a man, the only memories I shall keep for old age. Through you I have known the truest secret of love, it is that those who feel it most can least express it. That is the mystery of love. In every other thing, the more you know, the more you can describe it, but my love works the opposite way. That's why I can't tell you my love.'

Swooningly, Paula continued staring blankly at the floor. Panty shook her with agitated tenderness. She looked at him helplessly, returning her downward gaze.

Panty placed his hand lightly on her knee, an exploratory

manoeuvre, but again Paula boxed it away and smoothed the folds of her dress, closing her legs tightly. Anxious as she was to go, she lacked the will to move. Instead, she kept frequent watch on the door for GB's return.

The rapid surges of events weakened Paula, but everything conspired to increase Panty's passion, till it became a tidal wave sweeping away derelicts of reason and self-control.

Excess of passion produced a suppliant intonation in his voice as he asked: 'Tell me, dear Paula, do you love me? '

'I do not.'

'What do you feel in your heart for me, tell me! '

'Nothing. I never remember you until I see you.'

Panty inquired what she had felt for him in childhood and, laconically, Paula replied that it was pure curiosity incited perhaps because her mother had emphasized the difference between white and coloured people.

'So you never loved me! I wish I had not been told. I could have lived on the belief forever.'

Breaking his short reverie, Panty asked Paula if she had loved anyone and she promptly told him of Ronnie Carpin.

'It was only when I thought of him . . .' she did not complete the statement.

Panty now resumed pressure and tried to force a kiss. She turned her head away. Again he began his soothing: 'I forgive you for making me love in vain, but I'll never regret loving you. I will never stop. You could only light, you cannot extinguish love. Love you awaken in a heart you are powerless to take out again. Some hearts grow old with long-dead love enshrined in them, always giving them vitality. I will keep my heart, for in it I have my most precious possession, my love for you.'

Whilst Panty made his little speech, Paula allowed his hand to rest on her leg: this Panty interpreted as a favourable omen. He said more nice and sweet things and as the verbal perfume disseminated in the warm air, it was the speaker rather than the hearer who was being most affected by the fragrance.

Paula again resisted Panty's embrace, this time threatening him. He resorted to gentle blackmail again, then to humble pleas, eventually declaring that if he went to prison on her account, it were small price to pay for the fulfilment of his love for her. He swore that if the love caused his death, he would die indebted to her: 'I'd pay my life for my love but not relinquish my love even to save my soul. I cannot say more.'

Passion inflamed Panty's eloquence but diminished his sincerity. Lust burdened his cadence as he spoke, Paula began sobbing faintly, feeling as helpless as an ensnared mouse in a cat's paws.

She rose, but fell back on her seat. It was as if the earth had suddenly checked its rotation and flung her back in her seat, the din of the imaginary clash deafened her. Panty applied force. It was as if he had many hands touching Paula whilst she possessed only two weakened ones to defend herself.

The struggle, in which Panty planted an inflammatory kiss in Paula's mouth, did not last long. Although she bit him and shifted and wiggled like a hooked fish, her eyes were glazed with a film of overpowering desire and her voice sweetened in a submissive softness to plead rather than protest.

She was the centre of a confused conflict in which dignity was the first casualty, followed by reason. Inside her the fifth-columnist, that Goliath-strong sex-urge, the Judas of logic, assumed control and bargained with the enemy in spite of her grand effort to escape.

When Panty eventually lifted her up, she was as light as a feather in his passion-reinforced arms. He took her half dazed into the nearby bedroom, closed the door and turned the key.

On returning to the sitting-room, Panty was sad and Paula apprehensive: 'You'll be in trouble if you make anything happen to me!'

Panty allayed her fears and in extenuation of his recklessness told Paula that her beauty was her curse: 'You, like a rose, should have a thorn to protect you, but you only have charm, which is no protection for beauty.'

Paula took little notice of the adulation.

As if timing them, GB returned with profuse apologies for her absence, which she said was caused by a neighbour's sudden illness.

When Panty was leaving, GB followed him to the door and squeezed his hand approvingly. It was the touch of congratulation rather than good-bye.

Paula left soon after Panty, GB begging her to call again.

28

Commercial banks in Jamaica acknowledge no discrimination regarding race, creed or class amongst customers.

It is purely coincidental that bank clerks are white or very fair of skin, sometimes recruited abroad.

Bank clerk Ronnie Carpin, son of a late English clergyman, was engaged in England. Besides dealing very efficiently with the normal business of his institution, he conducted a large number of emotional transactions with the best-looking girls of all races.

He was now deeply involved with a nineteen-year-old Chinese beauty, petite Daisy Kai, the daughter of a wealthy merchant. After they had been secretly going steady for some months, she informed him that she was expecting his child.

Ronnie did not show the usual white man's proneness to retreat from this responsibility involving a racial outsider. He quickly and bravely agreed that they should marry, although he failed to name the date.

His terror increased as he contemplated the embarrassment of hearing a slanted-eye, yellow-skin hybrid call him Dad. Before, it had never even remotely occurred to him that he was race-prejudiced, having associated freely and intimately with all races. From childhood he had consorted with coloured people when his saintly, late father had taught him not to judge humanity by skin-shade. Now, however, he was quite chary of having an Oriental father-in-law who would certainly be a social encumbrance, and he thought he definitely lacked the resources to be paternally affectionate to a half-caste.

Daisy alone was all right; she was beautiful, educated, cultured, accomplished, besides being an heiress.

When Daisy pressed for action, Ronnie eventually suggested that they go to England to marry and reside. In England, he said, they could enjoy greater anonymity and English people in England were in any case more understanding than English residents abroad.

With a lark singing in her heart, Daisy prepared plans according to his instructions, telling her father that she intended to study in England.

Ronnie said that he would be ready to travel as soon as he settled his outstanding personal affairs. He showed Daisy a draft copy of his application for a transfer to an English branch of his bank.

'One important thing my late father taught me,' he told Daisy, 'was to be a man and never run away from my responsibilities. Were he alive now, I could tell him everything and he would help in every possible way. Great old man he was. He would be ever so pleased to have a grandchild of another race than his own. He deeply believed in human brotherhood; skin-shades did not make any difference to him. That is the only way in which I resemble him.'

'Was he English then?' Daisy asked facetiously. 'I would have liked to know him. My father believe in the brotherhood of the Chinese race. He firmly believes in the equality of men, so long as they are Chinese.'

Daisy believed in Ronnie with all her heart. To her he was the nonpareil of white manhood, the worthy scion of a saintly father. She was sure his children-to-be would be a blessing to mankind.

It would have doubtlessly been better if Ronnie had been an exponent of race-prejudice. His multi-racial sociability was certainly to the disadvantage of races other than his own. It enabled him to seduce, without compunction, the prettiest women of the darker races, from whom he received near adoration for his apparent innocence of racial discrimination.

Apart from perhaps one or two copper-coloured bastards, the coloured race gained nothing from Ronnie's favour, but he himself made an important discovery which was that all women were alike when in bed with a man. They had equality of demands for self-expression and demonstration of their partner's affection, even if it be spurious.

Three days subsequent to Paula's eventful visit to GB, she was sent to the bank where Ronnie worked. In the crowded bank Ronnie attended to her without taking any special notice of her. However, the moment Paula saw this handsome young man she made a lodgement in the account of affection and therein deposited the invaluable treasures of her heart. The interest of joy and security began accumulating instantly.

29

Anxious to achieve her highest earthly ambition, GB acted precipitously. With senile recklessness, she parcelled a number of five-pound notes and went to the rectory where she found Paula ill.

Mrs Allen expertly diagnosed Paula's ailment as a slight cold. Nothing more serious could affect her innocent daughter.

GB gave the money to Paula, begging her not to tell her parents. Paula was very cold to GB and showed less interest in the gift.

GB explained that she was sure that God would specially bless Paula and solve all her problems.

Before departing, she recommended marriage to Paula and hoped that the gift would be useful in such a case. Paula silently agreed that marriage was now a necessity.

When Panty again visited his grandmother, he found her in a grand state of happy excitement, her head over-crowded with schemes for becoming the grandmother-in-law of the beautiful Paula. For the very first time in her rugged life, GB was unselfish, desiring only the happiness of the young couple, upon which, of course, her own fulfilment was dependent. She again emphasized the love the Allens had for Panty and specially underlined how pleased it would make Parson Allen to know of Panty's love for Paula.

'Go to see Parson soon,' she urged; 'Tell him everyt'ing.' Nothing GB said could induce Panty to visit the rectory, so she suggested he should go to the church to have a 'man-to-man' chat with Parson after the service.

She offered to accompany him. Panty bluntly refused, for social reasons. He would never allow himself to be seen in public with such a churlish, half-illiterate person, no matter what benefit he stood to gain. She was too plebeian for his refined aristocratic company.

Panty found himself faced with another problem, that of speaking to Mr Allen without Paula's consent.

'You well know that the girl love you from long time. Child-love never change. You were her first man and now you must not be shame-faced. Go like a brave man!'

Panty agreed that he would like to marry her in order to spite her mother. GB assured him that instead of being displeased, Mrs Allen would welcome the match.

It was decided that GB should make a preliminary reconnoitre to ascertain the feelings of the family.

GB's heart expanded with pride when Panty acknowledged his long-overdue gratefulness to her.

A bright smile polishing her face to make it resemble a new patent-leather shoe, GB told Panty that God would put words in his mouth for the occasion when he appeared before Mr Allen.

Admitting that he felt no deep love for Paula, Panty might have been unaware that his heart was sterile, unable to conceive true and deep affection. He was deficient and deformed as far as affectionate emotions were concerned, his life so far having never provided the nourishment or atmosphere in which love could flourish.

'Whether you love or not, it don't matter. Love may come after marriage. If people waited for love to get married, there wouldn't be ten weddings a year in the world. People marry to get pickney, to settle down and make security against old age and loneliness.'

At the end of the visit, Panty was made to see success within easy reach. Just before he went, GB gave him a long gold chain which she had captured from Bill Toms. Panty thanked her, although he suspected that it was part of the legacy left him by his mysterious father.

Nattily dressed in his well-pressed suit, white shirt and coloured tie, brown-and-white brogue shoes, Panty went to church where he took the Holy Communion to imbibe courage and impress Parson Allen. After the service, he went with understandable diffidence to have a chat with Mr Allen in the vestry.

Genuine delight was bursting all over Parson Allen at the sight of his beloved boy Panty.

'Well, this is indeed a real pleasure. I'm ever so happy to see you, my son. I've been wondering what happened to you!'

This overwhelming cordiality accentuated Panty's diffidence. He was sensitive to the risk of breaking such good relationship.

'How d'you do, sir? I intended to come to see you long ago, but hard work prevented me.'

'You must be making a lot of money! You look prosperous as if you owned a town. Sit down, boy, and tell me all about yourself. We all think of you, in spite of the rather bad turn you have given us . . . by not coming to look us up.'

The last phrase relieved Panty from considerable perplexity. For a moment he had thought that Parson referred to the bedroom incident with Mrs Allen.

Continuing to praise Panty, Mr Allen said: 'An Englishman has special foresight in certain matters. I knew from the first time I saw you that there was something in you. Now I can say that there is absolutely nothing to stop an ambitious, honest young man who believes in God. You have everything for success. There's nothing to prevent you from becoming a leader of men. All you want now is to get married and lead a truly respectable life as an example. I suppose you have been thinking of that!'

Radiance from Parson Allen's face illuminated the room. Jets from the fountain of joy squirted from Panty's spine, bursting in rainbow sprays in his brain. He now saw clearly that Parson was tactfully indicating his complete acquiescence regarding Paula's marriage to him. Panty remonstrated with himself secretly for his unimaginative cowardice which had delayed his approach.

His grandmother was absolutely right, he thought, as he beheld the goddess of fortune in bridal gown awaiting him. Then and there he resolved to pay attention to GB's wise future advice.

Panty beamingly confessed that he WAS thinking of early marriage.

'I have been working hard and saving for it.'

'I knew you would have taken the right course. I'm glad. I suppose you have now come to your "father" for his consent. I hope you've found a true Christian partner. Religious background is very important for successful marriage. When I say Christian, I mean a person of your own religious denomination. The time is not yet ripe for the different faiths to inter-marry. A marriage between persons of different religious faiths carries seeds of its own destruction. Marriage, in any case, is not something which man can manage on his own. God has to enter it at some point to make it a success. No man and no woman are suited to each other as they appear to be on first blush. But you know all this . . .'

'Yessir. I realize all that, but I've found an angel, pure beautiful and sincere.'

'That's what I expected that the Lord would do for you, give you a deserving wife. You will make a good husband, I know that. No Englishman would say as much if he were not dead certain, as I am indeed.'

Caught in the delicate silken meshes of delight, Panty was too entangled to maintain a free flowing conversation. He thought of his good fortune in having the Reverend Allen for foster father and redoubled his already strong admiration for the English philanthropic character.

Parson Allen, with a kindly twinkle in his usually sad, severe eyes, resumed:

'I do not of course hold myself competent to advise you in

this matter. God is the maker of true marriages and you must seek his guidance. However, I can give you a few helpful hints. In marriage it is a mistake to rely on our own judgment; we are too prone to approve the better and choose the worse. I know that with the training I gave you, you will succeed and both yourself and your partner will train your children in the fear of God.'

Panty's respect for Mr Allen's sincerity was compounded. He deduced that, being a true Englishman, Mr Allen was a diplomat and was adroitly handling this matter involving his own daughter. Panty allowed him to continue uninterrupted:

'God was not thinking of man's physical enjoyment when he ordained marriage. God ordained it as a means of accepting man as a junior partner in procreation. It was not made for man the hunter, but man the father and protector of the family.'

Panty agreed totally, wishing there were a way of framing the spoken word. Mr Allen with philosophical unctuousness continued:

'After religion, what would you say is next in importance in marriage? Think deeply before you answer.'

Panty answered spontaneously. Profound thought was unnecessary for such an obviously simple question. He said that the husband and wife were the runners-up.

'Excellent, my son! You're an apt student indeed. God first and the human beings second. But you also know that in order for them to be happy, the couple must have as much in common as possible. Love alone by itself is not sufficient reason for contracting marriage. Beside, love is illogical in its possessiveness. There must be other stabilizing factors to anchor the good ship of marriage if it is not to crash on the rocks.'

Then he added with an air of profundity:

'I think a couple's social level, culture, education and back-ground are important considerations.'

'Sure, sir, quite true,' agreed Panty respectfully. 'I imagine marriage to be a series of confessions, expressions of sympathy, appreciation, mutual encouragement, sharing of mutual as well as common interests, and unless people have some similarity of background and culture latent discord and reciprocating agitation will result.'

'My boy, you speak with authority. You'll have a truly happy life. I know the Lord will endow you and your wife with many children and ʼother blessings to help your own people. They need men like you, well-trained, conscientious, honest and God-fearing.'

Panty did not entirely follow Parson Allen's reference about 'your own people'. It must have accidentally slipped out of Mr Allen's mouth, Panty thought. From that point he listened with some apprehension, his face becoming gradually gloomy and his eyes were like a test-tube denoting albumen in the blood.

'Your people,' Mr Allen stressed, 'need a new generation of intelligent followers. There are far too many leaders in your race, not enough followers. The result is the confusion you see around you. In fact the whole world needs more followers after righteousness and fewer leaders to glory. In two thousand years, mankind has produced one worthwhile Saviour. Your race is producing too many pettyfogging saviours who don't have the good sense to get themselves crucified. When you begin to have children, train them to follow Christ and they will become leaders of men. With fewer leaders you'll have greater progress in the right direction, more unity and less confusion amongst your people. You be the one to show them a good example so that they will not lead each other astray. I believe that is why God sent you to me for training. Maybe I should not be talking to you like this, but of course, you are as my son; there is no lack of confidence between us.'

Plainly inspired, the clergyman continued:

'I am one of the millions of open-minded Englishmen who do not believe in the nonsense called race-prejudice. I personally like your people and, as a clergyman, regard them all as God's children. But between us, I think that in marriage the question of race is most vital. That's why I said earlier that I didn't consider love by itself a sufficient reason for marriage. I know that it is possible for people of different races to fall in love. Love, as I said, is illogical. But marriage has a social significance as well as its other religious and emotional aspects. We marry in church to show first of all that it is a religious institution and then we have a secular celebration to show it is an event in our social life. I know that you, like myself, feel that mixed marriage is of the devil's creation. Race-difference was ordained by our loving Father in heaven and it is presumptious of some men to want to alter the divine plan and law. God could have made His dear son Jesus a half-caste, half-white, half-black, in order to demonstrate to the whole world for all time that race difference is unimportant to heaven. I believe that up in heaven, God has His beautiful mansions for the different races of His creation. Jesus said, " In my father's house there are many mansions ". All races are treated equally, God loves them all, but He has His own reason for making them different.'

Parson Allen evidently was unaware that Jesus was indeed a descendant of a mixed marriage contracted between Ruth and Boaz at a time when mixed marriage was almost forbidden. It was from this union that Jesse, father of David, was born. Jesus came from the line of David and was as much Moabite as he was Jewish—mixed.

Liquid from the river Styx poured itself miraculously into Panty's bloodstream, clogging his circulation with sludge.

He resisted the urge to hit Mr Allen and in any case, he needed his strength to keep from falling.

' Don't you agree with me, son? '

' Ye-yes, su-sure! '

Now Mr Allen congratulated Panty for his innate wisdom, He imagined it came from his grandmother.

Whatever else Parson Allen said was meaningless to Panty, but in politeness, which he had learned from the Allens, he maintained a running series of staccato yeses. He experienced a feeling which must have been similar to that which inspired the lamentation of Omar Khayyám—that man's worldly hopes turn to ashes or prosper, but like snow on the desert vanishes quickly.

Spiritually, from that moment, Panty became a life member of that society of rejects whose password is a moan, whose emblem a crown of thorns and whose staff is a cross.

A gushing spate of latent hatred for GB returned to his perplexed mind.

' 'Tis that damned old fool that cause me to get into this mess,' he silently but bitterly lamented. 'If she did not force me, this would never have happened.'

Observing Panty's pensive appearance, Parson Allen believed he had deeply impressed his student as well as inspiring him anew with the seriousness of his prospective undertaking. So then, in order to cheer him, he said:

'I know how you feel, my son. You're really suffering from the stress of a yet unrealized joy. Earth's joys as you know are never unmixed. I shall pray, however, that you increase in the grace and favour of God Almighty who has led you to this important point. God the true marriage-maker will always protect and guide you and your dear wife-to-be.'

'Yes!' Panty grunted, 'I mean thanks. I'll return to discuss the matter.'

'Good! Excellent, my son,' Allen beamed. 'I'm so proud of you. For me your success is a personal victory. I trained you. I'll tell Mrs Allen and Miss Paula, both of them will be glad to hear. Call anytime, our home is always open to you.'

Drunk with perplexity, Panty staggered to his feet. Simultaneously, Parson Allen rose to give a warm parting handshake and a pat of congratulation.

Passing through the deserted aisle, Panty felt free to be profane. In his retreat from Gethsemane, he anathematized everything and everyone connected with Christianity, the Church and its English God of prejudice.

'That goddamned lying, deceitful bugger, calling himself a Christian parson! He's just another white crow scavenging his living from coloured people. The vulture drinks the blood and tears of people he hates. I wish the damned church would fall on his head. Never will I put my backside on a pew again or listen to any other white preacher. God can keep his many-mansioned, segregated heaven for His English children. Parson Allen, his wife and whore daughter can all go to hell, if the devil wants them.'

Parson Allen happily hurried home to give his wife the good tidings concerning Panty.

Mrs Allen was not interested, but curious to know who was the fortunate lady of his choice.

'He's bringing her to show us. I feel sure she is a wonderful person, according to his description.'

There was a profound reason for Mrs Allen to comment: 'I hope he'll make a good husband. Young people in these days tend to be so rash and . . .'

Mr Allen interrupted with reiteration of his confidence in his former protégé. He gave his idea of what the girl looked like, saying that he was sure she was of light complexion and with high principles. He stressed that he did not think she was black because Panty was a very 'sensible lad'. Mrs Allen expressed considerable relief, saying that she had feared that the 'ambitious' boy would want to marry a white girl.

Paula sipped her tea without apparent interest in the conversation. Her inherent English self-discipline and euphoria were under severe bombardment as her criss-cross emotions of anger, jealousy, humiliation, dread, hate and many more flashed like forked lightning in all directions at once.

Parson Allen suggested that the family should get a very worthwhile wedding present for Panty. Paula was deputed to make the selection.

The dismayed girl jumped as if bitten by an adder, then, calming herself, accepted the responsibility trusted to her.

And now Mrs Allen found another opportunity to praise

Paula. She said that it was the duty of Mr Allen and herself to help young girls to be like Paula, although she realized it was a herculean undertaking. She stressed that it was not merely because Paula had special opportunities, but there was innate goodness which the girl inherited from her family. She did not think Paula's virtues typical of the age in which they lived. It was said to be high above the locally accepted norm.

Agreeing that they had good reasons for pride in their daughter, Parson Allen reminded his wife that the girl, rather the family, was God-guided. None of us can be pure and good without the constant help of the Almighty. Continuing, he quoted some of the many complimentary opinions he heard about Paula. 'The whole community esteem her.'

Mrs Allen claimed that the community was indebted to them for their efforts to reduce illegitimacy.

Mr Allen had the usual clergyman's outward abomination for evil and vice, but in a special way he hated the ugly social problem of illegitimacy in Jamaica, fearing that the indiscriminate production of coloured children was a threat to white hegemony and might eventually result in complicating God's segregated plans for mankind.

Mrs Allen voiced doubt about Panty's virtues. Her husband could not understand her scepticism and by way of reaffirming his complete faith in the boy said: 'Were it not for his colour, I would not have the slightest objection to being his father-in-law. The boy is intelligent, honest and ambitious, which we cannot fairly say all white people are. It is a real pity he has to be coloured, everything else is in his favour. But God has wise reasons for everything. Our Lord is particular on this racial matter. He said that it is not right to take the children's bread and cast to dogs .We must not try to alter the divine order. God made black people black for the simple reason that he wanted them to be black and stay black, not change into yellow, brown, pink, or green for that matter.'

'Thank heaven you have some reservations. I'd prefer my daughter dead than married to a coloured man. I would never be grandmother to a half-caste. I am loyal to my race, even if being so is a crime. God made me thus.'

Mr Allen expatiated about God's kaleidoscopic racial scheme. He said that every colour has its own use and its own beauty in its rightful place.

Mrs Allen complained that some races only created problems for other people to solve. She did not see much use in that.

Mr Allen now suggested that the human skin-colour may be God's wise way of making quick identification. In a twinkling of an eye God could point out all the evil-doers on earth by just looking at the colour of their skin. It made judgment so much easier and he said that he believed God could tell the degree of a man's transgression by the nuance of the man's shade, the darker, the more guilty.

'We read in the New Testament that there are those born that the works may be manifested. It means that God actually made some people for us to show them charity. All this talk about social equality is of political rather than religious origin. The Commandments decree that we must love our neighbour; they don't say that we must be equal to the rabble.'

It was decided at this point that time would be better spent in thanking God for the many blessings He manifested to them.

'We have no problems. We have one lovely daughter who has made us proud and happy. In this backward colony, she has upheld the highest English standard of virtue. Let us ask God to bless the couple about to wed. May they too be as fortunate as ourselves.'

Mr Allen descended waftingly into a reverie from which he spoke with inspiration:

'Too many people complain when they should be singing God's praises like the birds. Birds never complain about their difficulties regarding food and shelter or their colour. They all sing in all seasons to the glory of their Maker.'

It escaped the philosopher-clergyman that birds did not have colour-prejudice to contend with, hence had no reason to want their feathers changed in order to bring them social and economic advantage, or any right which they claim. He failed to see that birds did not force other birds to make slum areas in the trees or persecute each other because of difference of shades. Birds do not terrify and antagonize their fellows in order to prevent them from soaring to the greatest height their wings can bear them.

For all birds, the sky is free. The eagle, the hawk, the dove, the crow and the sparrow all enjoy their freedom according to their capacity.

30

'Take my place,' Paula offered, giving way to the man behind her in the queue at the bank. They were the only two awaiting attention. The short, dark man, obviously a messenger, thanked her with a jewel-smile, glad to encounter such a kind white person. He at once imagined that she was a newcomer to the island.

Bank clerk Ronnie, noting the switch-over, dispatched the male customer speedily. He took spontaneous interest in Paula, not yet aware of her real identity.

Taking the lodgement slip from her, Ronnie's mouth opened with surprise as he involuntarily muttered:

'Paula! Paula Allen! Don't you remember me? Don't you remember . . . ?'

Paula was ashamed to admit that she did not recognize the young man. She had faint promptings that the person was no stranger, yet she could not guess who he was. She did not know that Ronnie had returned to the island.

'Look at me Paula. Don't you remember Ronnie? Ronnie Carpin!'

A wave of delight engulfed Paula and nearly threw her over the counter into Ronnie's arms.

Only a short conversation was possible before other customers arrived. It was long enough for Paula to invite Ronnie home again.

From that instant, Ronnie began reconsidering his promise to the Chinese girl Daisy. He saw definitely that their relationship was impossible.

In due course, he visited the Allens, where Mrs Allen literally fell on his neck to kiss him. She was beside herself with joy at seeing him, but she remonstrated with him for not reporting sooner. Parson Allen's delight was expressed unmistakably in the firm handshake and the broad smile he offered Ronnie.

During the ensuing sparkling conversation, Ronnie cast a shadow of gloom upon the company by telling them of his intention to leave for England again. Mrs Allen begged him to visit them as often as possible during the remainder of his local stay.

Within the next few days, Ronnie found himself properly bewitched and haunted. Upon the closest self-examination, he discovered that this was true love. He wanted to propose at once, but there was Daisy to consider. He was truly perplexed.

In the welter of circumstances, Ronnie decided to confer with Daisy. He thoroughly hated himself for hurting this beautiful, trusting and loving girl, but the harm could not be undone. She had money to cover up any situation. She could go abroad to have her baby and return home when things were normal again with her. He thought he was doing the right and noble thing for a white man. The normal practice would be to spirit oneself away, without trace, leaving a half-caste to be dubbed ' coloured '. He hoped Daisy would concede him this point and understand the sincerity which directed him.

With a contrite and humble heart, he approached Daisy. He told her in a straightforward manner of his renewed affection for his childhood sweetheart with whom he had accidentally remade acquaintance. He begged her to face the hard position with courage and faith, pledging his co-operation in any way other than a marriage. He almost grovelled with repentance at her feet.

On finishing his earnest plea, he awaited Daisy's anticipated fury of jealous wrath. But he was positively startled when Daisy, instead of crying, burst out in rip-roaring laughter. It evidently was the sweetest joke she had heard in her life. She laughed until he believed she was becoming hysterical. He was really frightened, thinking she had become insane to be so jocund at such a serious moment.

Feeling every inch a fool, he waited for her to stop. Daisy's mirth ceased eventually, but her brilliant, slanted eyes were filled with contempt as she informed him that she had never been pregnant. She was just testing him when she told him so. She disclosed how strongly her father disapproved of Ronnie as a possible son-in-law. He would have disinherited her had they married.

Too petrified to move, Ronnie felt hopelessly ridiculous when he eventually followed his heavy feet in the direction away from Daisy, who resumed her mocking laughter which he could hear the louder, the farther away he went from her. He felt as if daubed with sticky mud, from which no water could cleanse away. He was ashamed.

In the next few days, he put pressure on an apparently reluctant Paula, to consider a speedy marriage. Nothing in the world did Paula desire more, at this problematic moment, than a quick marriage to the man she had loved ever since childhood. However, as a girl of breeding, she demurely procrastinated in order ostensibly to be forced against her will. She appeared not to be able to make up her mind so quickly, although she well realized that time was very important to her. With determination Ronnie prosecuted his quarry ardently with asseverations, pleas, promises and coercion. He was very pleased with his own convincing eloquence and successful technique which won Paula. Little did he imagine that had he been dumb, he would have accomplished the same victory in a much shorter time.

Paula's parents were extremely co-operative when they were informed. Indeed Mrs Allen agreed that it was best for all concerned. She and her husband would themselves soon be going to England—within the next year—so whatever the speedy marriage lacked could be put right later, when they all met in England. Mr Allen readily gave his blessing to the wedding, small and quiet with the minimum delay. He had the highest respect for the virtues he imagined Ronnie possessed. Having known Ronnie's saintly father, and Ronnie himself from childhood, Mr Allen supposed Ronnie to be the epitome of a truly fine, Christian English gentleman. He was very grateful to the wise and kind Almighty for finding such a well-born and faithful husband for Paula. He said this in his prayer.

The rectory was in a flurry of activity when an excited GB visited. She had received a banker's cheque for five hundred pounds from an anonymous donor, towards the Moral Welfare Society for helping young girls. On receipt of this, GB rushed to the bank where she attempted to cash the cheque to extract her commission. Finding that the authority of the society was necessary before the cheque could be cashed, GB was left with the personally unprofitable alternative of taking the cheque to Parson Allen. It was with forgivable immodesty that she told how her work had impressed a friend of hers who made the gift but wished to remain unnamed. Of course, GB had no idea where this money came from.

Parson Allen was not surprised with GB's success. He said it had always been patent to him that God would work wonders through her. A five-hundred-pound wonder was just a start.

'Even greater works shall ye do, if you only maintain your usual standard of faith in God. He is watching you, willing to bless you and prosper your works. Many are called but few are chosen. One day you will be surprised to see what God will do.'

Without compunction, GB drank copiously of the sweet praise and said that she would always trust in God no matter what.

'I know! I know! You have been a tried and proven servant of God.'

Mrs Allen was only mildly interested in GB's good news. She imagined that she had information which would cause GB greater rejoicing. She therefore hinted:

'GB, Miss Paula is thinking of something in the near future. The dear child!'

GB understood at once. 'That is wonderful, Missis. Me is very glad to 'ear. Me is really, really 'appy about it!'

'I knew you would be pleased to hear,' Mrs Allen nearly kissed GB. She herself was agog. 'I cannot give you all the details now, but we have decided on a very quiet wedding.'

'But of course! That is the rightest way!'

Spontaneous delight inflated GB's heart as if it were made of rubber. Her head, too, was big with pride. Mrs Allen needn't have told her. She thought as initiator of the scheme she knew even more than Mrs Allen did. One dark spot was now on GB's bright sun. Panty had not returned to tell her of his success. That was very ungrateful of him after all she had done on his behalf, she lamented. Mrs Allen swore GB to absolute secrecy, a responsibility which GB accepted unreservedly. Mrs Allen hinted that the couple intended to go abroad for the honeymoon. GB, in rapture, commended the excellent idea.

With Mrs Allen, GB worked out the details of plans to announce the grand news of the windfall to the Moral Welfare Society. A presentation ceremony was arranged to take place at the rectory where GB would formally hand over the money. All details finalized, GB went home happy as a clown. It was for her one of the best and happiest days in her fairly fortunate life. GB began at once to prepare the speech she would deliver on the grand occasion. She would have to be perfect this time because Allen had promised to get the whole matter in the newspapers. She looked forward to being 'worshipped' by a grateful nation.

It became necessary for her to moderate her almost unendurable ecstasy in order to preserve her sanity and prevent her heart from exploding. Thinking of Panty's ingratitude, therefore, was the means by which GB accomplished this desirable self-restraint.

'And to think of it,' she soliloquized, 'if it wasn't for me, 'im would be in Swine Lane up to now. But me t'ank Massa God that mi labour is not in vain. Excep' the Lord build the 'ouse, the labour is vain. Is Massa God alone who lead and guide me always.'

Somewhat painfully, GB recalled how often she had been warned of the propensity for ingratitude which was possessed by mulatto people. They were classified as ingrates, unsympathetic to people of dark hue.

In spite of all she said, she kept undiminished her hope for a visit from Panty. Expecting him momentarily, she prepared the table with drinks. Patience was increasingly difficult to exercise. She often went outside to look up and down the street for him. She volunteered many excuses for his failure to return, but as the delay lengthened, she tortured herself with the fear that something must have happened to him. Laboriously each morn, she rolled her huge stone of hope up the steep hill of time, only to watch it revert headlong at day's end to the bottomless pit of despair. In the agonizing suspense, GB was subject to violent changes of moods, sometimes cursing Panty scathingly and other times praying for him. At one time she decided to spite herself by keeping away from the wedding.

In her abysmal perplexity, GB anticipated the day for the presentation ceremony. Early in the morning of the joyous day, she started preparations, tediously perfecting the great speech she had composed and committed to memory. With a hot iron comb, she straightened her short mop of grey hair to make it resemble a bird's nest. She had previously attempted to dye her hair, but it was a wasted effort.

She spent a long time in her bath, singing happily, then she ironed her best gown, cleaned her best shoes and made selections from her abundant stock of costume and other jewellery.

The function was to commence at 4.30 p.m. GB had been preparing for it from 4 a.m. and by 2 p.m. she could stand the suspense no longer, so she began walking slowly to the rectory. This would also afford the opportunity to be seen in her splendour by many people. In her rimless brown-straw hat with a long peacock feather and a short veil in front, GB's face appeared to have suddenly increased in size and now resembled a flour cake with too much baking-soda. Her dress was gaudy, a veritable Joseph's coat; she also wore a long frilled-top pair of gloves, brown shoes and black stockings. As a special decoration, she wore the egg-shaped pair of spectacles inherited from Bill Toms. In her large black handbag was the draft of her speech. As she walked along, looking if she was admired by passersby, she collided with a handcart, but suffered no worse damage than getting her stocking badly torn. Her spectacles had encumbered her vision.

Under a large mango tree on the lawn, members and guests of the Moral Welfare Society sat on chairs and benches arranged in a semi-circle. The small number of men present, less than a dozen, was an indication of the lack of interest men took in the moral welfare of girls. More than one hundred and fifty women, mostly middle-aged, were in attendance. The back porch of the rectory was used as a platform, whereupon sat Parson Allen, GB and Mrs Jones, the president of the society. The table in front of them was beautifully decorated with flowers.

Following an opening prayer, Parson Allen extended welcome to all. He then paid tribute to the work of the Moral Society, pointing out that through its vigilance many secret sinners were exposed and deprived of the holy sacrament which he said, was not invented by Jesus to encourage illegitimacy.

He spoke of GB's special contribution to morality in the community and said that from the first time he met her, he knew that she was a power for good. After closely observing her for many years, he had proven that his English foresight and judgment of human nature were very efficient.

' It is said that we English are slow to make friends. That may be true, but it is no bad thing that we take time to make sure of other people's standards before committing ourselves in friendship. It is because we are a sincere people who think affection and friendship are too precious to be flippantly wasted on the undeserving.

' I find myself pardonably proud of the " Englishness " which makes me accept GB as a friend after keen and long observation.

' It is not the colour or state of a person that influences English judgment, as you know. The average Englishman cannot be fooled; he takes nothing for granted in his dealings with frail mortals.'

He briefly described his early encounters with GB and how she had proven always to be unselfish, loving, cheerful and altogether a good Christian. ' She has often inspired me in my ministry and many, many others have gained from her what money cannot buy. Tonight, we celebrate good fortune which is the result of her hard work and Christian enthusiasm. Even though I am aware that in her meekness and modesty she would prefer to be less prominent, I cannot but ask you all to giver her a big hand. I hope and pray that more people would follow her good example when I am sure the Lord would reward them openly as He is doing for her.'

Loud cheers.

GB coyly smiled benignly at her cheering flatterers.

GB, an avid Bible student, appeared now to be conveniently oblivious of the warning ' Beware when all men speak good of you. . . .'

Mrs Jones, the president, rose to address the group. Her dislike for GB originated when GB returned the gift-dog Rexi. Mrs Jones had never forgiven GB and would have liked to use the present opportunity to make her true feelings known. However, the occasion demanded a display of oratory and expressions of praise, hence Mrs Jones was obliged to meet the requirements of the moment.

With a most charming smile, this very attractive middle-aged coloured woman, obviously refined, and elegantly dressed in white shark-skin material, with an expensive brooch clasped on her right breast, began to speak in a deep, warm, sweet voice.

'As president of the Moral Society, I feel very proud tonight. We are a band which does not work for earthly praises and glory. We humbly endeavour to serve God by helping our fellow creatures. We find ourselves interested in the social problems besetting our younger sisters of the lower social classes. We go out to them in their plight. We give them valuable advice, but as our society is not a wealthy organization, we cannot give much in material assistance. We concentrate more on the spiritual help that we can give. We do our best to make young women conscious of sin; we try to make them understand the great dangers of illegitimacy. I strongly feel, however, that we should have a similar society for young men. I find that the young men contact the girls before we do and then trouble invariably results. We have reasons to believe that God is pleased with our efforts. Tonight we have special evidence of divine pleasure.'

Mrs Jones spoke freely of her own personal sacrifices on behalf of the society. She said she had given valuable lectures to many young women expecting their first illegitimates. During Mrs Jones's address, GB was ignored although she gazed intently on the speaker and almost called her attention with quick gestures. At last Mrs Jones caught a wink of GB's eyes which made her remember the presence of the guest of honour.

'And now,' she said, 'I must not forget to mention our guest of honour! As you all know, she comes from that great line which produced such women as Edith Cavell, Florence Nightingale, Joan of Arc, Madame Curie and other great women. I have the same love for her as I know she has for me! We are alike in many ways. We have the same righteous indignation when we see injustice. We love our people and hate to see misery and poverty, and more than all we are both great lovers of animals! I will always remember an incident involving a pet and how we both craved the animal.'

Mrs Jones spent the next few moments apparently praising GB, but really mocking her obliquely. Whenever she said anything really good about GB she included herself. But GB was glad to hear the few words of praise and to watch the approving faces of the audience.

When Mrs Jones finished it was time for GB to reply, she was suddenly seized with stage-fright. She forgot all about the speech which she had prepared and proceeded to extemporize. She developed increased confidence as she spoke, however, and eventually gave a good account of herself. With a few quite pardonable instances of *lapsus linguae*, she said that the government should take more interest in the problems of the poor, especially the young girls whose paramours abandoned them with illegitimate children. She said that she was pleased that her friends had from time to time given secret help and she made special mention of the nameless friend who had given the windfall which was the cause of the present cele-bration. She presented the cheque formally amidst tremendous applause.

This done, it was now refreshment time. Servers appeared with tray-loads of ice-cream, cakes and sandwiches. A few persons moved to the refreshment room for quicker and greater service. They divided into groups to discuss the origin of the mysterious gift.

It was claimed that it was stolen money given away to ease a guilty conscience. It was felt that the money should be held until more was known about its origin. Others invented means of using the money to bring the best results. There were suggestions to have regular parties to bring people together for talk and free refreshment.

One woman in this group suggested that the money be used to pay teachers to train girls in domestic science. In the course of further discussions, it was discovered accidentally that the wise lady making this suggestion, was herself a domestic science teacher. There were strong objections to her views because it was claimed that the training would not benefit the girls but their employers. In the arguments for and against the various proposals, permanent enmities were created. There were those who thought that someone should be imported

224

from England to investigate the social conditions and make recommendations. This fair lady said: 'In England, illegitimacy is not a social problem.'

A withering reply came from a malicious-looking dark lady, who said, 'Yes, I know! They make wider use of contraceptives there than is possible here. These people cannot afford to buy food regularly, let alone birth control equipment!'

Like a wounded animal, the fair lady retreated from the discussion and the group.

Another bright idea was that the money should be spent in helping illegitimate children.

'What is this amongst so many?' a voice asked. Then a prudish buxom lady with a nose resembling a flattened bread-roll, objected on the grounds that the society did not intend to subsidize immorality, making promiscuity profitable. 'We should try to invent means to make the operation unattractive and unprofitable at least.'

'And then the human race will perish,' opined a man speaking for the first time. The woman cut him sharply with her eyes as she replied: 'Better not to have a human race than a world packed with ragged, illegitimate brats. There must be a way to continue the human race without all this sordidness!'

'Which? Do you know of another way?'

This woman did not answer the embarrassing question. It must be said in her favour that she had lived a life of continence and abstention ever since she had to abort to avoid bringing into the world an illegitimate child years ago. She hated everything connected with sex-relations since.

The short dapper man in his late fifties repeated his question to other members of the group: 'What must the people do?'

'Nothing,' answered one woman. 'Just go to their beds and sleep soundly at nights.'

Then said another: 'If we cannot stamp out sexual promiscuity, we should try to get people to marry. Let it be easy and free. Divorces, too, should be facilitated when justi-

225

fied. Many people fear to marry because it seems so absolute in case the marriage turns out to be a mistake! '

' I hope you do not think that marriage diminishes sexual promiscuity in this country! '

' I'm no expert in this matter. I prefer to listen to you,' snapped a woman with finality.

' Let's close this discussion, it is getting us nowhere and breaking our friendship.'

Until after midnight, people argued about the use of the money. Some of them described GB as a fool. If they had received the cheque, the society would never have heard about it, much less have this big argument going on and on. Someone pointed out that it showed GB's honesty and devotion to her people. All agreed.

When the ladies retired some of the few men continued the discussion and agreed that tons of contraceptives should be purchased with the money over the period of years and distributed to the poor through a church committee. This would reduce the illegitimacy problem and give a much better moral picture—as in England.

31

Time sat still in her comfortable house while GB fidgeted.

She selected and rejected dresses, confusing herself as to how she should attire herself for the wedding. She tried on necklaces and beads, admired herself in the mirror for a few moments and then sadly decided that nothing improved her looks. She wanted to make herself attractive to be a credit to her grandson on his nuptial day. She wished he would come to advise her how he wanted her to dress.

GB persecuted herself with dark fears during the day, and at night she had frightful dreams.

When she was near to the very end of her hope, Panty at last visited. His arrival was to her a perfumed wind of pure joy. Everything became instantly all right.

GB gave him a hearty welcome, forgetting to scold him for his delayed arrival. She never inquired why he did not come sooner. She hurried to pour out drinks, a whisky for him and sherry for herself.

'Congratulations, mi son,' she offered as she raised her glass. 'God bless you and make the two of you 'appy. May He who carried you this far keep and guide you to the end!'

GB swallowed her drink with relish. Panty watched her angrily, feeling the urge to strike her for the mockery. He did not touch his drink. Suddenly, GB looked upon him with great surprise. She wondered if he was ill; it was hard to imagine what else could cause his gloom in this moment of joy and success.

'What make you so sad, son? It is not the responsibility you afraid of?'

'You got me into a proper mess! Everything is wrong, if you want to know!'

''Ow come! Why you talking like this, son? You not going to draw out now? You must go through with it. You can't let down the nice young lady. Imagine what the family would say!'

'I don't have to let her down!'

'That's better. Me is glad to 'ear you say that. Mrs Allen told me everything a'ready! She is glad about the wedding. Me never see 'er so 'appy yet from me know 'er!'

'What she said?'

'She tell me 'ow she like the choice Paula made. She said that the wedding is planned to be very quiet and that it will be very soon. You is really a lucky young man!'

Panty looked at her with contempt, feeling sure that she was out of her mind. 'I think you better go and get your head examined,' he recommended. 'You couldn't be in your right senses!'

She reiterated what she had said before, in a very calm and calculated manner. Panty listened while every cell in his brain caught fire so that he doubted his own sanity. It was hard to imagine who had been responsible for this terrible confusion.

In the meantime, GB begged him to be brave. She thought that the apparent good luck had gone to his head, making him temporarily unbalanced. Her words were like quick-sand to Panty. He sank deeper in confusion with every slight movement of his imagination. Perplexity sanded his throat, making it necessary for him to drink frequently to quench his burning thirst.

He disclosed what took place during his meeting with Parson Allen, particularly what the clergyman said about mixed marriage. GB was alarmed. According to what she knew of Parson Allen, she could not believe he would say such things. She said: 'But the man could not be such a damned fool to

228

say that! Moses married a black woman of different race and religion, so the Bible says. Parson know it better than me that God got vexed with Moses's sister Mariam when she mentioned about colour. Massa God burned 'er skin with leprosy until she repent for interfering into other people's business with her damned big mouth. God don't like colour-prejudice from those times!'

GB glanced at Panty while she spoke, and gradually her sorrow for him turned to fear. The drinks had reddened his eyes, but were not responsible for the cold, murderous look in them. GB begged him to go and have a rest. Panty staggered out of the house promising to return the following evening when GB would have better particulars after her proposed visit to the rectory.

Early next morning, GB gathered a bunch of flowers, dressed and visited the rectory. On her arrival, Mrs Allen received her with excessive cordiality and although glorying in the sight of the beautiful flowers, regretted that they had not arrived a day before.

'These would have been wonderful yesterday!'

'They are for Miss Paula. I know she loves them.'

'She would have liked them surely, but they arrived too late.'

'For what?'

'The wedding of course! I told you about it before! I told you it would be quiet. Parson insists that a wedding is a sacrament not a revelry. The two children themselves wanted it small and quiet.'

GB's smile stuck to her face, slightly disfiguring it. Mrs Allen saw the embarrassment.

'Oh, GB. Come, come! Don't be so surprised, as if you did not know. You must have expected it! I gave you fair warning! It is a pity you didn't see them before they left to catch the ship. You know her husband well—I think!'

'Me saw him yesterday! Funny!'

'No, GB! You must be making a mistake!'

'Not a bit. Me could not make mistake and me know the man so well!'

'That's extraordinary. He has changed a lot since you saw him, GB. Let me refresh your memory. He is the son of a parson. . . . Does that . . .'

'Don't tell me. Me know that of course! Me tell you that me know 'im.'

'Did you know that he had come back to the island then?'

This last question confounded GB. As far as she knew, Panty had never left the island. But in any case, she did not understand any more of what Mrs Allen said as she stood, feeling faint while horror stiffened her face.

Mrs Allen comforted her: 'Miss Paula didn't forget you though, GB. She left a letter for you and the last thing she did was remind me to give it to you soon. I'm so glad you came today.'

GB's heart pounded with new hope at this information. She knew that the letter contained the money which she had forced upon Paula. Whatever might have gone astray in the plans, at least the money was not lost, GB was glad to think. Yet for all this hope, she suffered frequent contractions in her stomach, which behaved as if packed with explosives.

'You see now that Miss Paula always had you in thought!'

'God bless 'er,' muttered GB by way of a curse. 'Me really sorry me didn't get a chance to see 'er for the last!'

'There was no time, GB. Everyone of us thought of you. But we all knew you would understand. You were always so kind to Miss Paula, she will never forget you. She loves you.'

The thoughts passing through GB's head were unsuitable for expression at a rectory, that was why GB remained silent.

'I've saved a small drink for you, and a tiny bit of cake.' GB was only thinking of the money.

Mrs Allen served a very small amount of wine and a crumb of cake, symbolic of the extreme frugality of the wedding. She then rushed upstairs for the important envelope.

When GB received the envelope, she had a heart-quake. She

230

had expected the envelope to be more bulky. Perhaps Paula might have enclosed a cheque. However, she could not open the letter in the presence of Mrs Allen, although she was obsessed by a pressing curiosity to see the contents.

She soon found an excuse for going, but before she left she promised to make another visit shortly. Mrs Allen begged her not to forsake them now that Paula had gone. Mrs Allen told her that during the next year she and Parson would be returning to England, when they would take all GB's good wishes to Miss Paula. Mrs Allen seeing the sad look on GB's face, sympathized by saying: 'I know how you feel when your best friend is gone. I almost want to cry myself, but I'm just pretending. We miss her very much indeed!'

Rushing out of sight of the rectory, GB opened the envelope. Tears prevented her from reading the hurried note inside. It was as if she had been injected with tear-gas. She decided that it would be best for Panty to read the letter and explain it to her.

When she reached home, anger fired her inside, smoke from which beclouded her eyes, while the sparks escaped from her tongue. She cursed, everybody and everything. Black and white were equally reviled, but Paula naturally, received extra vilification. 'A wicked li'l white bitch,' GB called her. To console herself she conjectured: 'Mi parents must 'ave done evil why this bad luck come down 'pon me 'ead. Me should know better than want to elevate myself. Mi mother always tells me that cockroach don't 'ave no business to attend fowl's dance!'

Confused as she was in her mind, she now clearly understood the mystery of the donation to the Moral Welfare Society. All that was said about her assistance to fallen girls turned out to be true. If heaven rewards unintended kindness, GB was sure of a bright star in her crown.

Greatest cause of her remorse was that Panty should be deprived of the inheritance she intended for him! 'The poor fatherless boy would 'ave been so glad to receive the money!

Poor people shouldn't plan not'ing. God always mash up our plans!'

A number of illnesses, including indigestion, hiccup, headache and diarrhoea, afflicted GB simultaneously. When she tried to rest in bed, she had the sensation of lying on a raft in a stormy sea. Eagerly, she wished for Panty to come to console her and share the grief.

In the tortuous moments, her lively imagination produced no anodyne for her pain. Panty's coming was all that could bring surcease from her mental agony.

In the evening the setting sun poured gold into GB's house for her to collect and hoard, but the frustrated woman only longed for darkness to help hide her sorrow.

At nightfall, dishevelled and haggard, a red-eyed Panty arrived. His presence ended GB's hope of consolation. It frightened her to see him as he was. She quickly placed a bottle of whisky in front of him as if making a sacrifice to propitiate an angry god. Panty poured a drink in silence.

'Well! What's the news now?'

'Mi son, you was quite right. Me is the fool!'

With funereal grief, she told Panty the whole story of what took place during her rectory visit.

Panty said that he was glad it was over. He cursed all white people and swore that none would cross the steps when he possessed the house.

GB winced. The house was still indebted to the Building Society. GB paid no attention to demands of the mortgage although she had money. She had intended giving the house to Panty and Paula as a present so that she could escape paying the debt. Of course, she expected to live there with them, giving them her devoted service.

Panty was never told anything about the house debt and therefore looked forward to outright possession of the legacy.

It was only now that he recalled Mrs Allen's bad treatment, that he condemned himself for being colour-prejudiced:

'If a black woman treated me like that, I surely wouldn't

want to marry her daughter. I would never forgive her. Yet, I was willing to get into Mrs Allen's family in spite of knowing she hates me!'

Remonstrating with himself, he claimed kinship with the moths which rise to burn their wings, for whom brilliant destruction has the greatest attraction.

'Don't worry, Massa Panty. Every disappointment is for a good reason. Man appoints but God disappoints. Big Massa God want you to marry a rich coloured girl and that's why 'im broke up this business. Trust in God, Massa P!'

Panty did not comment for a while. He said as if speaking to himself: 'Some of us don't know a damn what we want. We are even dissatisfied with the way God Almighty made us!'

There were shorter and shorter intervals between his drinks. In the meantime, GB kept still and even tried to escape into sleep, but Morpheus cast her from his kingdom.

As the drinks loosened Panty's tongue, he said: 'Our enemies often help where friends fail. I owe all my progress to Mrs Allen. I just wanted to convince her that being born in the slums of a dark race did not make any difference, if one gets the opportunity. If it wasn't for her, I don't know if I'd have any ambition.'

'You prove it to 'er over and over, mi son. She knew long time that you 'ave better brain than 'er wicked daughter. The two of them was jealous of you, me know that very well!'

Panty swallowed another drink and then, in his gradually increasing intoxication, addressed GB directly, as if suddenly becoming aware of her presence. 'I've an idea! Let's get rid of this god-damned house! It's full of bad luck.'

Panty had long been thinking of getting money to buy a motor-car to increase his social status.

GB shivered at the suggestion, simultaneously making a funny sound: 'Massa P, you is more intelligent than me, you can understan' t'ings quick. Read that note there and explain it to me.'

233

Panty read it over and over with increased perplexity. 'I don't understand! What money she is talking about?'

It was GB who had to do the explaining. After telling him all about the matter, she stressed that she was seeking his welfare chiefly when she took the rash step. She had thought the marriage was a certainty.

Panty's anger coiled serpent-like in his breast, ready to strike. GB squirmed under his cutting gaze and, in a cracking voice, meekly apologized. Panty, who had inherited his grandmother's lust for money, was too nonplussed to speak. GB began to sob: 'Massa P, it is the Lord's doings. This li'l sorrow will soon pass. God make sorrow and trouble for poor people to 'ave somet'ing to enjoy in this life!'

With a feline arch of his back, Panty appeared ready to spring on his prey, as GB waited helplessly for the hands of doom. She could not bear the torture of looking at him standing in silence.

'Say somet'ing noh, Massa P! Me know me is wrong this time, but don't be vexed with your gran'mother! Me is a damned fool. But it was because me love you and would like to see you 'igh hup in life why this 'appen!'

'Say something?' Panty at last exploded. 'Say something indeed! Well let me tell you that you are the damnedest dry-headed ass God ever made—if you can prove that it's He who made you. You should be in a mental asylum. You foolish bitch! Both God and the devil must have long forgotten all about you and that's why you are still here to cause trouble on earth. You better make sure you have funeral expenses, otherwise you'll walk to your own funeral.'

Hoping that the storm had now passed, GB sought to transfer Panty's anger to Paula: 'Massa P, me couldn't imagine that that innocent-looking gal was such a bitch. Me glad you don't marry 'er. You are a very smart man!'

'Shut you blasted ugly mouth. So help me God, if you talk any more rubbish I'll strangle you. You say you're in God's hands, well try and don't let me put my hands on you. Swine

234

Lane people should never have anything but trouble. That's all they can manage. You low-class people worship the white skin. You spread inferiority. Why the hell a ugly brute like you wanted a white grandchild! To frighten the child with your monkey-face, I suppose! You resemble an over-ripe sour-sop!'

'Listen, Massa P, please. Just one word!'

'Shut up and don't aggravate me any more.' Panty rushed up to her in a mad rage, shaping his hands as if to attack GB.

Stopping just in front of her, he asked: 'Tell me . . . tell me why the hell you didn't die long ago! What excuse you have to be here now when you could have killed yourself long ago! I don't know why I got mixed up with a ragged old bag of evil and idiocy like you!'

GB made a heart-breaking wail ending with a wish to die.

'Well go on now! Go and die! No one is preventing you!'

This was the last straw on the heavily laden back of GB's tolerance. She could take no more insults. She flared in wild temper. 'Damn it all,' she screamed, 'who give you the right to talk to me like that—you damned li'l stray'way bastard brute! Did you give me any money? Me been slaving for you since you was born in the gutter. I should have dumped you in one of the Swine Lane latrines where you belong. Now, clear your backside out of my house. God wasted time to create you, when the flesh and blood could have made pigs and hundreds of lice. Miss Paula was right not to want to marry a stinker like you. Your mother was right to run away from you. Get out! Get out, you saucy crow!'

With all her angry energy, GB rose up and pushed him violently. Panty held her, but like a wounded tigress, GB freed herself and hammered him with her fist, prepared to fight to the death. As she hit him she cursed simultaneously.

'You can never be a gentleman. You come from the slums, but the slums never came out of you. Swine Lane is inside you.'

'Because I'm your grandchild. I inherited Swine Lane from you.'

'Yes. You inherit Swine Lane, so the little govament job

235

cannot make you into a gentleman. It cannot take away Swine Lane out of your heart. You ill-treat your mother and your grandmother! A fine gentleman for a govament office.'

'A blasted cow like you should have respect for your superiors. You black bitch!'

Panty slapped GB in his uncontrollable temper. She staggered and crashed to the floor, hitting her head.

'Die! Die like a dog! It will be the end of an idiot. A fool is worse than a thief!'

Drunk with rage and whisky, Panty stormed out of the house.

32

To save Panty from prison, GB minimized the extent of her injury and declared that it was an accident.

In the few days she spent at hospital she had totally forgiven him, grieving personally for his disappointment.

When she recovered, however, she was filled with fear of remaining in her 'castle', so she sought sanctuary at the rectory with the Allens, who were preparing for their departure to England.

Mr Allen praised GB's loyalty, thinking that she had come chiefly to give assistance and share their company for the last.

When the Allens left, GB acting like a thief, collected few necessaries and made a bus journey to Montego Bay. She was sure of a welcome amongst the lowly.

Her unexpected arrival delighted Sue Browley, who considered herself flattered to be hostess of her successful friend. She begged GB to remain indefinitely and from the start treated her like a princess, without thinking of any prospects of reward. She did not know about GB's downfall. GB appeared normally cheerful always, saying nothing about her precarious state. Not incited by ambitious social or economic hopes, GB gradually found the precious peace of mind which so long evaded her. It had taken her a full lifetime to learn life's elementary lesson—'All is vanity.'

Occasionally, Sue repeated congratulations to GB for remaining humble, in spite of the social height she had reached. She reminded GB often enough: 'You get all your wishes, you is really blessed by the Almighty. Yours is the luckiest family ever to come from Swine Lane. Many envy you and pray to be like you! '

GB agreed she had many blessings and learned many things which would be very useful if she could relive her life. Somehow, she considered herself neither a failure nor a success. She had merely lived through the vicissitudes of life, rising and falling on the unstable waves of existence. She thought and prayed frequently for Panty's welfare.

With all passion spent at the jungle club, which he had optimistically foresworn at Ada's death, Panty returned in a rather confused state of mind to Watalow Road, intending to make some amends to GB and so save more serious consequences. Not finding her there, he was indecisive whether or not to contact the police before they came to him. After he reported to the police that GB was missing, he spent many anxious days in tortuous suspense expecting to be arrested. Indeed, during this period, the sight of a policeman was sufficient to make him think of suicide. He made frequent visits to the house and when to his great relief he heard where GB was, he simply took charge of his heritage.

It was just at this time that he was dismissed from his job for dereliction of duty and absence without leave for an inexcusable period. He was rapidly spent as a social fire, but, fearing a too precipitous fall and also to preserve his own life, he selected a nucleus from the jungle club to have their sessions at his house at Watalow Road.

One day he opened a letter addressed to GB. It came from the Allens in England to announce the birth of Paula's superlative baby. The letter blazed with ecstasy which the event brought the Allens. The baby girl was said to be of the most attractive complexion ever invented by creation's sensitive painter, who took special pains to cover this new human bloom with petals of velvet all over. Its premature birth, said Mrs Allen, was obviously due to Paula's illness on the voyage. Mrs Allen said that she never imagined anything earthly could make her so happy. She described herself as specially favoured amongst women to be grandmother of such a pretty baby. She ended by sending GB all Miss Paula's love and personally thanked GB for all she had done for the whole family.

Panty read the letter without much interest; he felt neither pride nor triumph to be a father by proxy. He knew that he would father a nice child in any case. He had always felt sure of this.

Poor GB never heard that her once dearest wish was fulfilled, but it would not have mattered to her now.

After reading the letter, Panty did get some satisfaction from the feeling that he had fulfilled the Christian injunction to do good to those who spitefully use you. Mrs Allen had been his lifelong enemy and now he took Christian credit for causing her such happiness. It all went to show that God could fulfil His purpose in rather strange ways. It must have been divine will for Mrs Allen to be a happy grandmother, so what if God had chosen the least of the apostles, so to speak, to bring His will to light? Mrs Allen did not like coloured people, yet it was through one of them that her greatest delight was to be achieved.

Panty felt no envy for putative father Ronnie Carpin, who by fate's facetious irony became the proud papa of a coloured girl. Panty also thought of Parson Allen who, believing in a colour-prejudiced God, would be unaware of his near kinship with the race he proscribed secretly but publicly approved.

From Mrs Allen's description of the baby as a little angel sent down from heaven's prize stock, Panty justly inferred that there were coloured angels up there crawling in the celestial playpens, who really were not fussy about the colour of their parents. Mrs Allen as a knowledgeable parson's wife must have been subconsciously aware of this, since she said such nice things about Paula's baby.

This baby would eventually transmit African blood through

white veins. She would pass it on so that it would run quickening unborn generations of racial purists throughout the endless ages.

To Panty, the baby was one of the incredible number of illegitimates born in Holy Wedlock whose surnames on the earthly registers were at variance with the identification in heavenly records. By what names they will be called on judgment day is known by God alone. Perhaps Mr Allen was indeed right to suggest that God intended skin-colour to be the means of identification, thereby mercifully saving from embarrassment many blushes from respectable mothers, and heart-breaks of shocked fathers. Good indeed it is that husbands and wives will not be known to each other in the resurrection, or some risen fathers would promptly die of shame or commit suicide after being resurrected to truth.

The friendship between GB and Sue sweetened and deepened into a mellow thing of beauty, now that there was no rivalry or jealousy. Sue, feeling as proud as if she had received the accolade by her friend's presence, showed an enthusiastic willingness to serve one she now considered her superior, but who deigned to be her equal. No doubt, had Sue not seen GB's prosperous position in Kingston, she would now have been taunting her guest with ostentatious displays, but now she was ever willing to accommodate GB's smallest request without even thinking of reward.

During one of their friendly conversations, they were talking about life, when in her rude philosophy, GB described it: 'Life is a trap, and if you escape from it, you die. It is not good to try to get free when you is in the trap of life. Just keep calm an' quiet.'

'Ah, GB. Don't me knows dat too! Me could be free from trouble long time ago, but as me want to live, me prepare to bear trouble an' pain.'

GB suddenly complained of a stabbing pain in her head: 'Me just feel like mi hairs turn into pins and needles.'

'Do you want some worm-grass tea?' Sue asked with

240

solicitude. 'Worm-grass tea is good for rheumatism, flu and 'eadaches as well as worms.'

'No, boil some Leaf-o'-Life-bush tea for me. Put a piece of ginger in it and drop a li'l strong rum.' The request was made obviously through the necessity of pain.

'Res' you'self, GB. Me soon come back.' Sue hurried to prepare the bush-tea.

GB whispered a prayer in the interim: 'Dear God, spare me to drink more bitter, black, bush-tea on earth before you call me up for the milk and honey. Amen.'

She was sinking. Her eyes blared with the haze of death. GB was fighting hard, granting no quarter to her enemy, tyrant Death. It had her by the throat, but she plunged her fingers into Death's eyes.

Amidst the battle, Sue brought a pint-can, full of hot Leaf-o'-Life-bush tea.

'Dis is very good, GB dear, drink it. It will soon make you feel all right.'

GB raised her hand eagerly for the elixir, but it weakly fell to her side again.

Wild with anxiety, Sue knelt beside GB and with a table-spoon began to baby-feed her dying friend. One, two spoonfuls went down GB's throat and then, no more. GB's need for earthly balm and friendly kindness ceased. She had now escaped from the 'trap' as she aptly called life. Success and failure could taunt her never again.

It took many moments for Sue to convince herself that GB now did not need any assistance or attention from her.

In spite of her stupendous efforts to amass worldly riches, GB now left only one thing of value—a true friend—Sue Browley.

Only Swine Laners attended GB's funeral. They were people of great experience in mourning and from their fund of grief they made generous contributions of tears to GB's funeral. Dead or alive, if anyone wanted sorrow, they could get millions of tons of it from Swine Laners in the twinkling of an eye.

241

Moanfully, they jerked out their heart's native agony as they sang in a minor key, slurred by tearful cadences and attractively embellished by tonal discords: 'Earth has no sorrows which heaven cannot cure.'

Thus, by wailing sounds they expressed their faith and again reminded the Almighty of their never-ending cares.

It would have been indeed a triumph for GB to watch the sincerity of their grief. She would have understood that some of the fairest flowers of friendship grow in the manure of adversity, constantly watered by tears in the perennial drought of poverty.

The former stonebreaker GB would have been pleased to see the hearts she had now broken with the hammer of her own death.

The occasion gave Sue ample opportunity for showing the profound affection she felt for GB.

Now at last was GB a complete success. She had always wanted appreciation, always wanted to know that people cared for her, loved and respected her. Her wishes were now all fulfilled in profusion.

But death, the mocker of all successes, refused her the opportunity to view her 'Promised Land'. The fact that GB had made herculean struggles on the winding path of life made no difference. Death is callous of human merit; in its economy there are no special plans to reward or show any favour to the deserving.

33

Less than a year following GB's death, Kate and her lawyer husband Harry Bernart returned to Jamaica.

Kate's charitability had at last been rewarded. In England she had shown great generosity and friendship to Harry when he was an impecunious student. Soon after his call to the bar they were married just before sailing home on a luxury liner.

The house at Watalow had considerably deteriorated and the garden was now all in weeds.

Panty and party were still engaged in a gambling session lasting all through the night when there was a knock at the door. Since the loss of his employment he was able to keep well in funds by using the premises as a common gaming-house illicitly.

The knock put everyone on the *qui vive,* and Panty rushed to see to the caller. Peeping through the keyhole he saw a sight which cramped his stomach: his mother and a tall, handsome man, evidently a policeman whom she must have brought to eject him. Panty ran back to the gambling room, urgently telling his pals to scatter and leave the house with all haste. In a moment they fled in all directions; those who could not get through the back door in time jumped through the window. Panty himself made his escape faster than the others.

After continuous knocking, Kate searched a small suitcase for a key which fitted the lock, thus letting her husband and herself in.

They saw abundant evidence of very recent habitation, yet

the house was mysteriously empty. There was no sign of GB anywhere.

Without losing time, Kate and Harry set out to find GB and Panty. The police, naturally, were contacted. Kate learned that GB was dead. It was heartbreaking news for her, yet she hoped to find consolation when Panty was found.

Panty kept low for the first few days and, fearing the worst, he decided to make a quick trip to England.

During the formalities of getting out his passport and ticket to travel, he was discovered by the police as the person they sought.

Panty was asked to accompany an officer to Watalow Road. On the way he kept strangely silent in the police car; he was anxious to make come confession although he did not know what charge exactly would be brought against him. He well knew that there were many points in his life which if known to the police would at least temporarily curtail his freedom.

Added to all his fears was his unwillingness to meet his mother face to face. He felt that he would have little chance if his mother was his accuser.

'I'll confess everything, I have nothing to hide,' he said, thinking aloud in his dire confusion.

'Be careful what you say,' said the officer rather unofficially. 'Never say too much to any woman.'

Panty winced. Now they reached the premises and the car stopped at the front door. Kate must have been listening for the arrival. She rushed out wildly.

For a brief moment mother and son gazed at each other without speaking. Kate's lips quivered, her soft eyes glistened with the sparkle of tears. Plain, ordinary terror filled Panty up to the brim. He did not know what to say. Before the car drove away, Harry came up fast behind Kate and, just as she was about to embrace Panty, she paused and said to her husband: 'Harry, this is my son—our son, I mean. You were so anxious to meet him. Well, here he is.'

The rest was easy. Panty was relieved when Harry shook his

hand and Kate fell upon his neck with the same parental affection with which the Prodigal's father greeted his errant son. The enmity or rather misunderstanding between mother and son instantly melted, forming a warm, clear pool of reconciliation deep enough to swallow all past hatred.

They all went into the house where Panty was literally put into the witness-box to give account of himself and, of course, GB. Luckily for him it was to a friendly jury that he gave evidence. They accepted everything he said, never questioning to create embarrassment, but such queries as were made sprang from deep interest and love.

When he gave evidence about GB, Kate broke down in tears. She was full of thoughts of forgiveness and understanding which now of course were useless to GB.

Kate had intended a great surprise for her mother. She had bought a number of dresses and other little presents which she knew GB would have liked very much.

Severely, Kate remonstrated with herself for the harsh way she had judged GB's rapacity, which she only now understood was inspired by healthy ambition for a better life on earth and in heaven. But now there was no opportunity of apologizing.

The following day, Kate, Harry and Panty went to Montego Bay.

Sue guided them to GB's grave, where tearfully she recounted the deceased's greatness and loyalty.

' Despite 'er great success and the big-shot people she could mix with, she came back to Swine Lane to die amongst 'er own people. She loved us all and we all loved her. Not'ing, no height could make GB scorn the poor and lowly.'

Sue recalled to her audience the visit she made to Kingston and how kindly she was entertained by GB who wanted her to remain.

Over the oblong pile of broken stones, GB's grave, the sad party stood. Through the magnification of tears, Kate examined the past. She observed: 'I remember when GB used to be on top of a pile of broken stones at Rockhill. Now she is under this pile of stones as if she had merely fallen from her seat. Stones were part of her life and now follow her to the grave.'

Pensively, Harry looked on the grave, observing philosophically, 'The world we live in is a stone. We all are stones. God Almighty is a great stonebreaker using some stones to make cathedrals and others to pave gutters. The making of some things is the breaking of other things. Broken stones build shelters, broken bones build nations and broken hearts build heaven. GB was a good stone.'